A Sugarloaf Adventure

ROSEMARY WHITTAKER

A Sugarloaf Adventure

Rosemary Whittaker

Also by Rosemary Whittaker

A Sugarloaf Valentine
A Sugarloaf Mix-Up
A Sugarloaf Surprise
A Sugarloaf Christmas
A Sugarloaf Easter
A Sugarloaf Secret
A Sugarloaf Summer
A Sugarloaf Appeal
A Tale of Two Christmases
A Boxful of Christmas
The Christmas Cookie Club
The Cinnamon Snail
Sunshine State
The Wattle Birds
The Feijoa Tree
The Villa Mimosa
Making the Effort

First printing, 2025

ISBN-13: 978-1-922651-71-6

This book is a work of fiction. Names, characters, places, and incidents are the product of the author's imagination or are used fictitiously. Any resemblance to actual events, locales, or persons, living or dead, is coincidental.

Stopwatch Publications

www.rosemarywhittaker.com

Coverdesign including elements from 100 Covers, Greylilac, petitelili, Goodlucky, Nicemonkey, LanaBrow and Lembergvector.

With thanks to the members of trauma fiction for their invaluable medical advice regarding broken legs!

Sharon - the butterflies are for you - x

Chapter One

'Isabella – we're going to be late!' shouts Georgia for the third time, and I sigh.

My sister's less than dulcet tones have become even more strident over the past few weeks. It isn't my fault I can't leap out of bed and run down the stairs at top speed as quickly as I used to. My broken leg has healed well, but I'm still a little wobbly at times. Nor is it my fault her employer is currently more demanding than usual.

If I were Georgia, I'd be grateful I still had a job. She isn't the most ideal employee. Not for the first time, I'm thankful she's never asked me to employ her at the bakery. Even if I sent a formal refusal on headed notepaper, signed by all our members of staff, Georgia wouldn't accept it. She's never been one to take no for an answer, especially from her sister.

I've told her a hundred times it's customary for younger sisters to look up to their older siblings and treat them with deference, but she always gives me one of those annoyingly blank looks of hers and carries on with whatever she's doing. I've given up worrying about it. I've known her for more years than I care to remember, and I doubt she'll improve.

'Isabella!' she yells again so loudly that I'm almost sure I see a chunk of plaster fall from the ceiling. 'If you aren't down here in exactly ten seconds, I'm leaving without you!'

What does she expect me to do – hurl myself at the banisters and slide down them or glide gracefully down the stairs on a tea tray?

'I'm coming!' I call back in a far sweeter tone than she deserves. She has the upper hand for two more weeks. She's my ride, so I have to stay in her good books.

I pick up my bag, walk as quickly as possible along the landing, and peer over the banisters. Georgia is standing in the hall, staring at her watch and scowling. I greet her with my friendliest smile.

'Good morning! I'm glad to see you're so punctual. Your employer is a lucky woman.'

She makes a sound somewhere between a snarl and a growl and gestures towards the door. 'Hurry up, if you're coming with me.'

'It should be obvious to you that I am. You told me we had to leave at seven thirty, and here I am at almost precisely seven thirty. It must be a great comfort to know my recent misadventure hasn't affected my impeccable sense of timing.'

She ignores this as she climbs into the car.

'That's ok,' I murmur, opening the passenger door. 'I'm happy to struggle all by myself.'

She barely allows me time to buckle my seatbelt before roaring off down the drive with a spray of gravel.

'Careful!' I say. 'You'll chip your paint.'

She gives me an annoyed look. 'I'll bill it to you.'

'I'm not an insurance company. And I'm not the one driving without due care and attention on an unstable surface.'

'You're the one who's made me late,' she says, turning onto the road without indicating.

'Only thirty seconds, which is a lot better than when I first broke my leg. It used to take me ten minutes just to get down the stairs each morning. You should be delighted with my improvement. You could even post about it on your blog.'

'I don't have a blog.'

'You could start one especially for the occasion. You could call it Georgia's Jolly Jottings.'

'No one has written a blog since the 1850s,' she says contemptuously.

'That's fascinating. You should write to the British Computing Society to let them know the Internet was in existence far earlier than is generally known. They'll be most interested. They may even invite you to write a blog post about it.'

Instead of looking impressed at my technical expertise, Georgia rolls her eyes and swings the car onto the road that leads to Honeywell. She's obviously not keen on displaying her lack of computing knowledge to someone who knows as much about technology as I do.

'Why is Cath making you come into work so early?' I ask.

'Because she's an idiot.'

'Possibly, but I don't see the connection.'

Georgia gives me an aggrieved look. 'When Cath bought the shop from Marcia, she told me and Lucinda she wanted to make some changes. Neither of us realised she meant our working hours.'

'What did you think she meant?'

It's interesting to hear about how other small business owners operate. Georgia has always refused to tell me much about her job and I haven't pressed her in case she decides she'd rather come and work for me instead.

'How should I know?' she asks. 'We thought she was planning to move the clothes racks around or offer us private health insurance.'

The workings of my sister's mind are endlessly fascinating. It's about the only work I've ever seen her do.

'Did you seriously expect her to offer you health insurance?' I ask.

'Why not? We stand around all day telling our customers how wonderful they look in our hideous clothes. It can't be good for our backs. Lucinda said the other day she thinks she's developing a varicose vein.'

'That's because she's about fifteen months pregnant.'

'That isn't the point,' she says. 'It wouldn't hurt Cath to show some consideration to her employees, whether they're expecting a baby or not. Last week, she was talking about introducing performance plans. Luckily, Lucinda's husband knows a good lawyer. They're planning to ask him about suing for pregnancy discrimination.'

'Would he sue on your behalf too?'

'I'm not pregnant.'

'That does present a difficulty,' I agree. 'Couldn't you come up with some other protected characteristic – terminal laziness or permanent inertia?'

'I could say I had you for a sister.'

I give her my most patient smile. 'That's a bonus, not a negative. Anyone would be lucky to have me as a sister.'

'I can't think of anything worse. How long before you can drive again?'

'Two weeks. I'm sorry it's such a short time. I know you've enjoyed these morning chats almost as much as I have. Perhaps we should aim to continue them once a week, even after I've recovered. We could take it in turns to drive.'

'Not a hope,' she says. 'The moment they hand your licence back, you're on your own.'

'They haven't taken it away. But my physiotherapist says it isn't safe for me to drive until I can perform an emergency stop if need be.'

'Speaking of which –' she skids to a halt outside the bakery. 'Hurry up and get out! If I lose my job because you've made me late, you'll have to employ me here.'

I snatch up my bag and jump out of the car. 'What a terrible thought. Off you go! Don't pay too much attention to the speed limit, and definitely don't stop for red lights.'

I heave a sigh of relief as I watch her drive away. That was rather too close for comfort. Georgia may be my sister, but if there's one thing I'm certain of, she'll never be my employee.

Chapter Two

Lily is making herself a coffee when I open the bakery door.

'Right on time,' she greets me. 'Did Georgia give you a ride in?'

'She did, but very reluctantly. She was her usual uncommunicative self on the drive over here. I don't think she appreciates the amazing bonding opportunity she's been offered.'

'Does she have to start work early again?'

'So early that she almost left without me. She was hopping around the hall like a cat on hot bricks, and I could tell she wanted to leave me behind. But the last time she did that, Mum made her come back for me. She stood at the end of the drive like Gandalf, telling Georgia she should not pass! She's the only person Georgia ever listens to. I don't know why. Possibly because my sister has never learned to cook, and Mum makes bacon just the way she likes it.'

'I'm glad she didn't leave without you,' says Lily. 'I need to run out for half an hour soon, and I didn't want to leave Abby in charge of the shop. She has a busy morning ahead of her.'

'Is it Bakewell tart day? You're very right not to interfere with that. I like her mind to be on the job on Bakewell tart and doughnut days. And eclair days. And cherry slice days.'

'So, pretty much every day,' she says. 'Would you like a coffee?'

'I'd like several, but I'll settle for a large cappuccino to start with. I'll inspect the out-of-date cakes while you're making it.'

'There are none. We check them every evening before we close up.'

'The almost out-of-date cakes,' I correct myself. 'Those with only one or two days to go. It's important to stay on top of these things. That's what differentiates an excellent bakery proprietor from a merely adequate one.'

'Leave the lemon tarts alone,' Lily warns me. 'Abby made them for the Silver Surfers. They're meeting here in an hour or so. I'm not sure why. Ivy wouldn't say. But she requested them specially. And don't eat the last plum slice either or Mabel will set Bernie onto you.'

'That doesn't scare me. I'll buy him off with a beef-and-basil-flavoured biscuit. He'd make a terrible guard dog. Any burglar could sneak past him as long as they brought food.'

'The same goes for you,' she says.

'That's why we have an electronic alarm system at home. My parents know better than to expect me to concentrate on possible intruders when I'm busy eating a midnight snack. As for Georgia, nothing short of a bucket of cold water wakes her.'

'She's been getting up early for weeks now,' Lily points out.

'That's true. I'm not sure how she does it. She must have invested in an alarm clock company and taken a supply of their products in lieu of a dividend.'

She smiles. 'Wouldn't you hear her alarms go off?'

I pick up the tongs and fill a plate with doughnuts and slices of caramel shortbread. 'I'm an overworked business owner. I need my sleep at night. I don't have the mental bandwidth to listen out for my sister's alarm clocks. Maybe she has something else rigged up in her room to wake her each morning.'

'Such as?'

'I wouldn't like to speculate. I never go in there unless I'm forced to. She may have got an idea from one of those cartoons we watched when we were children. You know the sort of thing. A fuse leads from an ironing board to a stack of baked bean cans, eventually burning through a rope and dumping a gallon of water on her head. But she would almost definitely sleep through it, so there would be no point.'

Lily hands me my mug and I carry it over to my usual table. I never used to have one, but I've been incapacitated for the past couple of months and have taken over the table in the corner at the far end of the cafe. It has a comfortable chair and gives me an excellent view of everything that's going on. Lily is good at her job, but she still needs overseeing, although I know better than to tell her that. She isn't the easiest person to manage, but I've learned how to get her to do what I want while believing it's all her own idea. I sometimes think I should write a book about stealth management. I could call it *The Invisible Hand – Secret Leadership in a Modern Environment.*

'Shelley popped in earlier,' Lily tells me. 'She saw I'd arrived, and she wanted to buy some custard doughnuts for their elevenses. Apparently, she and Victoria love them.'

'Sadly, we're fresh out of Sachertorte, which is Victoria's actual favourite.'

'We never have that,' she says. 'It isn't something that village bakeries usually stock.'

'This isn't just any village bakery,' I remind her. 'This is The Sugarloaf Bakery – world famous in The New Forest and parts of Bournemouth and Southampton. It's bursting with prestigious awards –'

'One award,' she corrects me.

'And runner up in the New Forest Bake-off. And we have our very own canine mascot!' I finish triumphantly. 'How many other bakeries in the area can say that?'

'You have me there,' she says. 'Bernie is unique.'

'He is. Speaking of whom, I can see him coming along the high street now with Mrs Ogilvie. She's wearing a sedate grey twinset and tweed skirt, whereas he's looking very smart in a bright green Argyle tank top. That must be where the term *dapper dog* comes from.'

Lily cranes to peer over my shoulder. 'Mrs Ogilvie says it's Bernie's favourite outfit. But Mabel says he has to be bribed with a biscuit to stand still whenever she wants him to wear it.'

'It's definitely worth it,' I say. 'The full effect is quite something.'

Bernie catches sight of himself in a shop door and spins around several times to see whether a strange dog is peering over his shoulder. Then he notices the bakery and takes off towards us, with Mrs Ogilvie tugging on his lead and expostulating.

'You may need to open the door and untangle Bernie before he pulls Mrs Ogilvie off her feet,' I tell Lily.

'Heaven forbid you should put down your doughnut and do it.'

I give her a hurt look. 'It has nothing to do with my doughnut, although it's only half finished. But you know I'm less quick on my feet than I used to be.'

She opens the door. It takes her a moment to sort out the lead, which Bernie has managed to tangle around both his front legs as well as Mrs Ogilvie's shopping trolley.

'Good morning,' I greet them when they're finally inside the shop. 'Isn't it a lovely day?'

'And doesn't Bernie look smart?' adds Lily.

Mrs Ogilvie looks pleased. 'It's his favourite top. He couldn't wear it yesterday because it was in the wash. He was most disappointed. But I hung it on the line this morning, and it was dry by the time we set out.'

'No Mabel today?' I ask.

'She's joining us later with Phyllis and Ivy. We're meeting about the community centre. But Bernie was so full of beans, I thought I'd bring him here a little early.'

'Nathan says the committee has decided to replace the roof entirely,' I say. 'They got the quote to replace all the missing tiles and the torn waterproof membrane and realised it would only cost another couple of thousand pounds to do it properly. He says the roof is so old they thought it would be the best option.'

'I believe Mabel mentioned something of the sort,' says Mrs Ogilvie. 'I think Bernie would like a biscuit. He knows where the basket is, don't you, darling? What a clever boy!'

I'm about to point out that if he doesn't know where it is by now, there's no hope for him. But I catch Lily's eye and think better of it.

'We have some pork-and-apple flavour biscuits,' I tell Mrs Ogilvie. 'Abby has been experimenting with new flavours. She said she's been making beef and basil and lamb and rosemary for long enough.'

She looks alarmed. 'I hope she doesn't stop making those entirely. Bernie is very fond of them. He has a sensitive stomach and doesn't adapt to change well. I doubt he'll want to try these new-fangled biscuits.'

'Let's see, shall we?' says Lily. 'I'm sure we have a couple of the original ones left at the bottom of the basket if Bernie doesn't like these.'

She holds out a biscuit to Bernie, who snatches it out of her hand and retires under the nearest table to make its better acquaintance.

'I hope it doesn't disagree with him,' says Mrs Ogilvie anxiously.

'I doubt it will say anything at all to him,' I tell her. 'It's too busy being eaten.'

She looks confused. 'I'm talking about his stomach.'

Lily shoots me a warning glance, and I grin back at her. 'His stomach will be fine. It's too late, if not. He's finished it.'

'Oh, Bernie,' she chides him. 'What have we said about chewing our food several times and not taking too large bites?'

Bernie tips his head on one side as he considers this. He gives a quick shake of the head as though to say he doesn't believe such a conversation ever occurred, lays his head on his paws, and goes to sleep.

'We'll keep an eye on him,' Lily assures Mrs Ogilvie. 'But Abby checked all the ingredients with the vet before trying the new recipe.'

Mrs Ogilvie's face relaxes. 'Robyn?'

'That's right. She was in here last week, and Abby stopped by her table to ask her advice.'

'Robyn is an excellent vet,' pronounces Mrs Ogilvie. 'I took Bernie to see her when he fell into a ditch recently. She was most reassuring. She checked him all over and said he only had a couple of scratches. She gave me a tube of ointment and told me to apply it twice a day until they were healed. Bernie didn't like me doing it, so Mabel fed him bits of chicken to distract him. I thought he might have been suffering from shock, but Robyn said he's a very resilient dog with great strength of character.'

I cram the last piece of doughnut into my mouth so I'm not tempted to make any of the amusing comments hovering on the tip of my tongue.

'Bernie's a real character,' agrees Lily. 'That's why we chose him as our mascot.'

'We're thinking of having his portrait painted for the bakery wall,' I say.

Mrs Ogilvie looks delighted. 'What a wonderful idea! I don't know whether he would sit still for long enough to be painted, but I have that beautiful photograph of him that Will took for my eightieth birthday. Perhaps the artist could use that for inspiration?'

'Great idea!' I say. 'Do you think we should have him painted full length or just a headshot?'

She purses her lips. 'That's difficult to say. A headshot might be more dignified. And Bernie has a lot of dignity.'

'He does,' agrees Lily before I can speak. I'm not sure what she thinks I'm about to say.

'But he's also very lively, with a big personality,' adds Mrs Ogilvie. 'It's very difficult to decide.'

Bernie opens one sleepy eye and grins up at us. He appears to debate with himself whether it's worth summoning up the energy to trot over to the counter and demand another biscuit, but obviously decides it isn't and falls asleep again.

Lily gives me another of her looks – the one that says I should refrain from making the sort of suggestions our customers take seriously and that make extra work for her. It's a look she gives me fairly often, although I'm not sure why. I'm a huge fan of providing an enhanced customer experience, and my suggestions and ideas are an important part of that.

I've been working with Lily for eight years now, and I like to think I can read and interpret her looks pretty well. There's her mildly concerned expression that means she's considering calling in reinforcements to subdue me by force if need be. And her look of intense concentration that means she's planning her next holiday.

In her turn, she's learned to take my written warnings more seriously and never to bother me with difficult conversations before my first doughnut of the day. It's like being an old married couple, except she doesn't help me pay my grocery bills or keep my feet warm at night.

Chapter Three

The bakery door opens, and a group of women enters. They're led by Mavis Sotherby, who looks like a sheepdog herding a flock of badly-behaved sheep. My uncle has two working dogs at his farm, both of them well-trained and hardworking, but neither of them is half as efficient as Mavis. She heads up the Silver Surfers and keeps them in order by the sheer force of her personality.

I take great care to stay on her good side. She has plenty of excellent qualities, but she doesn't like unnecessary humour or time-wasting. I'm rarely guilty of either of those things, but it's best not to take any risks.

'Good morning,' says Lily when the last sheep has been safely herded inside. 'We've been expecting you.'

'I've told you before that you should say that while stroking a white cat,' says Mabel.

'We don't have any cats,' I tell her. 'Lily and I thought about getting one a while back – at least, I did – but we didn't want to leave it alone in the bakery overnight.'

'If I remember correctly, you offered to sleep here each night to keep it company,' says Lily. 'But I told you our profits are small enough with you eating half the stock during the day. We'd be bankrupt within a week if I let you move in entirely.'

'It would lower our insurance premiums,' I say. 'Our broker would be delighted to know there was a responsible caretaker on our premises both night and day.'

I wave to Bernie. 'You could come and join me. I could train you as a security guard.'

'I don't think he'd like that,' says Mrs Ogilvie. 'He's never slept away from home.'

'He wouldn't be sleeping,' I say. 'He'd be on patrol. We could buy him a peaked cap and a high-vis vest. He'd look very smart.'

She visibly wavers, and Mabel gives one of her infectious chuckles. 'You have my vote. I can barely remember how it feels to get a full night's sleep. The mutt is either scratching at my door at 3 a.m. looking for something he's convinced he left in my room, or he's barking at imaginary mice. It's like living with a badly-behaved toddler.'

Mrs Ogilvie's face turns pink. 'I might say the same of you. A packet of biscuits used to last me at least two weeks before you moved in. Nowadays, I'm lucky if it lasts for two days. And don't try to blame that on Bernie. He's a clever dog, but he can't reach the top shelf of the larder.'

'Neither can I,' says Mabel. 'Why do you think I keep that step ladder handy? Although if you don't believe dogs can climb, you're wrong. I went to the circus in Melbourne once and saw a whole horde of dogs dancing up and down a flight of steps, barking the national anthem.'

'I could train Bernie to do that,' I say. 'Not the Australian one. That would confuse everyone who heard him. But I'm sure he'd learn the British one very quickly. It would give us both something to do during the long night watches.'

'You're welcome to him,' says Mabel. 'I think it's an excellent plan.'

Mrs Ogilvie opens her mouth to answer, but Lily forestalls her.

'Why don't we push these two tables together?' she asks. 'Then you can all sit in one place, and Bernie won't have to move.'

She smiles at Mrs Ogilvie and holds out the chair for her. 'Bernie wouldn't enjoy being a security guard, but I agree with Isabella he'd look lovely in a little cap. And I'm sure he'd learn his duties very quickly.'

Mrs Ogilvie's flush subsides. 'He knows a lot of tricks. He's a very clever dog.'

'You call everything he does a trick,' says Mabel, taking a seat opposite her and leaning down to scratch Bernie's ears. 'But I won't insist on the security guard thing. I daresay you and I would miss him if he weren't there at night, running around the house making a nuisance of himself by growling at rodents.'

'Isabella, why don't you take the cake orders?' asks Lily. 'And I'll make the drinks.'

'What's today's meeting about?' I ask. 'Are you here to discuss the latest thing in computer software?'

'We did that at last week's meeting,' says Ivy. 'Graham gave us a most interesting talk about spreadsheets.'

'I still need one of you to lend me your notes,' says Mabel. 'It was extremely warm in the village hall, and I almost nodded off.'

'Almost!' scoffs Barb. 'I was sitting four rows behind you, and I was tempted to throw something at you. It was worse than Geoff's chainsaw. I could hardly hear what Graham was saying about printing reports.'

'That was the mutt,' says Mabel unblushingly. 'He'd slept for the entire afternoon, but he never says no to another nap. I think he needs his adenoids seeing to. You might mention it to Robyn the next time you see her, Edie. She'll probably give you something to squirt up his nose like that stuff you use when your sinuses are playing up.'

'There's nothing wrong with Bernie's adenoids,' says Mrs Ogilvie. 'He had his annual check-up last Friday. Robyn said she'd rarely seen a dog in such perfect health.'

'She has to say that. You single-handedly keep that practice in profit. You and the mutt are in there almost every week.'

'The staff likes to see him,' says Mrs Ogilvie. 'And Bernie loves to pop in when we pass so he can jump on the scales.'

Mabel rolls her eyes. 'That's because they give him a treat whenever he goes in. Although they won't do that for much longer. He'll be breaking their scales soon with the amount of snacks he eats, and you'll get the invoice. Equipment like that doesn't come cheap. You and Bernie will be on bread and water for months until the bill's paid.'

'Won't you be joining them to show solidarity?' I ask.

She gives a shout of laughter. 'Not a hope! It's the mutt's solidarity that's the problem here. And that has nothing to do with me. I put up with him as a housemate, but only because I have no choice in the matter. I refuse to be put on starvation rations because he can't stay out of the biscuit tin.'

'My sister would say much the same thing,' I agree. 'She'd allow me to go in rags and live in a cardboard box before she'd lift a finger to help me. But I doubt it will come to that in your case. Bernie looks the perfect size and weight to me.'

'He is,' says Mrs Ogilvie. 'Robyn is very pleased with him. Which is more than I can say about Dr Mitchell and Mabel. He said her cholesterol was too high and told her she needed to watch her diet.'

'Traitor!' says Mabel. 'That's confidential medical information. I could sue you for making it public.'

'You told us all about it at our last meeting,' says Barb. 'Why don't you two call it quits and agree both you and Bernie are perfect just as you are?'

I smile at Lily as I put the various cakes onto the plates and carry them over to the table. The Silver Surfers are some of my favourite customers. They're just as good company as the Poker Club, and they've never relieved me of a week's wages.

'Do you have a written agenda for today's meeting?' I ask Ivy, handing her a cherry slice.

'We're here to discuss the budget for the arts centre,' says Mavis. 'We're having a few difficulties with it.'

Bernie lifts his head and gives a hopeful bark when I set Mabel's plum slice in front of her.

'Don't even think about it,' she tells him. 'I have no doubt you've already talked my sister into buying you a biscuit. Probably several. Now it's my turn.'

'He was testing out our newest flavour,' I tell her. 'Pork and apple. Abby is feeling creative, and she's decided we should start offering a wider selection again. We used to change the flavours each week, but we're so busy these days there never seems to be enough time for all the things we want to do. But nothing's too good for our mascot, is it, Bernie?'

Mrs Ogilvie looks up from her cup of tea. 'Bernie is having his portrait painted.'

Mabel almost chokes on her slice. 'What did you say?'

'His portrait. Isabella was telling me before you arrived that she and Lily were planning to have it done.'

'I did say that,' I agree, as everyone turns to look at me. 'But I'm not sure when we'll have time to arrange it. As I say, we're always so busy in here.'

'Bernie's schedule is flexible,' Mrs Ogilvie assures me.

'I've never met anyone less flexible,' says Mabel. 'And I've lived with you for years. The mutt rules our household with a rod of iron. He has to have his walk at the same time every day, and we all know the fuss he makes if his meals don't arrive exactly on time. Which wouldn't be too bad if there weren't so many of them. My entire life is ruled by his timetable. I can't even watch my favourite programmes in the evenings without having them approved by the mutt first.'

'Bernie's very sensitive,' Mrs Ogilvie defends him. 'He doesn't enjoy all those nasty violent things you like to watch, especially right before bedtime.'

I look at Mabel with interest, wondering what she's been watching. Knowing her, it could be anything from a programme about taxidermy to a documentary on serial killers.

She gives another crack of laughter. 'It was an Agatha Christie film! You didn't even see the murder happen. It was all over by the time Poirot arrived and found the body.'

'Bernie doesn't like that sort of thing,' says Mrs Ogilvie. 'He prefers travel programmes. He loved the one he saw last week about Portofino.'

Mabel rolls her eyes. 'No one would ever take us for twins.'

'Apart from the fact you look exactly alike?' I ask.

'We used to,' she agrees. 'I'm not sure we still do. Edie has a permanently worried expression, whereas I'm carefree and spontaneous.'

'You'd look worried if you had to deal with all your nonsense,' says Mrs Ogilvie.

I raise my hand to give her a high five, remember she doesn't know what they are and may think I'm about to assault her, and lower it again, trying to pretend I was scratching my ear.

'You seem to get along very well,' says Lily, always the peacemaker. 'It's lovely having Mabel living in the village. And Bernie is certainly delighted. He loves company, don't you, Bernie?'

He isn't listening. He's sitting next to Mabel's chair, watching her eat the plum slice and trying to give the impression of a dog who hasn't been fed for days but is far too well-mannered to deprive anyone of their food unless they really, really want to share with him.

Mabel grins at him and flicks him the last few crumbs. 'You're like the church bells – annoying on a day-to-day basis, but we'd miss you if you weren't there. Are you really thinking of having his portrait painted?'

'It was Isabella's idea,' says Lily. 'I'm leaving all the details to her.'

'We can talk about that some other time,' I say. 'I'd hate to interrupt the flow of your meeting.'

'What sort of portrait did you have in mind?' asks Mary with interest. 'And who's going to do it?'

All eyes turn to me. I'm about to brush off the question with a light comment when I see Mrs Ogilvie's face has lit up, as it always does at any mention of Bernie.

I try to catch Lily's eye, but she's carefully not looking at me. I make a note to have a word with her later about her lack of collegiate spirit. Maybe I'll give her a written warning.

'We haven't finalised the details yet,' I say when it becomes clear she isn't about to dig me out of the hole into which I inexplicably appear to have tumbled. 'But we'll let you know once it's all settled.'

'Will you ask someone from the arts centre to do it when it opens?' asks Barb. 'Are any of the volunteers professional artists?'

I assume my most sphinx-like expression. 'As I say, nothing is set in stone yet.'

'Will they be offering sculpture lessons too?' asks Mavis. 'Sign me up if they are! I've wanted to try my hand at that ever since I saw a programme about Michelangelo's David.'

Her eye falls on Bernie. 'I could try making a sculpture of you, only you wouldn't sit still for long enough.'

'You aren't making an indecent statue of Bernie!' protests her sister.

'Who said anything about an indecent statue? Not that David is anything of the sort. He's art, which is a very different thing. Anyway, dogs never get fully undressed, so you don't need to worry about that.'

'I wouldn't mind having a go at pottery if it's on offer,' says Barb. 'I've always wanted to try that.'

'Have you been watching Ghost again?' asks Phyllis, and the pair of them collapse into giggles.

'I don't know what kind of classes they'll be offering at the arts centre,' I say before Mrs Ogilvie can demand an explanation of this, or Mabel can offer one. 'But I'm glad you're all so enthusiastic. The village has worked so hard to raise the money to buy that building. It would be a shame if no one signed up for any of the classes.'

'No fear of that,' says Mabel. 'I intend to sign up for everything. It will get me out of the house, and I'm keen to unleash my inner creativity. I've been convinced for a while now that I have hidden artistic talents. This will be the perfect opportunity to find out. If I have to start with a sculpture of the mutt, so be it.'

'You aren't using Bernie as a subject,' says Mrs Ogilvie. 'I won't sign the release form.'

Mabel grins. 'Listen to you talking as though he's some famous model. You'll be telling me next he has an agent.'

'I'm sure he could get an agent if he wanted to,' says Lily, noticing Mrs Ogilvie's flushed cheeks. 'But why would he? He's much happier just as he is, aren't you, Bernie? The showbiz life isn't for everyone.'

'Chance would be a fine thing,' says Mabel. 'They only use properly trained dogs in the movies. Can you imagine Lassie digging in her heels and refusing to rescue the person who'd fallen down a well until she'd been offered a beef-and-basil biscuit?'

Mrs Ogilvie's cheeks are turning pinker by the moment. Their argument is interrupted by a musical chime. The bakery door opens again, and a tall, fair-haired man walks in.

I wink at Lily. 'Yet again – saved by the bell!'

Chapter Four

'Good morning,' says Lily, setting down the last cup and wiping her hands on her apron.

I wait for her to add, 'Welcome to The Sugarloaf Bakery. How may I help you today?' But she doesn't. I'm not sure why. It's in the staff handbook. But none of my colleagues ever appears to read it, much less consult it daily and treat it as what it is – the compilation of all the wisdom I've gained from so many years in the bakery industry.

Nor does she add each time our customers leave, 'Thank you for visiting The Sugarloaf Bakery. I hope your experience was everything you hoped for.' Sometimes, I wonder why I bother. Working with me must be like spending the day alongside Sheryl Sandberg, yet no one ever seems to take advantage of it.

'I was told I might find some doughnuts if I came in here,' says the man.

I fight the urge to tell him I have no idea what put such a ridiculous notion into his head, and he should try the hardware store. Lily doesn't like it when I do that kind of thing, although I can't think why not. It might teach people not to say stupid things.

But I don't need the hassle, so I point to our display of doughnuts. 'Not just some doughnuts – the best doughnuts in town.'

'You mean the village,' says Lily.

'I do not! I mean town. But that's being modest. I could easily have said in the New Forest area, or the whole of Hampshire. Or,' I continue, warming to my theme, 'the entire south of England.'

'That's a bold claim!' says the man with what I hope is an impressed smile.

'But it's one I can very easily make good. Buy half a dozen of our doughnuts. If they're not the best you've ever tasted, we'll refund your money. No questions asked.'

I catch Lily's eye. 'Half your money. And no more than five questions asked.'

He laughs. 'How can I resist such a tempting offer? But we don't need half a dozen doughnuts. There are only three of us.'

'A dozen, then.'

'I mean, I only need three doughnuts.'

'I don't understand,' I say. 'You told me there were three of you.'

'That's right.'

'But you went on to say you only need three doughnuts. I'm an accountant, which means I have an exceptionally deep understanding of numbers. But this particular calculation has me in a puzzle.'

Lily picks up the cake tongs. 'Please don't listen to my colleague. Which flavours would you like?'

'Dealer's choice,' he says.

I try again. 'We have six flavours. If you plan to give our product a fair trial before exercising your right to make a claim on our extremely generous refund policy, you need to buy at least one of each. Personally, I'd have said all three of you should try all six flavours before making a judgement, but I'm aware not everyone sees things the way I do.'

'I'll give you an apple, a strawberry, and a blackcurrant,' says Lily, placing them in a paper bag. 'If you want to try our other flavours at any point, you know where to find us.'

He taps his card on the reader. 'I'm Simon, by the way. I'm working just down the road at the new arts centre. If these doughnuts are as good as you claim, I'm sure I'll be seeing you again.'

'They're better than we claim,' I say. 'That's the secret of all good businesses – over-promise and under-perform. Actually, I think that might be the other way around, but you get the general idea.'

He smiles at me. 'I do indeed. Maybe I'll see you sooner rather than later to claim my refund.'

'Partial refund,' I correct him because it's as well to get things straight from the outset. 'And you won't be claiming any sort of refund. You have my word as a doughnut connoisseur.'

'Isabella is absolutely right,' says Mabel loyally.

'Right about what?' Simon asks her.

'She eats a lot of doughnuts.'

I wait until he's left before giving Mabel a reproachful look. 'That was uncalled for.'

'What was?'

'Telling him I ate a lot of doughnuts.'

'It's true, isn't it?' asks Ivy.

I turn my head slightly so I can include her in my reproachful look. 'In my capacity as small business owner and quality control tester for a baked goods emporium, I may possibly –'

'Give it up,' advises Lily. 'Everyone is fully aware of the hundreds of reasons you're forced to eat so many cakes and the daily sacrifices you make to keep this business running.'

'That's very true,' says Barb.

'Thank you,' I say.

'You tell us almost every time we come in here,' she adds.

I shake my head more in sorrow than in anger. 'I've said it before, and I'll say it again. It's no picnic running this sort of business.'

'I'd have said it was a permanent picnic for you, Isabella,' says Ivy, and they all burst out laughing.

'Does anyone need a refill?' Lily chips in before I can make any of the more than justified comments hovering on the tip of my tongue.

'I saw Simon at The Red Lion this morning,' says Barb. 'He was standing at the bar talking to Nathan.'

'Day drinking is a terrible thing,' I say. 'Do you think that's why he needed the doughnuts – to mop up the alcohol?'

'He didn't look drunk to me,' says Mabel. 'And believe me, I've had plenty of experience.'

'None of us has any difficulty at all in believing that,' says Ivy.

'I'm not referring to myself!' says Mabel. 'I may have had the odd rowdy night out in my youth, but I'm talking about my restaurant in Melbourne. It was situated right between the pub and the main train station. We did a brisk trade in takeaways on a Saturday night, I can tell you.'

'I'm never sure how many of your stories about your time in Australia are true,' I say. 'Do they still require you to possess a criminal record before you can apply for a visa?'

She gives a snort of laughter. 'How old do you think I am? Next you'll be saying you think I went over on one of the old transportation ships.'

'Mabel flew British Airways,' says Mrs Ogilvie. 'We went up to London to see her off.'

'To make sure she left, you mean,' says Barb. 'I don't blame you. I'd have done the same thing in your place. Yet here she is – as large as life and several times as loud. It's a mystery.'

'Planes fly both ways,' says Mabel. 'And so did I. Don't change the subject, Isabella. We were talking about the young man who was just in here, not my life history. He was very good looking, wasn't he?'

'Trust you to notice that,' says Barb.

'I'm eighty-five not dead,' says Mabel. 'I can appreciate a handsome, well-proportioned man as well as the next person. More, in fact. I think it may have something to do with that dormant talent for art I was telling you about earlier.'

'I didn't notice how good-looking he was,' I say. 'But that was because I was distracted by his appalling mathematical skills.'

'What mathematical skills?' asks Lily.

'Exactly! And he didn't even have the grace to be ashamed of his ignorance. One might have thought a man of his age would be aware of his weaknesses and attempt to hide them from complete strangers. But he seemed quite happy to announce he was buying for three people, yet he only wanted three doughnuts. Someone ought to buy the poor man a calculator for Christmas.'

'Not everyone feels the need to eat their food in multiples of five,' says Lily.

'I know what I meant to ask,' says Phyllis. 'What was Barb doing at the pub earlier? Surely she hasn't started morning drinking too?'

'I have not,' says Barb. 'I popped in to give Victoria my aunt's recipe for barmbrack. I was telling her about it last week, and I promised to write it out for her.'

'Write it out?' scoffs Mabel. 'Anyone would think you hadn't been a member of the Silver Surfers for the past ten years. What's wrong with sending the girl an email with a PDF attachment?'

'No one emails any more,' says Phyllis. 'It's all instant messaging nowadays. You may as well ask why Barb didn't pick up the phone, call the exchange, and ask them to put her through to The Red Lion.'

'Ladies!' says Mavis.

She never raises her voice, but the group immediately falls quiet – even Mabel. I wish I knew how she does it. I'd love to control the staff of The Sugarloaf Bakery with nothing more than a lift of an eyebrow and a single quiet word. It's as much as I can do to maintain order by the force of my sparkling personality. It's most dispiriting. Still, practise makes perfect, and I hope one day to learn the trick. I must ask Mavis sometime whether she went to management school or whether she was born with it.

'I would appreciate it if you could save this discussion for another time,' she says. 'We are meeting today to talk about the finances for the arts centre. As most of you know, we are having difficulty in balancing the books. The roof was in a worse condition than we expected, and we had to spend rather more on it than we'd budgeted for. That means we have less money available for the rewiring and decorating than we'd hoped.'

'Aren't we getting it all done at a discount?' asks Ivy. 'Bob told me his friend at the council had recommended a firm who were willing to give you ten percent off.'

'We are,' says Mavis. 'But the extra for the roof still leaves us more than two thousand pounds short. Either we have to raise the extra money or negotiate ourselves a better deal.'

'That would be the easiest thing to do,' I say. 'The village is pretty much tapped out by now. Everyone has worked so hard to fund-raise. I'm not sure anyone is in the mood for yet another sponsored event. And my uncle's garden is still recovering from the ball. I doubt he'll want to hold another large event before his annual garden party.'

'Quite so,' says Mavis. 'So, we need to persuade the contractors to lower their costs. Does anyone have a suggestion as to how we can do that?'

'I could go and talk to them,' says Mabel. 'I could pretend to slip on something on the building site and threaten to sue them for everything they've got if they don't bring down their price.'

'No, you couldn't,' says her sister. 'That would be dishonest.'

'I wouldn't go that far,' says Mabel. 'But if it makes you feel better, I could actually slip and hurt myself.'

'How would that make me feel better?' asks Mrs Ogilvie. 'I don't want you lying in bed for months, making me run around after you.'

Mabel grins. 'I don't see why not. You run around all day after the hell-hound, pandering to his every whim. I wouldn't make much more work for you.'

'If you do that, you'll have to find somewhere else to stay until you're better. I mean it, Mabel.'

'Oh, very well,' sighs Mabel. 'I don't suppose any of you would like to put me up for a while?'

She glances around at the assembled company, who all shake their heads.

'Fine set of friends you've turned out to be,' she grumbles. 'I'd have done it for any of you. What's wrong with my idea? No one said anything when Isabella did it.'

I feel impelled to chip in here, if only to clear my reputation. 'I had a genuine accident. I didn't deliberately tangle my foot in a wire so I could claim compensation. Surely you can see the difference?'

'Not really,' she says. 'But I can tell there's no point in arguing. Does anyone have a better idea?'

'I do,' says Phyllis. 'Let's send Isabella.'

'Send me where?' I ask.

'To The Red Lion to talk to whoever's managing it all.'

'I'm not sure I follow. If you need someone to talk to the manager, Shelley or Nathan are the obvious choices. They're living on site, and they must have a much clearer idea than I do what's going on.'

'I think it's a wonderful idea,' says Ivy. 'Isabella has the gift of the gab. If anyone can persuade the company to lower their prices, it's her.'

'I don't know anything about building works,' I object.

'You didn't know anything about running a bakery when you started, but you picked it up quickly enough,' says Lily.

'Et tu, Lily?' I ask. 'If there was anyone I might have counted on to support me, I thought it would have been you. I expected you to tell these good people that I'm too indispensable to the business for you to allow me to leave the premises for even ten minutes.'

'You went to have your hair cut yesterday afternoon,' she reminds me. 'And the building didn't fall down.'

'And you've already met one of the people concerned,' adds Barb. 'So, it isn't as though you'll be talking to complete strangers.'

'The man who was in here just now?' I ask.

'That's what I was trying to tell you all. I saw him at the pub this morning. Shelley told me he's the architect. She said he's here for a few days to liaise with the project manager. You've already had a pleasant conversation with him about doughnuts. All you have to do is pick up the threads and move the discussion towards plumbing and electrical bills. Nothing could be easier.'

'I don't see the connection,' I say. 'Doughnuts are doughnuts. Plumbing and wiring is a completely different thing.'

'I thought you'd be glad to help out,' says Barb. 'You're always so community-spirited.'

They all turn to look at me, and I feel myself waver.

'I *am* community-spirited,' I say. 'But I usually confine myself to offering refreshments and wise advice. However, if you're all so set on it, I'll give it a go.'

'I knew we could rely on you,' says Mavis with an approving smile, and I wonder whether this was all planned in advance.

'I feel a little ambushed,' I tell her.

'Nonsense,' she says. 'It was just fortuitous that someone suggested it, and you happened to be here. Are we all finished, ladies? Then we should leave Lily and Isabella to get on with the rest of their morning in peace.'

Chapter Five

I set off from the bakery the following morning carrying a pink-and-white- striped box. Lily and I have decided to open negotiations with cake. It's always my weapon of choice. Once there, it will be up to me to use my ingenuity to direct the conversation into the appropriate channels.

'I feel like Red Riding Hood,' I tell Lily as I close the lid of the box.

'I'm not sure why. She didn't wear jeans and a bright yellow T shirt.'

'I mean the modern day equivalent,' I explain, wondering for the thousandth time why everyone around me has to be quite so literal.

'And isn't it Little Red Riding Hood?' she asks, opening the bakery door for me.

'What is?'

'The thing people always call her. Not just Red Riding Hood.'

'But I'm not little,' I say. 'I'm quite tall.'

'I know you are.'

'So, the people in the fairy tale would just have called me Red Riding Hood.'

She doesn't look convinced. 'Why do you feel like her, anyway?'

'Because of these cakes. She went skipping through the forest without a care in the world, carrying provisions for her grandmother. I believe the story says it was a basket, but a box would have done just as well.'

'Not if she tripped and fell,' she says. 'A basket would have been better in that case.'

'I have no intention of tripping and falling between here and The Red Lion. My leg is back to normal now. I met Matthew and Victoria for a drink last week, and he told me he'd never known anyone recover so quickly from a broken bone. He said I was a medical miracle.'

'I was there,' she says. 'You might not have noticed my presence because you were too busy studying the bar menu. What Matthew actually said was that you were doing fine.'

'That isn't how I remember it. Anyway, I can't stand around here all day talking about your false memories. I have a long journey ahead of me and a box of cakes to carry safely through the perils of Honeywell High Street.'

She holds the door a little wider and motions me through. 'Give my regards to your grandmother.'

'My grandmother is in Corfu for a month. She's staying with my Great Aunt Tabitha. But I'll be sure to pass on your greetings the next time I see her.'

I set off along the high street, careful to hold the box level. It would be a terrible thing if any of the meringues were to be crushed. Abby took them out of the oven earlier this morning and filled them with Chantilly cream. I hope the recipients are grateful. I was tempted to fill the box with lesser cakes, but Lily and I agreed the situation is grave enough to warrant bringing out the big guns. If Abby's meringues and eclairs don't do the trick, nothing will.

I reach The Red Lion a few minutes later.

'Good morning!' Nathan greets me as I open the door. 'Have you come to visit Victoria? She's in the kitchen with my mum.'

'I'd love to have a chat with her later,' I say. 'But I'm here to talk to whoever's working on the new building.'

'I don't know who's in today. I usually pop over around eleven o'clock to ask whether anyone would like a drink.'

'That seems a little early,' I say, and he grins.

'I'm talking about tea and coffee. I know better than to offer alcohol to people working on a construction site. To do them justice, I don't think they'd take me up on the offer. They're very strict about rules over there. They don't let anyone near the place unless they're wearing a hard hat.'

I look down at the box of cakes. 'I'm hoping they'll make an exception for me. I've brought some of Abby's famous meringues.'

He shakes his head. 'Not a hope. But I have a spare hat behind the bar if you'd like to borrow it.'

I hesitate. The whole idea of coming here is to charm whoever's in charge into offering us a reduction in the price of the repairs. And a hard hat isn't the most glamorous of accessories. I dressed more carefully than usual this morning. I even allowed Lily to fasten back my hair with a sparkly clip.

If I hadn't made a dart for the door, she might have insisted I leaned more fully into the Little Red Riding Hood theme. Not that we have any cloaks hanging around the premises, but I saw her old red duffle coat hanging on its peg, and I wasn't taking any chances.

'Fine,' I say. 'I'll wear your stupid hat if it makes them happy.'

'Here you are,' he says, reaching over the bar and producing a bright yellow construction hat. 'It should fit you alright if you bundle your hair inside it.'

This was definitely not the idea when I carefully brushed my hair this morning and allowed Lily to decorate me like a Christmas tree. But I can see I have no choice, so I set down the cakes and cram the hat onto my head. So much for Lily's hair clip. I'm not sure why she was so insistent on me wearing it unless she thought it would flash and sparkle in the light and dazzle the unwitting construction crew into submission. It's certainly an idea – just not a very good one. For one thing, it would depend on there being a suitable light source. For another, I'd have to hold my head at exactly the right angle for the sparkles to entrance the onlookers without causing permanent damage to their eyesight.

'I won't be long,' I tell Nathan, picking up my box of cakes.

'Wouldn't you prefer to leave those here?' he asks. 'I could keep a close eye on them for you.'

'I'm sure you would. Like the wolf.'

'What wolf?' he asks, puzzled.

'The one in the forest,' I say enigmatically and make my way towards the garden door before he can ask any further questions.

It's a beautiful June day, and I pause for a moment to enjoy the sunshine. One of the worst things about working in a bakery is that you can't drop everything and wander outside whenever the sun shines. I often suggest closing the shop on sunny days, but Lily always vetoes the idea, saying our customers can't be expected to restrict their bread- and cake-buying to grey and rainy days. I'm not convinced they couldn't be trained to do that, but Lily is the most stubborn women I've ever met, and it's never any use arguing with her.

'Don't kick it over the fence!'

A ball flies over my head, and two young boys appear from nowhere. One minute, I'm peacefully minding my own business and enjoying the cry of the lapwing and the beautiful tortoiseshell butterflies fluttering around my head. The next, I'm almost knocked off my feet by a low-flying ball. I'm all for constant variety in life, but I prefer it not to involve more than one broken bone per year.

'Sorry!' gasps a fair-haired boy as they rush past me.

'Ollie, Toby!' shouts a man's voice from somewhere nearby. 'Don't go near the water!'

'We won't!' they call back in unison.

I wait to see what will happen next. When nothing does, I abandon my observations of the local wildlife and continue walking through the pub garden towards what should soon be our new arts centre.

I was expecting to find a swarm of tradespeople milling around with axes and hammers, busily knocking nails into window frames. I've seen enough movies about barn-raisings to know how it's done. But either they've all gone off for their coffee break, or today is national don't-take-your-tradesperson-to-work-day. There's no sign of anyone working on the building, which is disappointing. Lily and I toil ceaselessly each day to make a success of our business. It would be nice to see other people doing the same with theirs.

I walk towards the main entrance. Far from looking like a work in progress, it looks much as it always has – an L-shaped brick building standing a little way from the pub, with a small courtyard in front. I peer in at the nearest window and see three people studying a roll of paper spread out on a trestle table. One of the two men is pointing to something as he talks. I recognise him as the man who came into the bakery yesterday – the one with the surprisingly poor appetite.

A red-haired young woman is holding another roll of papers and looking bored. I don't blame her. It wouldn't be my ideal way of spending a morning. I can't see much of the third person. He's half hidden by a stack of boxes. They're brown and square and don't appear to contain anything interesting. Not like my pink-and-white-striped cake box. Even before you look inside, you can tell it's full of something exciting.

Lily says they used plain boxes when she first started working at the bakery, but she persuaded Mr Mason to order some pretty striped ones, and the business never looked back. Those increased profits also coincided with the pair of us buying the bakery, so you can't necessarily make the connection, but I'm sure the new cake boxes had something to do with it.

Time to do what I came here for. I walk around to the door, which has been propped open with a fire extinguisher. There's no need to lock it as there's nothing here to steal. The entire space has been gutted to prepare for the renovations. So, unless someone is interested in stealing a stack of empty boxes or a couple of ceiling rafters, there isn't much to attract burglars. I'm carrying the most valuable thing in the place.

I walk along the narrow passageway towards the room where I saw the three of them working. I tread as softly as possible in order to make the surprise I'm bringing them seem even more unexpected and wonderful. I remember my mother telling me when I was younger that you only get one chance to make a first impression, so you should always make sure it's a good one.

I'm not too worried. It's impossible not to make a good impression when you arrive bearing cakes. I reach the doorway and step inside, holding out the box with my most winning smile.

Something catches my foot and twists around my ankle. I lose my balance and start to fall. I fight to maintain both my equilibrium and the precious cakes, but it's no good. My leg is mostly healed now, but I'm still having physiotherapy, and my reflexes aren't as quick as they used to be.

Three startled faces turn towards me as my leg buckles, and I topple forwards. I hit the ground with a crash, and the box flies out of my hands. I can only watch in horror as it rises in a graceful arc before crashing to the floor – all the beautiful meringues, eclairs and turnovers landing in a creamy mess right in front of my eyes.

Chapter Six

'What on earth is going on?' says a man's voice.

I peer up to see who's speaking, but his face is nothing more than a blur. For a moment, I wonder whether I've hit my head. Concussion can cause loss of vision. I learned that when I ended up in the hospital only a few months ago, after being knocked unconscious in a bakery accident. I prefer not to think about it in too much detail, which is fortunate because I couldn't if I wanted to, having banged my head and passed out cold at the start of the incident. When people ask me what happened, I tell them I was injured in the line of duty and glare at Lily whenever she attempts to offer more details.

'Can I help you up?' asks a second voice I recognise as Simon's.

'I mustn't move,' I tell him. 'I can't see properly, so I may have brain damage.'

'You have cream in your eyes,' says the first voice. 'You can't possibly have a brain injury because you didn't hit your head.'

'Are you a doctor?' I ask.

'I'm Jon, the project manager.'

I wipe my eyes on my sleeve, relieved to find my vision miraculously restored. But that doesn't mean this man is correct.

'Unless you're a medical project manager,' I say, 'you have no right to tell people whether or not they're injured.'

Simon bends down to look at me. 'Where does it hurt?'

'Nowhere,' I admit. 'But that isn't conclusive. I may be numb from paralysis.'

The flicker of a smile passes over his face, but he quickly composes himself. 'Can I get you a chair?'

'I'd prefer you to rescue my cakes. Where did the box go?'

'Over here,' says the woman.

She lifts the lid and looks inside. 'There are a couple of cakes still in here – a little squashed, but nothing too serious. The rest of them are scattered around the room.'

I sigh. 'And we packed them all so carefully.'

'Didn't we meet at the bakery?' asks Simon. 'It's difficult to tell under all that cream, but I'm almost sure I saw you when I came in yesterday to buy doughnuts.'

'That's right,' I say, scrambling to my feet and holding out my hand to him. I think better of it when I realise it's covered with jam. 'I'm Isabella Campbell – one of the bakery owners.'

'The one who offers free cakes,' he says. 'I remember.'

'Not free cakes! Refunds if our customers aren't satisfied.'

'Isn't that the same thing?' asks Jon.

'Not at all. Our customers always are satisfied, so we never need to make good on our pledge.'

Honesty compels me to add. 'Except for one customer, but she'd complain whether or not we made the offer, so she doesn't count.'

The woman has picked up the stray cakes while we've been talking and disappeared with them. Perhaps she plans to eat them before I can demand them back. She returns a minute later holding a cloth. 'I thought you might like to clean yourself up a bit.'

'Thank you,' I say, taking it from her and scrubbing my face and hands.

'So, what's the story behind these particular cakes?' asks Jon.

I'm about to tell him they're a bribe but remember in time the conversation I had with Lily before I set out.

'Don't let them think these cakes are anything more than a welcome-to-the-village gesture,' she instructed me. 'If they get the idea you're after a quid pro quo, they'll never give us what we want.'

'They're a gift from The Sugarloaf Bakery,' I tell him. 'Our way of saying how grateful we are that you're doing something so nice for the community.'

'We're just doing our job,' he says.

I'm starting to dislike this man. He didn't seem worried that I might have hurt myself when I fell. Even worse, he doesn't seem remotely concerned about the cakes. How can someone remain so indifferent after witnessing the tragic destruction of so many culinary works of art?

'It was extremely kind of you,' says Simon. 'I'm sorry they didn't arrive in perfect condition, but we can take the thought for the deed.'

I'm not sure I agree with this. I can imagine no circumstances under which the idea of cake could equal the actuality. But he's making the effort to be polite, which is more than his colleague is doing.

'Which of the cakes survived?' I ask the woman.

She lifts the lid and surveys the contents. 'Something with chocolate and a triangular pastry.'

'An eclair and an apple turnover,' I say. 'You'll have to share them between the three of you. That makes two-thirds of a cake each.'

I wait for one of them to say, 'But there are four of us.' Sadly, none of them does.

I wipe a smear of apple puree off my sleeve and fold up the cloth. 'I should find a mop and a bucket. Shelley's bound to have one in the kitchen.'

'Don't worry about that,' says Simon. 'One of us can do it later. They've stripped off all the old carpet, and they'll have to prepare the wooden floor properly before we can stain and seal it.'

I glance at the battered floorboards. 'I thought they might re-carpet it. I'm glad that isn't the plan. This wood seems to be in good condition. It should look lovely when it's finished.'

'They'll do the floor last,' he says. 'First, we have to finalise the plans for knocking down a couple of interior walls and throwing the rooms into one. That's what we were looking at when you arrived.'

I walk over to the table and study the blueprint. 'I like what you've done with the two larger rooms.'

'You shouldn't be looking at that,' says Jon. 'It's proprietary information.'

I turn to face him. 'This is a village project, and I'm a village resident. Well, almost. I live in Compton, but I work in the village. And I've worked as hard as everyone else to raise the money for this project, so I have as much right as anyone to know what you're doing. No taxation without representation!' I finish triumphantly.

He raises an eyebrow. 'Who's trying to tax you?'

'That's hardly the point. What I'm saying is that there's nothing secret about these plans.'

'Nothing at all,' he agrees.

'Then why did you tell me there was?'

'Just to see what you'd say.'

Simon interrupts before I can think of a cutting reply. 'This section here will be the main function room. And the three rooms upstairs will become art and craft rooms. We'll keep the kitchen where it is and add a second toilet where the current bathroom now is. We don't need to keep the bath and shower in place as this will no longer be a residence.'

'It looks like an excellent plan,' I say, because there's no harm in starting off on a positive note, and the plan does seem well thought out.

'The committee approved it yesterday,' he says. 'I was just running Jon through the basics so he can draw up a timetable and organise the work. Jon, this is Isabella from The Sugarloaf Bakery.'

Jon smiles at me. 'It's a good thing you didn't throw your cakes at the blueprint or Simon would have had to start all over again, and he might not have remembered what he'd drawn. You would have been single-handedly responsible for a far inferior design.'

'Didn't you prepare it on a computer?' I ask Simon.

'Of course, I did. It's backed up in the cloud and on my hard drive. Jon is just joking.'

I'm about to suggest that Jon would be better off using the time for which the village is no doubt paying him in doing his job rather than making flippant comments to complete strangers. But I remember in time why I'm here. I was expecting to talk to Simon about our budget, but he'll only direct me to the project manager. I may as well make my request directly to him. Remarks about his job performance, however well-deserved, won't achieve my objective.

So, I give them both my sweetest smile. 'Very droll. It's nice to see you're enjoying your work. I think that's so important, don't you?'

'Do you enjoy your work?' asks Jon.

'I've just told you I own a bakery. Who wouldn't enjoy that?'

'Me, for one,' he says, ignoring my shocked gasp.

The woman glances at her watch. 'I'm sorry to interrupt you, but it's eleven thirty.'

'Already?' asks Simon. 'I suppose it must be. I'd lost track of time in all the –' he looks at me with a faint smile – 'excitement.'

'I could order a taxi,' she says.

'No need. I'll take you.'

'I'd offer,' says Jon, 'except that I have to stay here with the boys.'

'I'm taking my intern over to Christchurch,' Simon tells me. 'Sorry, I should have introduced you. Isabella, this is Anne Goldberg. She's working on a project with my senior partner this afternoon. I promised to give her a ride back to the office by noon. But I think we're about done here, anyway.'

Anne smiles at me. 'Nice to meet you, Isabella.'

'You too. I'd offer to shake your hand, but mine's a bit sticky. Thank you for coming to my rescue. I hope you didn't get any cream on that lovely suit.'

'Not at all,' she assures me. 'I jumped back the minute I saw you fall. I was too far away to catch you, so –'

'Very wise,' I say. 'You must have excellent reflexes. I used to have them too, but I've been a little slower than usual since I broke my leg three months ago.'

'Was that why you tripped just now?' asks Jon.

'It was not. My leg is fine for everything except the most strenuous of exercise. I won't be rock climbing or skiing in the near future. Other than that, I'm completely healed. I tripped because of that bundle of wires next to the door. It's a complete safety hazard. I'm surprised you're allowed to keep it there.'

'We don't keep it there,' he says. 'I laid it down for a few minutes when I arrived. And it isn't a bundle of wires. It's an extension cable. I bought it on my way over here today, and I'll be taking it home with me when I leave.'

'That's no reason for you to leave it lying around where anyone could trip over it,' I argue. 'It constitutes a health and safety hazard. I know that because my partner and I have to keep our training up to date.'

'I have to keep my training up to date too,' he says. 'Speaking of health and safety, what's with the hard hat?'

I clap my hand to my head. I'd completely forgotten about that. It must have flown off when I fell over. So much for keeping my head protected.

Simon picks it up and hands it to me. I consider putting it back on my head, but there seems little point now. If this were a movie, my hat would have fallen to the floor, allowing my flowing locks to tumble becomingly around my shoulders, to the stunned admiration of all onlookers. However, judging by the amount of cream I had to wipe off my face, there will be a good amount in my hair too, acting as a kind of hair mousse. I'll have to wash it out as quickly as possible before I reach my expiry date.

'Why were you wearing the hat in the first place?' asks Jon, a smile tugging at the corners of his mouth.

'Nathan gave it to me. He said I wouldn't be allowed onto the site without it.'

'Is that so?' He looks even more amused.

'Come to think of it, where are your hats?' I ask them.

'We don't have to wear them until construction starts,' says Simon. 'As Nathan very well knows. We met with him and Shelley the first day we were here and ran them through everything that would be happening. We wanted to get their input. As I understand it, the building no longer belongs to them. But they're kindly granting us access, so we'd like to minimise the inconvenience to them.'

'You should still wear your hard hats,' I say. 'You never know when you might walk into a room to find someone has left something dangerous lying around. In fact, that's exactly what did happen –'

I remember I'm supposed to be staying on message and doing my best to charm them. There are several things I'd like to add, but now is not the time.

I summon up my most gracious smile. 'You mustn't allow me to hold you up. I'm sorry you didn't get your morning tea. You could take the leftover cakes with you. They may be a little battered, but they'll taste just as good. You could eat them on the drive over to your office.'

'That's very kind of you,' says Simon, 'but I don't want to spoil my car's interior. And it's only a short drive.'

I don't quite understand his logic. I can get hungry between the bakery and the post office. Still, I'm aware not everyone shares this view, and I'd prefer not to start an argument, so I don't press the matter.

'I'll call you this afternoon,' Jon tells him. 'We need to finalise the building regulations submission. Nice to meet you, Anne.'

'Thanks, Isabella,' says Simon. 'I hope to see you again under less … unfortunate circumstances.'

'What are the chances of you recognising me?' I ask. 'I don't intend to remain covered in cream and chocolate curls for long.'

'I don't imagine you do. But I doubt I'll have much trouble recognising you.'

He smiles and holds the door open for Anne. A moment later, they walk past the window on their way to the car park, leaving me alone with Jon – the man who puts the grump into Mr Grumpy.

Chapter Seven

'Do you plan to clean that hat?' he asks me.

'I do not. I intend to return it to Nathan exactly as it is. It serves him right for playing a trick on me.'

'Maybe it wasn't a trick,' he says. 'That was my assumption too, but having seen you in action, I've changed my mind. If he knows you well, he may have realised how accident-prone you are and done his best to protect you.'

'I am not accident-prone! Quite the opposite. I took ballet lessons as a child. My teacher said I could have taken it up professionally if I hadn't grown so tall. And if I could learn to stop talking for ten seconds and stand still,' I add in the interests of full and frank disclosure.

'I wouldn't have thought standing still was a required element for a professional ballerina,' he says. 'They're always leaping and twirling across the stage. It looks exhausting. Why they can't just walk from one side to the other is beyond me. I mean, does anyone in real life notice a friend standing at the far end of a field and start skipping and spinning their way over to them?'

'My accident had nothing to do with my grace, or lack of it,' I say, attempting to bring his mind back to the point at issue. 'Even Anna Pavlova would have come crashing down if someone had stretched a wire across the door the moment before she came in.'

'Anna who?' he asks. 'Is that a friend of yours?'

'Anna Pavlova! You must know who she is.'

'Judging by her name, I'd say she's someone big in the bakery world. Is that how you came to meet her?'

'She was a famous ballerina,' I say. 'We were talking about ballet when I mentioned her. Why would you think my mind had skipped away to the giants of the culinary scene?'

He looks from the crushed cakes on the floor to my face, from which I suspect I haven't removed the last traces of cream. 'I can't imagine.'

'Nor can I. We can try another example if it helps. What kind of sport do you watch?'

'I rarely watch sport.'

'You must watch some,' I say. 'All men do.'

'Is that right? Every single one of us?'

'Yes,' I say stubbornly. 'It's an accepted fact.'

'All four billion of us?'

'I suppose a small minority has to play,' I admit. 'Or there would be nothing for the rest of you to watch.'

'I enjoy crazy golf,' he says.

'Crazy golf?' I repeat, unable to believe my ears.

'Yes, the boys love it.'

'The boys out there?' I point towards the back of the building.

'That's right. I left them kicking a ball around while we discussed the plans. Did you meet them when you arrived?'

'We weren't formally introduced. We certainly didn't get to the stage of discussing what we enjoy doing at the weekend or exchanging tips and tricks for conquering the haunted windmill in fewer than three strokes.'

'So, you like crazy golf too?' he asks.

'I've swung the odd club in my time. Occasionally in the wrong direction. Our staff visited the local crazy golf facility for our last team-building day, but it wasn't as successful as I'd hoped.'

'I'm sorry to hear that. Did it rain?'

'We could have coped with rain,' I say, 'although not a thunderstorm. I read somewhere it's dangerous to play crazy golf in a storm. The lightning is attracted to the metal clubs.'

'That night be true on a windswept golf course with nothing else for miles around. But I doubt you'd be in too much danger playing crazy golf. If you weren't rained off, what happened?'

'Our pastry chef slipped and sprained her ankle. Or that's the story she gave us at the time. She seemed fine to me, but she insisted she was in far too much pain to continue.'

There's a distinct tremor at the corner of his mouth. 'Does that mean your staff remains unbonded, or did you make up for it by booking something else?'

'I wanted to, but Lily and Abby dug in their heels and said they'd had quite enough of team-building for the year. So, we went to the pub instead. You can't have fun with people who refuse to be had fun with. It's disappointing, but it is what it is.'

He's looking at me with a good deal of amusement. 'Forgive me if I'm speaking out of turn, but you strike me as someone who's fairly used to getting her own way.'

'Almost never. You must be thinking of my sister.'

'As I've never met your sister –'

'You can't know that for sure,' I say.

'Is she anything like you?'

'Only physically. Personality-wise, we're like Sainsbury's own-brand chicken-flavoured pie product and Shelley's game pie.'

'With you being …?'

'The game pie, of course! I thought we'd already established that.'

'My mistake,' he says. 'I'm doing my best to follow these pie-based analogies, but it's difficult. I'm not a huge pie fan.'

I might have known it. Anyone who considers it reasonable behaviour to leave fifty-metre coils of cable lying in doorways to ensnare kind and thoughtful local bakery owners would be capable of anything. Although disliking pie feels like a step beyond that.

'It may be a good thing most of my cakes ended up on the floor,' I say. 'I'd have hated you to eat them out of a misplaced sense of politeness.'

'I said I wasn't too fussed about pies. I love cakes.'

'Me too!' I say more enthusiastically than I intended.

'Again, that doesn't surprise me,' he says. 'You seem quite invested in your products. Maybe that's why your bakery does so well. If it is doing well?'

'It's the most successful business in the village. When Lily and I took it over, it was on the verge of going bankrupt. The previous owner hadn't made a profit for years, and almost no one bothered to go in there.'

'I gather that isn't the case now?' he asks.

'Not at all. People come from miles around to shop at our bakery or eat lunch at our cafe.'

'Miles?' he says. 'That's a bold claim. How many miles are we talking about – one or two? Surely, not as many as three?'

'I'm almost sure you're poking fun at me, but it won't work. I'm excellent with numbers. I was an accountant in a previous life, so I know the integers you've just used are extremely small ones.'

'Tell me about your previous life,' he invites. 'Was it an important posting – at the court of Henry the Eighth or one of the Pharaohs, perhaps?'

'Why would Henry the Eighth need an accountant?' I ask, confused.

'You just told me you were an accountant in another life.'

'I meant before I bought the bakery, not in some previous existence.'

'What a shame,' he says. 'It would have been a great opportunity to change history entirely.'

'Now, there's a thought. I could easily have smudged one of the scrolls or put a decimal point in the wrong place. Those quills aren't as easy to use as you'd think. I tried making one out of a duck's feather when I was younger, and it didn't work at all. And my uncle was angry with me because it was one of his ducks.'

'You pulled out a duck's feather?' he asks in a stunned voice.

'Of course not. I merely followed it around all day with a bag of bread, waiting until one of its feathers fell out on its own.'

'You aren't supposed to feed bread to ducks. It's bad for their health.'

'It wasn't for them,' I explain. 'It was for me. Do you have any idea how long it takes for a duck to lose one of their feathers?'

'I really don't.'

'A long time. It was almost an hour before one of its duck friends came over for a chat and started grooming it. When the pair of them finally wandered off, I saw a tail feather lying on the grass and was able to wade out and collect it.'

'Wade out?' he asks. 'Where exactly was this duck?'

'On the little island in the middle of the pond. My uncle put it there so the ducks had somewhere to build their nests.'

'I hope it was worth it?'

'Not really. As I say, the feather didn't make a good quill, and I dropped half my bread in the pond while I was wading out to get it.'

'A truly tragic tale,' he says. 'But not as tragic as if you'd messed up Henry the Eighth's accounts. There could have been all sorts of unforeseen consequences. He might not have had enough money to fund the navy, and major battles could have been lost as a result.'

He looks at his watch. 'Fascinating though this discussion is, I should be getting on.'

I'm glad he's found our conversation fascinating. It may warm him up for the conversation to come.

'I didn't only come here to bring you cakes today,' I say.

His eyes crinkle slightly. 'I'm pleased to hear it because you didn't do a very good job of that.'

'I came to talk to you,' I say with my sweetest smile.

He doesn't look as flattered as I'd hoped. 'Are you sure? You've never met me before.'

'I'm aware of that. Nevertheless, you're just the person I've been looking for.'

Too late, I realise how this sounds. 'I don't mean for my whole life.'

'What?' he asks.

'I'm not trying to say you're the person I've been looking for my entire life, and now that I've found you, I don't want to let you go. Like they do at the end of romantic movies. Just when the audience has given up all hope of the pair of them seeing sense and realising they were meant for each other, one of them has some sort of epiphany.'

'Epiphany?' he asks.

'A sudden realisation,' I explain. 'A moment of clarity and understanding.'

'I know what an epiphany is. I just don't understand is which one of us is supposed to having one, or why. To be honest, I'm unable to grasp the skein of this increasingly tangled conversation or unravel it.'

He gives me a patronising smile. 'A skein is a ball of thread. Other synonyms may include a coil, an entanglement, or a complication.'

'I know what a skein is,' I say, annoyed by his assumption that my vocabulary is more limited than his. 'The word can also be applied to a group of geese in flight.'

'Or swans,' he adds. 'As a student of ornithology, I thought you'd have known that.'

'What makes you think I'm a student of ornithology?'

'You once spent half a day stalking an innocent duck. Naturally, I assumed you were a keen student of our feathered friends. But we're wandering away from the original subject. You started this rather confusing conversation by informing me you hadn't come all this way in order to launch a volley of cakes at me. A fusillade of cakes? I'm not sure what the collective noun is.'

'A batch,' I say. 'How do you not know that? It's one of the first words children learn. But that isn't relevant to what I'm here to discuss today.'

'I'm relieved to hear it. As you seem unable to get to the point, maybe you'd prefer to present it to me in written form? Or would you like to start again from the beginning?'

I had my speech all prepared when I arrived at work this morning. I rehearsed it with Lily before I left the bakery, and I repeated it to myself while I walked down the high street. But all this talk of ducks and monarchs has driven it out of my head. That and the almost fatal accident I incurred on first arriving here.

'I've been sent here by the Silver Surfers,' I begin at last. 'They're one of our village societies.'

'Like the Da Vinci code?'

'They're nothing like the Da Vinci code! They're our resident computer experts. They're led by a woman called Mavis Sotherby.'

'Tall woman with grey hair?' he asks.

'That's right. Have you met her?'

'She popped in yesterday to see what was going on.'

'Very likely. Anyway, she runs the Silver Surfers and generally keeps the village in order.'

'Does it need keeping in order?' he asks.

'Not me, obviously. But yes, but there are members of the community who benefit from a certain amount of oversight. Anyway, the Silver Surfers held a meeting in the cafe yesterday afternoon to discuss the budget for our project. They seemed quite upset.'

If I'd been hoping to awake his sympathy and appeal to his better nature, I'm disappointed. He doesn't appear to have one.

'Upset about what?' he asks.

I assume my most mournful expression. 'You.'

'Me personally?'

'More in your role as representative of this project. You're the face of the company we've employed to do the work for us.'

'I'm an independently contracted project manager,' he says. 'Simon's company has hired me to oversee the work and make sure it comes in on time and doesn't go over budget.'

I seize on this last word. 'You've put your finger right on the problem. The projected expenses are too high.'

'They're about right for the scale of the work that needs to be done. If anything, I'm surprised by how low Simon's quote was.'

'Price is relative,' I tell him. 'What may be seen as high in some contexts would be seen as low in others. I could talk to Simon, but you seem like the best person to deal with this extremely minor issue.'

'You keep talking about slight problems and minor issues, but you haven't yet told me what yours is.'

'We've had some unexpected additional expenses since we first agreed the price. So, if you could adjust the budget slightly to reflect that fact, I'll get out of your hair.'

He puts down the bag he's just picked up. 'Adjust it how?'

I'm tempted to ask whether he undertook any formal education at all before accepting his current job. But that might prejudice my chances of achieving a favourable outcome.

'I'm asking you for a reduction in your bill,' I say. 'Just a small one. The actual amount is negotiable.'

He swings around to face me. 'Let me get this straight. You're here to ask me to charge less than the agreed amount for the work we've undertaken to do for you?'

'That's right!' I say, pleased with his comprehension and willing to overlook the fact it took him so long to grasp the point.

'The amount written on the contract that was signed three weeks ago?' he pursues.

I feel the faintest stirrings of unease.

'I don't know how long ago it was signed,' I say. 'I wasn't a party to the official side of things.'

'But you are aware it was signed?' he asks, brushing this aside.

'I suppose it must have been if you've all arrived and started work. But it's quite a common practice to revise contracts as the work progresses.'

I relapse into silence to give him a chance to think about the wisdom of what I've just said. He may need a few minutes to fully absorb it.

He doesn't seem to. 'No.'

'What do you mean no?' I ask, caught off balance.

He rolls up the blueprints and stuffs them into a cardboard tube. 'It's a clear enough word. It refers to a negative answer or decision.'

'I know what the word means!' I exclaim. 'I just don't understand why you're using it.'

'To communicate my intentions.'

He gives me a considering look. 'Possibly, it isn't a word you've heard too many times in your life.'

'I hear it all the time, but I'm not sure why you're using it now. You haven't given my proposal even a second's consideration.'

'Nor do I intend to. It's out of the question. If that's all you came for, I need to see what those boys are up to. Can you find your own way out without tripping over anything?'

'Wait!' I say desperately.

He turns to face me. 'What now?'

I take a deep breath. 'I didn't want it to come to this. I'd hoped to find you more reasonable. But if this is your attitude, you leave me no choice. Are you aware that you have obligations under the Management of Health and Safety at Work Regulations of 1998?'

'No,' he says. 'Neither do I have any under the actual act of 1999.'

'I think you'll find you're wrong. When I run this past my lawyer, I –'

We're interrupted by the slamming of the outside door and a rush of footsteps along the passage. A second later, two small boys appear in the doorway, red-faced and out of breath.

'We've kicked our ball onto the roof,' gasps one of them. 'It's fallen down one of the gaps in the tiles, and we don't know how to get it down!'

Chapter Eight

Jon raises a hand. 'Slow down! I can barely understand what you're saying.'

'It sounds quite clear to me,' I say. 'They've lost their ball, and now it's on the roof.'

The boys have skidded to a halt in the doorway. The fair-haired one looks around at the carnage. 'What happened here?'

'Just a minor accident,' I say. 'Speaking of which, be careful of that extension cord. It's been placed in an extremely dangerous position.'

He glances down. 'No, it hasn't. I saw it the moment I came in.'

I feel Jon's amused gaze on me but decide to take no notice.

'You have sharp eyes,' I say. 'But I'm more interested in hearing how your ball came to be up on the roof?'

His brother has been staring at the mess, fascinated, but this brings him back to the original subject. 'Ollie kicked it, but he can't aim for toffee.'

'Can too!' says Ollie, elbowing him in the ribs.

'That's enough!' says Jon. 'I'm sure we can get your ball down from the roof somehow. Although I'm not sure we should. If Ollie can't learn to aim better than that, he'll never become a professional footballer.'

'I imagine any junior team would sign him up at once,' I say. 'According to my friend Jack, half the professional footballers out there are incapable of hitting a barn door from ten feet away. He says it's the only pre-requisite for giving most of them a contract.'

'We'll fetch the ball later,' says Jon. 'In the meantime, I'd like you to say hello. Ollie, Toby, this is Isabella. She came to see how the work is going here.'

'And to bring you all some cake,' I remind him.

'Cool!' says Toby. 'I'm starving.'

Jon points to the floor. 'I'm afraid that's all that's left of it.'

Both the boys' faces fall. They look almost ludicrously disappointed. I know how they feel.

'It wasn't my fault,' I say. 'I tripped over the extension cord someone carelessly left in the doorway.'

'Which reminds me,' says Jon. 'Weren't you about to ask me something when the boys interrupted us? You were raising some sort of legal issue, if I remember correctly.'

'It will keep,' I say.

It seems to me there are more important issues to be dealt with, such as getting that ball down from the roof. And I'd prefer not to quote laws and legal precedent until I've checked my sources. By which I mean Uncle Harry. He's done all the legal work for my family for as long as I can remember, and he's forgotten more about the law than most high court judges ever learned.

'What's in that box?' asks Ollie.

'All that's left of the cakes I brought with me,' I tell him. 'Would you like them?'

The boys pounce on it eagerly and peer inside.

'Bags I the eclair!' says Toby

'I saw it first,' says Ollie.

'No, you didn't. We saw it at the same time. But I called shotgun, so it's mine.'

I snatch up the box before they can send it flying. We've already had one cake-based tragedy here today, and I can't bear the thought of a second. There's only so much a person can take in one day.

'I'm afraid the shotgun rule doesn't apply to cakes,' I say. 'They're a special case. It isn't like sitting in the front seat of the car. You have to divide them fairly. Unless either of you has any allergies, each of you gets one half of the turnover and one half of the eclair.'

Ollie looks as though he's considering claiming to have a severe apple allergy.

Jon interrupts before he can frame the words. 'Isabella's right. And you can trust her to have done the maths correctly. She's told me several times she's an accountant.'

'You're the one who couldn't stop talking about it,' I say. 'I merely mentioned it in passing.'

'Who's going to divide them?' demands Toby. 'Ollie always takes the bigger piece for himself.'

I pick up a metal ruler lying on the table. 'I am.'

'Are you planning to measure them first?' asks Jon.

'I don't have a knife with me, so I thought this would be a suitable alternative. Is that alright with you?'

'The ruler doesn't belong to me,' he says. 'I think Simon brought it.'

'I'll wash it before I leave. He'll never know.'

I slice the cakes neatly in two and hand the box to Ollie. 'You choose the first piece, then Toby can choose the second. And so on until all the pieces have been eaten.'

'You've done this before,' says Jon.

'Many, many times. I know from bitter experience what it's like to have a sibling who refuses to play fair. Not that I'm accusing either of these two of cheating, but my younger sister would eat anything that wasn't nailed down. Even that didn't always stop her. My mother instituted the rule very early on that one of us had to cut and the other one choose. It's amazing how accurate the cutter can be when they know their sibling will get first choice.'

'Your mother is a wise woman,' he says.

'She is indeed. She had to be with Georgia for a daughter.'

The boys aren't listening. They've finished the turnover and started on the eclair.

'There's nothing wrong with their appetites,' I say.

'No, just their aim. I'll have to ask Nathan whether he has a ladder.'

'I know he has. The pub was re-thatched last year, and I remember him telling the thatcher he needn't bother getting his ladder out of his truck because there was one in here. This place has been used as a storage unit for years. I never knew why the previous owner didn't do something with it. I suppose he thought it would cost too much.'

'Are we back to the subject of money?' he asks.

'I wouldn't dream of it. I've asked you to lower your price, and you've said no. The fact you said it without giving it the slightest consideration to my proposal is neither here nor there.'

'I'm glad you realise that.'

'Of course, I do. It means we'll have to find another way.'

'I look forward to hearing all about it.'

'You won't hear about it or even see us coming,' I inform him. 'The first you'll know is when we've succeeded in our aim.'

'Have you finished your cakes?' he asks the boys. 'If so, we should find that ladder. I need to have you home by lunchtime, so we don't have much time.'

'Isn't today a school day?' I ask.

I'm generally a little hazy about the days of the week. Lily and I are so busy, they seem to run into each other. But I'm sure this isn't either a Saturday or a Sunday.

'It's the school holidays,' he says.

'Already?' I ask. 'I've been so busy at work that I've lost track.'

'The boys are usually at holiday club on weekdays, but it was closed today, so they're with me. We should get going. They have a football game this afternoon.'

'I should be going too,' I say. 'I'd love to stay and help you retrieve the ball. There's nothing I like more than clambering around on roofs. But if I try that today, Victoria will hear about it.

She's a chef in this pub and an ex-employee of ours. She's dating my orthopaedic doctor, and she's bound to mention it to him.'

'Why would a doctor care about you climbing up ladders?' asks Ollie.

'I broke my leg recently.'

'Climbing a ladder?'

'Not exactly. But it was ladder-related. Or should I say ladder-adjacent?'

'What does that mean?' asks Toby.

'I was climbing on something. Just not a ladder. It's a long story, and I'm sure you aren't interested in hearing all the boring details. The point is that I'm popping into the pub to see Victoria before I go back to the bakery, and I don't want to put her in the position of having to withhold the truth from her new boyfriend. So, I'll let you two have the fun of scrambling over the roof today, and you can tell me all about it when I see you again.'

'You boys will have the fun of holding the ladder,' says Jon. 'I'll be doing the actual climbing. Your mother would never forgive me if she heard I'd allowed you to do anything so dangerous.'

The boys set up a protest, but Jon remains unmoved. Personally, I'd have great difficulty in resisting those pleading faces. But, as I've discovered to my cost, this man appears to have no difficulty in refusing to perform even the simplest of favours.

'You never let us do anything fun,' says Ollie.

'He shared his cakes with you,' I say.

'They weren't his cakes.'

'Yes, they were. At least, partly. I work at The Sugarloaf Bakery, just down the high street. I brought the cakes over for the people working here. It was our way of welcoming them to the village.'

I catch Jon's sardonic look and turn away. 'Two of them had to leave, which meant your dad had the unsquashed cakes all to himself, and he chose to share them with you. That calls for some gratitude.'

Ollie seems about to speak, but I carry on. 'Did you enjoy the cakes?'

They both nod vigorously.

'I'm glad to hear it. If you come to our bakery and give the secret codeword, you can both have a free cookie of your choice.'

Their faces light up.

'How about me?' asks Jon.

I point to the empty box. 'I'm afraid that was a one-shot deal. If you want one of our cookies, you'll have to buy it.'

That will show him he's not the only one able to say no to perfectly reasonable requests.

'Why is the codeword secret?' asks Toby.

'Because if she told it to everyone, she'd run out of cookies,' says Ollie.

'Exactly,' I nod. 'Also because super-secret passwords are much more fun than only half-secret ones.'

I beckon them closer and lean down to whisper in their ears. 'The password is Jammy Dodger. If you mention it to anyone, the password is automatically cancelled and never works again.'

They both glance at Jon.

'Even him,' I say. 'You have been warned. And don't think we won't know, because we will. My business partner has two children of her own, and she always knows when they're telling the truth. It's your choice whether or not to accept this top secret mission.'

They grin at each other, then at Jon.

'If you've finished with all these secrets, shall we look for that ladder?' he asks.

'I'll mention it to Nathan when I see him,' I say. 'I'm sure he'll want to know what's going on. It may no longer technically be his building, but he likes to keep an eye on things and make sure no undesirables try to access the property.'

'That's very kind of you. I won't say goodbye. Something tells me you and I will meet again.'

'Au revoir, then,' I say. 'Goodbye, boys. I hope you get your football back.'

I pick up the empty cake box and carry it across the strip of grass that divides the building from the pub. I was going to ask Victoria for a mop and bucket so I could clean up the smooshed cakes. But after the way Jon has behaved today, he can clean it up himself.

Chapter Nine

I put my head around the kitchen door, where I find Victoria pinching together the edges of a pie.

'Is that what I think it is?' I ask, and she jumps.

'You startled me! What are you doing here?'

'I was hoping to have lunch. I assume that's what all these preparations are for?'

'Not for you in particular, but yes.'

'You can't imagine how hurtful it is to hear that,' I tell her. 'When I arrive for a meal, I like my hosts to tell me how pleased they are to see me and how they'll make their best table available.'

'Of course, I'm pleased to see you. But I wasn't expecting you.'

'Always a mistake,' I say, dumping the empty cake box into a nearby bin. 'If you insist on making game pie each day, you must expect to see me here on a regular basis. But if I'm not welcome, I can eat somewhere else.'

She laughs. 'You're always welcome. You know that. We'll give you the best table in the house. I don't imagine many people are ordering lunch yet, so you can take your pick.'

She glances over at the bin. 'Is that a Sugarloaf cake box? Did you bring it with you in case you felt faint during the long trek over from the bakery?'

I lean against the counter and watch her roll out a second strip of pastry.

'As it happens, I did not. Although low blood sugar can strike at any time, with catastrophic results. I once almost passed out at the theatre during the interval. Someone messed up the peanut order, and they were all sold out by the time I reached the counter. It was a close thing. Luckily, I'd brought a few provisions with me in my handbag, so I was able to stay until the end of the play.'

Victoria doesn't seem as fascinated by this anecdote as I'd hoped.

She looks at the clock. 'Five more minutes before the first batch comes out, and I can put this next one in. So, if those cakes weren't for you, who were they for?'

'They were to welcome the contractors to the village and establish friendly relations between them and us.'

'That's nice,' she says, trimming the edges of the pastry and squeezing them into a ball. 'I've met the architect. He seems very pleasant. And the project manager stopped in this morning with his boys to ask whether we had any objection to them kicking a football around for an hour. I don't imagine it would have been much fun for them to have to sit through a business meeting.'

'Not at all,' I agree. 'They had a wonderful time out there, culminating in them kicking their ball onto the roof.'

She opens the oven door and lifts out a couple of pies. 'That's a shame. Maybe it will come down by itself.'

'How?' I ask, intrigued.

'I don't know. The wind might pick up later. Or a squirrel might kick the ball down on its way past.'

'Or mistake it for a giant nut,' I agree. 'If it were an exceptionally strong squirrel, it might try to take the ball back to its tree all by itself. Or it could call all its squirrel friends to come and help it. I wish I'd thought of that before I told Jon where he could find a ladder. Still, it's too late for that now. I expect he's perched on the roof at this very moment, wishing he'd had the forethought to wear a hard hat.'

I lay Nathan's hat on the table. 'Please thank your boss for this when you see him. Tell him it was a thoughtful gesture, but quite unnecessary. And if you could remember to warn him there may be traces of cream and jam inside the brim, he'll be grateful to you.'

'Stand back while I put these pies in the oven,' she says, not appearing to hear a word I've said.

I've become used to this over the years, but it's still hurtful when my staff members and ex-staff members fail to treat my words with the awed respect they deserve. On the other hand, she's dealing with the lunchtime game pies, and I'd hate to cause even the smallest lapse in concentration. Terrible consequences could ensue.

'I'll leave you to your essential work,' I say. 'I just thought I'd stop by and say hello. Perhaps you could call in at the bakery one morning, and we can catch up properly.'

'Won't you be working?' she asks.

'As you doubtless remember, I have the place running like a well-oiled machine. I consider it the duty of every small business owner to keep everything organised to a pitch of perfection. That way, should an unexpected crisis occur, such as my recent hospital stay, the customers won't even notice the difference.'

'You mean Lily and Abby can work longer hours?'

'If need be. They know I'd do it for them.'

'If they broke their legs standing on mixing bowls on top of chairs?' she asks.

I wave this away. 'It's unnecessary to go over all the details again. It was months ago. Who can remember with any degree of certainty exactly what happened?'

'Not you,' she says cheerfully. 'You were unconscious.'

That's the downside of people who work alongside you. They think they know everything about you, and they always put the worst possible slant on it.

'I should find myself a table,' I say. 'This will be the first time I've eaten your game pie. Don't let that worry you too much. I'm willing to make every allowance for your inexperience. Even the most talented chef has to go through a learning phase.'

'It's game pie,' she says. 'How much learning can there be?'

'This isn't just any game pie!' I say, shocked. 'This is Shelley's game pie. It's legendary. If it were me, I wouldn't dare attempt to follow in her footsteps.'

'Then it's a good thing I'm not you. If you'd like to find yourself a table and place your order, we'll have your lunch with you in a couple of minutes.'

Half an hour later, pleasantly full of game pie and chips and a portion of really excellent crème brûlée, I wander down the high street to the bakery.

'I expected you back here ages ago!' says Lily as soon as I open the door. 'I've been holding the fort all by myself for hours.'

I'm about to give her the same speech I gave Victoria about the importance of any business worth its salt being able to operate on a reduced number of staff when she looks at me more closely.

'What happened to you?'

I raise a hand to my hair and realise it's still rather sticky. 'I had a slight accident.'

'What did you break this time – your arm?'

'Nothing so minor,' I say in a tragic tone. 'The cakes. All but two of them. And even they weren't quite so pristine as when they set out. But I'm reliably informed they were still delicious.'

She sighs. 'You can tell me the whole story once you've washed your face and I've had some lunch. I've been rushed off my feet all morning. I haven't even stopped for coffee.'

'You poor thing. You should go over to The Red Lion. Victoria has now been let loose on the game pie all by herself, and I have to say she's making an impressive job of it.'

'You've been sitting in the pub while I've been here all by myself?' she asks. 'Please tell me you spent your time there in a high-level meeting with all the contractors and secured us a fifty percent discount?'

'Not quite,' I admit.

'What, then – forty percent?'

'You're getting closer.'

She frowns. 'Thirty?' Then, as I shake my head, 'Twenty-five?'

'This could take a while,' I say. 'It's like playing hide-and-seek with the children when Ethan insists on counting to twenty very slowly, occasionally getting lost on the way and having to start again. Perhaps I should just tell you.'

She pours herself a drink and sits down. 'Hit me!'

'Zero percent.'

She stops with her cup halfway to her mouth. 'Zero? As in nothing? The number that comes directly below one?'

'That's the one!' I say as cheerfully as possible.

'Then I have two questions. What kept you at the pub all this time, and why are you covered in bits of cake? Not necessarily in that order.'

'It's a long story, and you're hungry. I'll tell you after you've eaten. Things will seem less bleak after a piece of quiche or a sausage roll. It's important to understand this was just the preliminary skirmish. It would have been nice if I'd popped in and asked for a ten percent discount, and they'd beamed back at me and asked whether I wouldn't prefer twenty? But I wasn't really expecting that, so I wasn't disappointed.'

'You weren't disappointed?' she asks. 'I imagine Mavis will be.'

'I didn't anticipate such an uncompromising attitude from the project manager,' I admit. 'But I may not have to deal with Jon next time. The last I saw of him, he was off to find the ladder so he could climb onto the roof of the building.'

'Why would he want to do that?'

'Who knows? I can think of several reasons off the top of my head. It could be one thing. It could be another. People are complicated, and some of them have motivations most of us could never understand. The important thing is that he was planning to climb onto the roof. Once up there, anything could happen. He could fall off or he could decide to make his home up there. Victoria suggested he might meet a posse of giant squirrels and be carried off to their nest.'

'Dray,' she murmurs.

'That too. All sorts of things may happen to Jon. The next time I'm sent as an envoy to reopen negotiations, we could be dealing with someone entirely different. The architect, for instance. You remember Simon, the man who came in here yesterday to buy doughnuts? I met him again today, and he seemed a lot more reasonable than Jon. I'll bet if I'd asked him for a discount, he'd have given me one without even thinking about it.'

Lily doesn't look convinced. 'His architecture firm is already charging mates' rates. Your only hope is that the project manager can find a way to cut costs some other way.'

'He still may, although it's possible he won't. I only met him briefly, but he didn't seem to understand the duties of a project manager as well as one might hope. We may have to bypass him and look for another way.'

'Such as?' she asks.

'I'm not quite sure,' I admit. 'But I refuse to give up. There's a solution to every problem, and I intend to find it. In the meantime, I suggest you stop worrying about it and allow me to heat up one of Abby's delicious pies for you. And I promise not to throw this one on the floor.'

Chapter Ten

'So, what did happen this morning?' asks Lily when the last of the lunches has been served, and things are relatively quiet again.

'I enjoyed a larger than usual portion of game pie and chips. I expect Victoria was responsible for that. I visited her in the kitchen after my meeting, and she persuaded me to stay and have lunch at The Red Lion. I think she was nervous about making her debut.'

'She's been working there for more than a month,' says Lily. 'She has nothing to be nervous about. Shelley's very pleased with her. She told me the other day she's hoping to drop down to working three days a week by Christmas.'

'Then it may have been the realisation her ex-employer was in the vicinity. It's understandable that Victoria should be anxious to make a good impression on someone who's been both her mentor and a huge part of her professional life.'

Lily doesn't look as impressed as I'd hoped. 'She worked with us for twelve weeks.'

'Twelve days with me is enough to change the course of someone's life,' I say. 'Or twelve hours. Or –'

'Spare me the minutes and seconds and milliseconds,' she begs. 'I'm sure she had a great time working here. I certainly enjoyed having her. But I doubt she was too worried about serving you a meal.'

'She's only just started making the game pies by herself,' I say. 'Anyone would be forgiven a few jitters under those circumstances. When you add the fact she was being judged by someone she's been accustomed to look up to, you can see what a big occasion it was for her. I wouldn't be surprised if Shelley had to give her the afternoon off to recover.'

Lily hands me a tray. 'Can you clear tables eight and nine while you're talking nonsense?'

I pick up a cloth. 'As you're already aware, I'm a superb multi-tasker, so of course I can. As for talking nonsense – it's no such thing. I'm making my usual excellent good sense.'

'If you say so. But that isn't what I meant when I asked you what happened.'

'I thought it might not be, but I hoped I was wrong. It would have been far simpler to discuss what I had for my lunch than to talk about this morning's meeting.'

She fixes me with a steely gaze. 'Nonetheless …'

I sigh. 'None,' as you very rightly say, 'the less.'

'It's a shame things didn't go as well as you hoped.'

'I wouldn't say that. It started very well. I enjoyed a pleasant walk down the high street in the early summer sunshine. My thoughts were occupied with the topic of Little Red Riding Hood and her many and various exploits during the course of a single morning. Things continued to go well as I exchanged a few friendly words with my friend Nathan and accepted the hat he pressed upon me due to his very natural concerns about my safety. My spirits were still high as I walked across the grass towards what will shortly become our new village arts centre …'

My voice trails off, and I sigh again – more heavily this time.

'Thank you for the blow-by-blow account of the first ten minutes of your expedition,' says Lily.

'You think I don't know when you're being sarcastic, but I do. I've developed all kinds of skills after living with Georgia for more than three decades, and that's one of them. I know what you're asking, but I thought it would be better to discuss my journey and marvel at how well I accomplished it, and how safely

I arrived, than to dwell on the unpleasantness that awaited me at the end of it.'

'You may as well tell me,' she says. 'Mavis Sotherby will be in soon to hear all about it. You won't be able to fob her off like this.'

'Especially not if she's accompanied by her usual posse of thugs and enforcers,' I agree.

'And Bernie,' she reminds me.

'He could give my ankles a nip if he wanted to, but he's easily distracted. I can handle him. Besides, why would he want to harm me? He's our bakery mascot, and he knows who provides him with an inexhaustible supply of biscuits.'

'No problem,' she says. 'I'll wait until Mavis drags it out of you. And don't think I'll lift a finger to save you, because I won't. Remember to check the salt and pepper pots.'

'I'm quite aware of what goes into servicing a table. I've wiped this one down so well that our next customers will be able to see their faces in it, although I'm not sure why they'd want to. I've also changed the flowers, checked the condiments, and straightened the chairs.'

'And folded the napkins into swans?' she asks.

'Paper airplanes, actually. And I'll throw one at you if you don't stop telling me how to do my job.'

She grins at me. 'I'm sorry. I should know better by now. I won't do it again. Please don't give me a written warning.'

'Only because I don't have a pen. Maybe I should get my story straight before Mavis arrives and shines a light in my eyes, and I end up confessing to all my childhood sins.'

'I'll hide all the lamps,' she promises.

'That wouldn't stop her. She'd only use the torch on her phone. Don't forget she's the village's technical whizz kid. She knows how to use all the apps on her screen, and most of mine too. I've never worked out what that green squiggly logo is.'

'You can ask her to explain it to you right after you've told her how badly you've failed her,' she says unkindly.

'She's already met Jon. That's the project manager. She'll realise I did the best I could, and none of this is my fault. And don't forget I did this as a favour for everyone. I didn't need to go at all.'

'Not because you were afraid to say no to Mavis?' she asks.

'The point is that I didn't have to do your dirty work, but I did – much in the same spirit with which our ancestors sailed to Dunkirk.'

'I'm looking forward to being here when you explain all that to Mavis,' she says. 'Especially if you do the rowing motions to illustrate.'

She looks out of the window. 'Here they come now. Bang on time.'

'I've just remembered I have something urgent to do in the office,' I say. 'It's time-sensitive, so I'll have to leave you to look after things in here.'

'No problem. I'll send Mavis to have a chat with you in there. It should be very cosy with just the two of you, and no way of escape.'

'Can you remind me why I ever agreed to partner with you?' I ask.

'Because you knew no one else would put up with you?'

She opens the bakery door. 'Here you all are! Isabella was just talking about you.'

'And then we turned up like the proverbial bad penny!' says Mabel, pulling off her jacket and sinking into the nearest chair. 'My goodness, it was a warm walk up here. I didn't notice the time until it was almost too late. Edie was distracting me. She's taking Bernie on a play date with Olive this afternoon. You wouldn't believe the fuss she was making about it.'

'Didn't she want to take him?' asks Phyllis.

'It wasn't that. She was delighted when Olive's mum called and invited Bernie over so he and Olive could play in the garden together. But you know what Edie is. First, she had to go through every outfit in his wardrobe. Believe me, that takes some time! He has a closet all to himself where she keeps his outfits and toys and spare leads. It's absolutely enormous. I half expect to get lost in there one day and find myself face to face with a fawn prancing around in the snow. Anyway, she finally chose the perfect going-on-a-casual-play-date outfit, but that was only the beginning.'

'What was the outfit?' I ask, fascinated to discover what the well-dressed dog about town is wearing these days.

'Some sort of checked shirt thing. Personally, I thought he looked as though he was off to a hoe-down, but I wasn't about to say that or Edie would have started again from scratch, and I'd have arrived here even later.'

'My children love having play dates,' says Lily. 'It's the only time either of them ever tidies their room. I use the word tidy in its very loosest sense, but it's better than nothing.'

'The mutt doesn't understand the meaning of the word either,' says Mabel. 'Edie is always running around after him, picking up his toys and making sure his bowl is clean and shiny. She doesn't do any of those things for me, and we're related by blood. This isn't his first play date, but they're usually held at our house, and I make myself scarce the moment I get wind of them. He had a party for his last birthday I wasn't allowed to get out of, although I tried hard enough. My sister said she'd never forgive me if I missed such a momentous occasion.'

'A dog's birthday party?' asks Lily. 'You can't be serious?'

'I wish it were a joke. I had to spend half the morning cleaning the cottage while Edie wrapped the gifts for pass-the-parcel. Why the place needed to be so clean is anyone's guess. It looked as though a tornado had been through it by the time those dogs left. And there were only four of them! They finished with a pinata in the shape of a bone. Four sets of teeth, and none of them had the wit to get the thing open. I had to bash it open with a steak mallet in the end. I hit it a little too hard, and hundreds of tiny dog treats exploded everywhere. We were still hoovering them up three weeks later.'

Ivy gives a shout of laughter. 'Pictures, or it didn't happen!'

'No pictures,' says Mabel gloomily. 'Apparently, one of the dogs doesn't like mobile phones. He tries to pounce on them and eat them. But I took several photos of Edie and the mutt once all his little friends had gone home clutching their party bags!'

'Party bags!' exclaims Lily. 'Now I know you're teasing us.'

'If only! They had all the dogs' names printed on them. Blue for the boys and pink for the girls. My sister hasn't yet realised we're in the age of gender equality. They each got a ball, an engraved tag for their collar, and a selection of treats. I tried lining up as they left in case there was a bag for me too, but no such luck. The only thing I was given was a list of instructions about what needed cleaning up. It really is a dog's life!'

She heaves an enormous sigh and relapses into silence. If she's expecting a murmur of sympathy, she's disappointed. Everyone knows Mabel is almost as fond of Bernie as Mrs Ogilvie is. But if she enjoys her self-appointed role as the village's version of Cruella de Vil, that's her business.

Lily and I take everyone's orders. It isn't until we've served the final cup of tea that Ivy turns to me.

'How did it go this morning? Bob said he drove down the high street on his way out of the village, and he saw you carrying the largest cake box he's ever seen.'

'It wasn't that big,' I say. 'We have much larger ones. But we didn't want it to look like a bribe, so we chose a modest-sized one.'

'Very wise,' approves Phyllis. 'So, did they go for it?'

I consider how best to answer this. 'The apple turnover and eclair were definitely enjoyed.'

She peers at me over the top of her spectacles. 'That's a rather equivocal reply. Didn't they like the rest of the cakes?'

I look over at Lily, whose lips are twitching.

'Those were the only two cakes anyone tasted while I was there,' I say.

'I can't imagine why,' says Mary. 'If someone brought me a box of Abby's cakes, I'd be all over them like Mabel on a plum slice.'

'Me too,' agrees Barb. 'Don't say they took them home instead of eating them at once? That would defeat the purpose of the exercise. As I understand it, the idea was to send them into sugar shock, then pounce while their mouths were full and talk them into doing what you wanted.'

'That's almost what happened,' I say. 'I did the pouncing bit. Or near enough.'

Lily gives a meaningful cough.

'Fine,' I say. 'I tripped and fell before I could hand them the box, and the cakes went flying across the room. In my defence, it wasn't my fault. Jon, the project manager, had left a massive extension cable lying in the doorway. Anyone would have tripped over it. I'm not sure he didn't do it on purpose. He seems like the sort of person who might do something like that.'

'For what reason?' asks Phyllis.

'It's hard to say. Possibly, he was making sure no one crept into the building and took them all unawares.'

'Like a burglar?' asks Ivy.

'Or someone engaging in a spot of industrial espionage. The three of them were huddled over a set of plans on the table. Simon told me it was the plans for the art centre, but I didn't get close enough to make sure. Jon rolled them up and stuffed them into a cardboard tube before I had the chance to get a good look. But what if they were working on something far more important, like secret government plans for turning Honeywell into a covert operations centre?'

'Why would they be looking at top-secret plans in the building behind The Red Lion?' asks Phyllis.

'Think about it!' I say. 'It would be the perfect cover. You're involved in a top-secret operation to bring down the country. Where would people expect you to be discussing it? In some dusty old vault in Whitehall. So, that's where the authorities would plant their listening devices. Meanwhile, the actual spies choose somewhere no one would ever think to look.'

'Like the Honeywell Arts Centre?' asks Lily.

'Exactly! They could search the entire country for somewhere to hold secret meetings without finding anywhere half so good. And they could pop in for some of Shelley's game pie afterwards. I'd be surprised if we weren't on to something here. I'm not even sure Jon was a real project manager. He didn't seem to know much about negotiating prices, and he was quite curt when I asked. It all makes sense now. It's in his best interest to keep everything looking as normal as possible, rather than rocking the boat by changing the prices for us. Knowing what we now know, we shouldn't be surprised my negotiation with him went poorly. We should just be grateful I got out of there in one piece.'

I beam around at them all. Sadly, Mavis Sotherby doesn't look as stunned by my brilliant theory as I might have liked.

'So, you didn't get a reduction?' she asks.

'Not exactly. But I did get my hands on some potentially important information. What a shame Honeywell no longer has its own police officer. We could have sent them over to reconnoitre.'

'We could set up round-the-clock surveillance,' suggests Mabel. 'I'd be happy to take a shift. I won't volunteer to bring the mutt. He'd be sure to bark at the wrong time and give the game away.'

'I can always rely on you for support,' I say. 'How about the rest of you?'

'This is extremely disappointing,' says Mavis. 'I was relying on you to negotiate more effectively on our behalf. Not to throw cakes at the staff before concocting some ridiculous theory about them conducting a clandestine operation out of a derelict building.'

'Not derelict,' I say. 'It just needs a new roof and some interior decoration.'

Lily nudges me, and I subside. There's no point in arguing with Mavis when she's in this mood. I'll bring up the subject another time when she isn't here.

Mavis looks around at the Silver Surfers. 'Don't just sit there! I need you to come up with alternative courses of action.'

Somewhat to my surprise, they all nod meekly. Even Mabel looks more serious than usual, although she does treat me to an enormous wink when Mavis isn't looking.

I can think of several alternative courses of action. But, as they mostly involve hiring a private detective to trail Simon and Jon, I decide to keep them to myself.

Silence reigns for the next few minutes, broken only by the occasional chink of a teacup in its saucer. I'm just wondering how long this is going to go on for when the shop bell rings, making us all jump.

Chapter Eleven

The door opens, and Simon walks in. He stops and looks around him with a confused expression. I'm not surprised. It isn't every day you walk into a crowded yet silent bakery to face a barrage of accusing looks. He seems unsure whether to stay or turn around and walk straight out.

Lily steps forward to greet him. 'How nice to see you again.'

He looks relieved, if a little cautious. 'I thought I'd drop in and buy myself something to take home with me this evening. And perhaps get myself a coffee.'

He catches sight of me and smiles. 'Hello, Isabella. I told you I'd recognise you again if I came in here.'

'I'm surprised,' I say. 'It's almost as though you've had some sort of espionage training – facial recognition despite heavy disguises, that sort of thing.'

I glance at Lily, who doesn't seem as impressed as I'd hoped.

'What can I get for you?' she asks.

Simon walks over to the counter and inspects the cakes. 'Those apple tarts look delicious. And I'd love a cappuccino, if you serve them.'

'We serve everything,' I say. 'The coffee hasn't yet been invented that Lily doesn't know how to prepare. Isn't that right, Lily?'

'I wouldn't go that far,' she says. 'But I can make all the usual things.'

'She's being modest,' I tell him. 'Lily was runner-up at the Europe-wide coffee-making competition a few years ago. She was the youngest medallist in their history. It usually takes decades for someone to reach the dizzy heights of Maîtresse de l'Infusion, but Lily managed it in her early thirties.'

'I'm impressed,' he says, sitting down at a table next to mine.

'Me too,' says Lily, switching on the coffee machine and pouring the milk into a jug. 'I look forward to hearing more about my fictional exploits sometime when we aren't so busy.'

'She's just being modest,' I say. 'Notice the speed with which she's manipulating that steamer.'

Lily finishes making the cappuccino and carries it over to his table.

'And look at the finished product,' I add. 'The consistency of the foam and its even spread. Don't tell me that wasn't made by a European champion. She's even put a picture on your foam. Not strictly necessary for a non-competition hot drink, but always a welcome touch, and the mark of a true professional.'

I lean over to look at his cup more closely. 'What is it – a heart?'

Lily laughs. 'It isn't a picture at all. It's just the way the chocolate happened to fall.'

'No need to play it down,' I encourage her. 'We all have our areas of expertise, and this is yours. One of many, I should say.'

'It isn't a heart,' she insists. 'It's a … smudge.'

'It would be an excellent way for researchers to conduct personality tests,' I say thoughtfully. 'It could replace the Rorschach test. How much more pleasant for the psychologists to conduct their meetings over a nice, foamy mug of cappuccino.'

'What if they're lactose intolerant?' asks Lily.

'Then they'll have to use lactose free milk, just as we do for our puppuccinos. If we can offer our customers a choice of eight different milks, I'm sure they could manage three or four. I wonder why I've never thought of it before? The Sugarloaf Bakery is always trying to expand into new and exciting areas. A couple of large contracts with prestigious medical institutions, and we'd be set for life.'

'It sounds intriguing,' says Lily. 'Although I doubt our future financial success will come off the back of contracts to administer dairy-based psychological tests.'

Simon takes a sip of his drink. 'I'm also sceptical about that. But this is the most delicious cappuccino I've had in a while.'

'Thank you, but I'm sure you're exaggerating,' says Lily.

'Why are my staff members unable to accept a compliment?' I ask. 'I never have the slightest difficulty in accepting the praise that is my due, whereas most people seem to struggle with it. It's a mystery.'

'She's right,' Simon tells Lily. 'This is an excellent cappuccino. I'll be coming in here more often now I've found you.'

Mavis catches his eye. 'Hello again.'

Instead of shrieking in terror and making a run for it, as many people are prone to do when she fixes them with her gimlet eye, he smiles back at her.

'Hello, Mavis. Nice to see you again.'

'Where are my manners?' I ask. 'I didn't want to scare you off by introducing you to so many formidable women all at once. But I can at least make a general introduction. These are the Silver Surfers. They're doing most of the organisation for the arts centre. Most of you saw Simon when he came in yesterday. He produced the design for the arts centre.'

'How's the work going on the new building?' Ivy asks him. 'Do you think it will be completed on time?'

'That isn't really my department,' he says. 'But Jon seems confident everything will be ready by the date specified.'

'That's good,' says Phyllis. 'It would be a shame to have to move the grand opening.'

'When is it?' asks Lily.

'The August bank holiday. It seemed the most suitable date. There's still the chance of warm weather, and most people won't be working.'

'What do you have planned?' asks Simon.

Phyllis ignores the warning look I shoot her as she starts to describe all the activities. Sometimes I despair of our customers. I've only just finished laying out my theory about the goings-on at The Red Lion, and here she is blabbing about our top secret plans for the grand opening. Am I the only one who remembers the motto that loose lips sink ships?

'What do you think of the building?' Ivy asks Simon. 'I was surprised to hear how old it was. We assumed it had been added after the pub, but Mr Barker told us they were both built in the late 1800s.'

'It's a lovely building,' he says with enthusiasm. 'It's been a pleasure to draw up the plans for it. I was glad to hear you wanted a few of the previous interior changes reversed. I'm not sure how they even got planning permission for some of them. It was the sixties, but still ...'

'We're lucky it isn't a listed building,' says Phyllis. 'The pub is, which means they need permission to make any changes, even to the window frames. But they didn't add the second building to the list. I doubt the village could have raised enough money to buy and renovate a listed building. And the council might have been less keen to give us our grant.'

'They would,' agrees Ivy. 'Bob's friend insisted on going into all that very thoroughly. There were no covenants on our building, which was a surprise. But it would be unfair of us to take advantage of that, which is why Mavis asked your firm to draw up the designs. She said you have a reputation for sympathetic restoration.'

'She's right,' says Simon. 'We've done a lot of this sort of work. Our senior partners were quite keen to take on the project. The building has some interesting features we're keen to preserve.'

He finishes his tart and pushes away his plate. 'I should be going. I have a meeting back at the office in half an hour. I didn't mean to stay so long, but your wonderful cakes delayed me. And the excellent company.'

I carry his plate and mug to the kitchen. He follows me.

'Can I get you anything else?' I ask. 'Something to take with you for a midnight snack if your meeting goes on longer than you expect?'

He lowers his voice so only I can hear. 'I didn't just come in here today to assess your coffee making skills or try your world-beating apple tarts. I wanted to see you.'

'Well, here I am.'

It isn't my snappiest comeback, but he's taken me by surprise. Has he heard how my meeting went with Jon and come to tell me I was treated most unfairly, and he'd like to offer us a fifty percent discount and a grovelling apology? That would be one in the eye for Mavis and teach her not to make snap judgements about my negotiating abilities.

'Here you are,' he agrees. 'I was wondering whether you'd like to have dinner with me sometime this week?'

Over his shoulder, I see Lily giving me a thumbs up. I can't think why. For all she knows, Simon is telling me he intends to report us to the food standards authority for violating some code or other.

'Isabella?' he says. 'You appear to have gone into a coma.'

'Sorry! My mind was elsewhere.'

'Just what you want to hear when asking a woman out on a date.'

I can't help laughing. 'Alright – why not?'

He gives me a quizzical look. 'I applaud your enthusiasm.'

'I mean, that would be very nice,' I say with a quick glance at Lily, who's grinning at me. She'll pay for that later.

'How about Saturday evening?' he asks. 'I'd like to lock down an actual date before you change your mind or slip back into that coma. Would you mind giving me your number so I can text you with some suggestions?'

'Saturday evening sounds good,' I say. 'But if you don't mind, I'd prefer to choose the actual venue.'

'Of course! Just text me and let me know what time I should pick you up.'

He says goodbye to everyone and takes his leave.

'Well, well, well!' says Mabel as soon as he's gone.

'Well, what?' I ask.

'Do I detect an incipient romance?'

'You do not. Any other questions?'

'Where will you suggest he takes you?' asks Lily. 'There's an Italian place in Christchurch that Jack and I have been hoping to try. You could scope it out for us and suggest what we should order.'

'You shouldn't have told us that,' says Phyllis. 'Certain members of our group might think it fun to book a table there too.'

'Not me!' says Mabel as all eyes turn to her. 'I can't abide most Italian food, apart from pizza.'

'It looks as though I've dodged a bullet there,' I tell her. 'And I didn't say we'd be going to the Italian restaurant. That was Lily's idea.'

Ivy grins at me. 'Even if you go further afield, you're almost bound to bump into one of your customers. We're everywhere. Mavis runs one of the most efficient spy networks in the country. No matter where you end up eating, someone will get wind of it and let us know. We'll know exactly what you've ordered before the kitchen has had time to fire up the oven.'

'I'm sorry you have nothing better to do with your time,' I say. 'I, on the other hand, do. Hand me that cloth will you, Lily? I need to clean up the tea Mabel spilled while she was trying to eavesdrop on my private conversation and not paying attention to what she was supposed to be doing.'

Chapter Twelve

I wipe up the spilled tea and am about to switch on the coffee machine to make myself a latte when the shop door opens again. Maybe Simon has forgotten his wallet or keys in all the excitement of asking me out. Some men find that kind of thing surprisingly difficult. It doesn't seem that complicated to me. All they have to do is mention they've found a new restaurant and prefer not to eat alone. But even that seems to be beyond many of their powers.

Simon didn't do too badly, although I'd have preferred him to ask me in a more private setting. It's never the best idea to allow the Silver Surfers to get wind of personal details. They're like the proverbial elephants who never forget – particularly things like someone's failure to secure a large discount.

But Simon wasn't to know that. And he didn't blush, stammer, or forget my name. I doubt anything will come of Saturday's date. But he's friendly and pleasant, both of which make him a more than acceptable substitute for Georgia, who's more than usually grumpy at the moment.

I've asked her several times why, if she hates her job so much, she doesn't find herself a new one, but she always tells me to mind my own business. She tends to prefix the word business with the word 'failing', which is hurtful. She has no understanding of the sterling work Lily and I do here each day. Equally obviously, she has no intention of finding out.

'Find yourself somewhere to sit, boys, and I'll bring you a menu,' says a voice.

It isn't Simon, back to retrieve his lost keys or take one last look at the woman he couldn't wait to ask out. It's Jon, and he's brought his boys with him.

I wave at the pair of them as they rush past me. I don't think they notice me as they tussle with each other for the corner seat at my favourite table.

'We're here to redeem your promise of cookies,' says Jon as I turn to face him.

'I haven't forgotten. I just didn't expect to see you again so soon.'

He smiles. 'You can't offer free cookies to nine-year-old boys, then expect them to wait for several weeks to redeem it.'

'I know that. I was once a nine-year-old myself. Not a boy, but I'm not sure that makes much difference. In fact, I know it doesn't. My sister and I wouldn't have waited for even this long.'

'I hope you haven't run out of cookies?' he asks.

'The Sugarloaf Bakery never runs out of cookies. There would be mass firings should such a thing occur.'

'There are only three of us working here,' says Lily. 'You'd be bankrupt within a week if you fired all your colleagues. You'll have to make do with written warnings instead.'

'Lily, this is Jon,' I say. 'He's the project manager for the arts centre. You remember me telling you how I bumped into him this morning.'

'I do indeed,' she says. 'Although bumped into him may not be the best phrase to use under the circumstances.'

I gesture towards the two tables of women. 'And these are the Silver Surfers. Ladies, this is Jon. He's liaising with the contractors and making sure everything comes in on time and doesn't exceed our budget.'

I lay particular emphasis on the word budget, in case any of them haven't made the connection.

'The one who tripped you up?' asks Mabel.

'Is that what you told them?' Jon asks me.

'And was rude to you,' adds Barb.

I try to remember what I told them about our conversation, and whether I exaggerated in any small way.

'Not rude, exactly,' I begin.

'Not rude at all,' says Jon. Is it my imagination, or is his tone the tiniest bit exasperated?

'Are you aware we sent Isabella to talk to you?' Phyllis asks him.

'Which we wouldn't have done if we'd had the slightest idea how badly you would treat her,' agrees Irene.

I try not to catch Jon's eye. This is his fight, not mine. I wonder whether now might be a good time to slip into the office and work on some of those urgent emails.

'Don't forget our cookies!' calls Toby, and the tension breaks.

'Coming right up!' I call back. 'I'll check which kinds we have in stock.'

Jon lays a hand on my arm before I can move. 'One moment. Perhaps you'd like to clear this up first. These women appear to believe you and I quarrelled this morning.'

'Quarrelled?' I say lightly. 'Not at all. I'd say it was more of a slight misunderstanding. On your part, rather than mine.'

'I don't remember any misunderstanding. As far as I'm concerned, you asked for a discount for your building work. I told you it was out of the question, and we left it at that.'

'Not if I know Isabella,' says Mabel. 'No one refuses her anything and gets to leave it at that.'

Jon's face relaxes. 'I was giving you the condensed version. There may have been some back and forth between us. But, as I explained to Isabella, there's absolutely no wiggle room in this contract. We've already negotiated favourable terms for you as this is a community project, and we've kept the profit margins to a minimum. There's no room for further movement.'

I give him my most enigmatic smile. 'We'll see.'

'No, we won't. That's my final word on the subject.'

I'm tempted to argue further but remember in time he has his children with him. As small boys go, they're on the more acceptable side, which is surprising, considering they have such a stubborn, pig-headed father. Maybe they have their mother's genes.

'I was about to tell your boys which flavour cookies we have in stock today,' I say. 'We have cherry and walnut, salted caramel, and white chocolate. The cherry and walnut are my particular favourite, but the white chocolate cookies are larger. It's a difficult decision, and I'm glad it's not one I need to make.'

Ivy laughs. 'I've never seen you make any cake-related decisions.'

I interrupt before she can expand on this. For some reason, our customers are under the impression that cake plays a far larger role in my life than it really does. I'm not sure how that rumour got started. But, like all rumours, it's almost impossible to dispel.

'We're not talking about my choice of cookies,' I tell her. 'This is about Ollie and Toby. Take your time, boys. This is an important decision and one which may affect the rest of your lives. At least, the rest of your afternoon. Choose wisely!'

'Our cookies may be good, but they aren't the holy grail,' says Lily. 'Although there's no point telling you that. You and cookies are like –'

I cut her off mid-speech before she can do her bit to destroy my reputation with my adversary as well. What is it with people in this village and cake? Anyone would think I had an unnatural cake obsession instead of a healthy appreciation of the finer things in life.

'I'd like a salted caramel, please,' says Ollie.

'Cherry and walnut,' decides Toby.

'Excellent choices,' I say. 'I don't think you'll regret them. I never have, and I've been working here for the past eight years. Could you do the honours, Lily? You'll need to ask the boys for the special password.'

'I didn't know we needed a password to order things,' says Mabel. 'Is this a new rule?'

'Is it like those supermarket loyalty schemes?' asks Barb. 'You collect points each time you buy something, and you get money off your next shop?'

'Or periodic special offers,' suggests Mary. 'What a good idea.'

'Will you give us all a card?' asks Ivy. 'Or will there be an app for our phones? Is it alright if Bob and I share an account? It doesn't make sense for us both to save separately. It would take us far too long to build up enough points for the really large bonus products.'

'I hope I can get enough points to collect an entire tea service,' says Phyllis. 'I adore the china pattern you use in here.'

I throw an anguished look at Lily, who's bound to be annoyed with me. It will take some time to persuade her I haven't been developing a secret marketing plan without bothering to include her. It's amazing how little faith people have in me sometimes, and how prone they are to suspect the worst.

To my surprise, I see she's smiling. Does she think this is a good idea? Because it very definitely isn't. It's all very well for the supermarkets to offer loyalty programmes so they can harvest huge amounts of information about their customers and advertise to them more effectively. A business of our size can't possibly offer that sort of scheme and still expect to make a profit. Leaving aside the fact we already know all there is to know about most of our customers.

How will the knowledge that Mabel gets irritable if we run out of plum slices and likes lemon in her earl grey instead of milk enable us to market anything to her? And, given the amount of time and money most of our customers spend in here, they could bankrupt us in a week if we offered free gifts, especially if they banded together to pool their points. The bakery might have to close down by the end of the month.

I take a deep breath to explain some of this to Lily when I realise our customers are watching me intently. To my annoyance, they all have broad grins on their faces.

'I never thought I'd get the better of Isabella Campbell!' says Mabel delightedly. 'I've been trying to do that since the day I met you, and I'd almost given up hope of succeeding.'

'The look on your face when I mentioned free sets of china!' adds Phyllis with a splutter of laughter. 'I must tell Rose about it the next time I see her.'

'You don't really expect us to set up loyalty cards?' I ask.

It's disappointing to discover our customers have so little respect for me that they're happy to make frivolous jokes at my expense. But it's a huge relief to think we may still be in business six months from now.

'Of course not,' says Ivy. 'Although you might like to consider offering those coffee cards. Buy ten, get one free. That sort of thing.'

'Isabella hands out enough free stuff as it is,' says Lily. 'Please don't encourage her to make it a formal practice.'

The boys have been conferring all this time with worried looks on their faces.

Ollie nudges Toby, who looks at Lily with a hopeful expression. 'Jammy Badger?'

'Dodger,' I tell him. 'But close enough. Lily will bring your cookies as soon as she's finished behaving in a most unprofessional way towards her friend and colleague.'

Lily hands the boys their plates. 'I won't say make them last because I have a boy of my own. So, I'll just say enjoy!'

They beam at her and make a grab for the cookies.

'How about me?' asks Jon. 'Don't I get one too if I remember the password?'

He smiles at me, but I harden my heart, remembering he's made me look a fool in front of all the people here today. He may even have been responsible for them losing a certain amount of respect for me, which would be annoying after several years of being the person they've all looked up to.

'You can't refuse to accede to the very minor request I made of you, then expect me to offer you a favour,' I tell him. 'That isn't how business negotiations work. Or personal ones. I was strongly tempted to tell the boys the password was Your Father is a Grump. But I didn't want to lessen their respect for you, so I went with Jammy Dodger.'

He stops smiling. 'I'm not their father.'

'I'm sorry,' I say. 'I just assumed –'

'You assumed wrongly,' he says, but doesn't elaborate.

'You know what they say about the word assume?' Mabel asks me.

'I do. It makes an ass out of you and me. My mother has been saying that to me ever since I was a child.'

She shakes her head. 'You can't spell it without a double s.'

'That makes no sense,' says Ivy. 'There are plenty of words you can't spell without a double s, but we don't turn them all into sayings.'

Mabel shrugs. 'I don't know what to tell you.'

I change the subject before they can start on one of their interminable discussions about something completely irrelevant. These arguments only end when I intervene to act as peacemaker and offer them free cake. I wonder whether that's the reason they do it.

'How are you getting on with those cookies, boys?' asks Jon.

'What cookies?' asks Toby, and they both snigger.

'Don't try to persuade me there were never any cookies on those plates,' I warn them. 'You have crumbs all over your faces.'

'At least it isn't cream,' says Ollie, and they both give a snort of laughter.

'That's enough!' says Jon. His voice is quiet, but there's a note of authority in it I recognise from my childhood when Georgia and I pushed our mother that bit too far.

'Sorry, Uncle Jon!' chorus the boys.

'I'm glad you enjoyed them,' I say. 'Our pastry chef makes the best cookies in the world. She's the one who made the cakes you ate this morning.'

Their eyes dart hopefully towards the counter.

'Another time,' says Jon. 'We just came in to redeem your free offer and for me to –'

'You should buy something,' Mabel tells him. 'This is a business, after all.'

I'm surprised she can say this with a straight face after the number of plum slices she's blagged off me over the years. But I appreciate her supportive attitude.

'Simon bought an apple tart,' agrees Ivy. 'And a cappuccino.'

'Simon was in here?' asks Jon.

'You just missed him,' says Phyllis. 'He said he was here to try out the cakes, but none of us believe that. He came to ask one of these very attractive staff members for a date.'

Jon glances from me to Lily, who laughs. 'Don't look at me! I have enough on my hands with a partner and two young children.'

'I know the feeling,' he says. 'Not the partner bit, but young children take up quite a bit of time.'

'Simon appears to have plenty of spare time,' says Mabel.

She winks at me, and I'm annoyed to feel myself blush. I'm glad Georgia isn't here. She'd never let me hear the end of it.

'We're laying bets on where Isabella decides to take him,' Phyllis tells Jon.

'I hope it's somewhere nice,' he says. 'Are you ready, boys? Bring your plates back to the counter and say your goodbyes. I need to get you home for dinner and a bath. And don't forget it's your piano lesson tomorrow. Your new piece won't learn itself.'

'I advise you to invest in earplugs,' I tell him. 'My sister learned the piano for one excruciating year when we were young. I had to threaten to take up the violin in order to put a stop to it.'

'We must get going,' he tells the boys. 'Strange though it seems after those enormous cookies, I'm convinced you'll be hungry again within the hour. Tonight's chicken can cook to the accompaniment of Three Blind Mice.'

Mavis gives him a considering look as he walks past her table. 'I'm sure we'll be meeting again in the near future.'

Instead of looking as though he's been turned to stone and babbling excuses and apologies, Jon gives her a pleasant smile. 'I look forward to it.'

Wonders will never cease!

Chapter Thirteen

I'm waiting at the end of the drive when Simon arrives on Saturday evening. I wave, and he pulls into the grass verge next to the gates.

'Thanks for picking me up,' I say. 'I'm technically allowed to drive, but I'm a bit rusty. I need to take my car out and practise a few emergency stops in a secluded place before subjecting the world to my driving again.'

'No problem,' he says. 'It seems pointless for us both to take our cars if we're going to the same place. Where is that, by the way? I forgot to fill my car on the way over here, so I only have half a tank of petrol.'

'You won't need more than a couple of litres,' I assure him. 'Even if you get lost on the way, which you won't because I'm superb at giving directions – unlike my sister, who once drove with me to Edinburgh to see my mother's family. I mistakenly allowed her to read the map, which was a mistake I won't make again. It was only once I started seeing signs for Newhaven that I insisted on stopping the car and checking for myself, only to discover she'd mistaken Newhaven for Newcastle. If I hadn't intervened, we might have found ourselves on the ferry heading for the Isle of Wight, with only a drop of petrol in the tank and limited internet connection.'

'Do we need a map this evening?' he asks.

'No need. I have the directions in my head. We're going to the industrial estate on the other side of Christchurch.'

'The one with the escape rooms?' he asks. 'I love escape rooms.'

'You'll love what I have planned for you even more,' I assure him.

'Did you meet me at the bottom of your drive because you wanted to avoid me meeting your family?'

'Not at all. Although most people prefer to avoid meeting my sister, given the choice.'

'Would your father have met me at the door carrying a shotgun?' he asks.

'I doubt it. He rarely wanders around the place with a twelve-bore slung over his shoulder. Quite the contrary. He's been heard to say the sooner someone takes both his daughters off his hands, the better pleased he'll be. It takes the budget of a small island nation to keep my sister in bacon sandwiches. And the length of her showers is legendary.'

'Is your house a part of Compton farm?' he asks.

'It used to be. At one point, all the land in Compton belonged to the Wyburn family. The Squire lived in the Manor House, and some of his hangers on and dependents lived in the lodge. When my grandfather bought the farm, he rented out the Manor House and lived in the lodge until he'd paid off the loan he'd taken out. By that time, he was close to retirement, and my uncle took over the farm. My father had no interest in joining the family business by that point and trained as an actuary. When my grandfather died, he left the farm to my uncle, along with the Manor House. He left the lodge to my father, along with a small share in the farm profits.'

'That seems a little unfair,' he says.

'On the contrary, it was the best way of doing things. You can't leave a farm to several different people, especially if some of them aren't interested in keeping it running. The farm would end up being sold off, and everyone would lose out. My father was quite happy with the arrangement, and my uncle has been more than generous to our family financially. So, we've lived in The Lodge ever since. I plan to move out in the not too distant future, but it would take an atom bomb to dislodge my sister. She's burrowed in, and nothing short of demolishing the house will have any effect.'

He smiles. 'You talk about her a lot.'

'That's odd, because I rarely think about her. It isn't possible to ignore her completely while I have to sleep in the bedroom next to hers and share mealtimes with her. But I'm hoping to put an end to that in the next year or so.'

'I'd be interested to meet her,' he says.

'I can't think why, although you'd be very welcome to. You should drop into Martine's clothing store in Christchurch any day between 11 a.m. and 2 p.m. Georgia is the tall, blonde woman with the scowl. You can't miss her.'

'Does she only work there part time?' he asks.

'Technically, the answer is no. She has a full-time contract. But unfortunately for everyone, she hasn't inherited my admirable work ethic, which comes from our Scottish ancestors. Somehow, the hard-working gene missed my sister. She must be some sort of genetic throwback. It happens in the best of families, I believe. It's a burden we all have to bear as cheerfully as possible.'

'I'm even more eager to meet her,' he says.

'You know now where you can occasionally find her. Although I can't guarantee she won't greet you with a twelve-bore. My sister lives by her own rules.'

'Thanks for the warning,' he says. 'But you told me your family has nothing to do with the farm, so I'm not too worried.'

'Not quite nothing. I still help out during lambing season, but that's only for fun, and it never involves firearms. The sheep are skittish enough without that. My uncle keeps a couple of working sheepdogs, and they manage things for him.'

He turns off the roundabout and heads towards the industrial estate. 'I'm intrigued to discover where you're taking me tonight. Am I allowed to guess?'

'If you like.'

'You've already told me we aren't visiting an escape room, and we aren't driving into the town centre, so it's unlikely to be a restaurant.'

'You'll be able to eat,' I assure him. 'I never take anyone out without ensuring there's plenty of food available.'

'Which rules out dropping me off in the middle of nowhere as part of a survival course.'

'That isn't the plan,' I say. 'Although it's an excellent idea, and one I wish I'd thought of. Have you ever taken part in one of those?'

'No, but my brother has had to do a few. He's a member of the Territorial Army, and one of their favourite activities is to abandon their volunteers in random places without access to food and water and see how long they last.'

'No food at all?' I ask, horrified.

'Only what they can hunt and scavenge. And they have to build their own shelters.'

'I'd bring several days' rations along with me in my backpack.'

'According to my brother, plenty of people have the same idea, but their bags are carefully searched beforehand. Is that why you run a bakery – to ensure you're never more than ten metres away from something to eat?'

'It's a reason,' I say, 'But not the only one. I really love what I do. The Sugarloaf Bakery may not be the largest bakery in the world, but it's just the right size for where it is. I love that we're a central part of our community, and that we know all our customers, and they know us. I like to think we provide a service far beyond providing the inhabitants of Honeywell with bread and cake.'

'Here we are,' he says, pulling off the main road. 'Where would you like me to park?'

'Over there.' I point to the rows of cars at the far end of the tarmac strip.

He pulls into a parking space and looks at the building in front of us. 'I still have no clue.'

'What do you mean? I know you can read because I've seen the plans you've drawn up for the arts centre. And you've managed to follow all the road signs this evening.'

'I am, in fact, literate,' he agrees. 'What am I missing here?'

I gesture to the sign on the building. 'I don't understand the confusion.'

He peers at it more closely. '*Bouncy Benny's Spring'n'Swing.* Very funny.'

'Lots of fun,' I agree, unbuckling my seatbelt and climbing out of the car. 'Come on! It opened ten minutes ago.'

He follows me over to the big double doors. They've been propped open, and we can hear shouts and shrieks of laughter coming from inside.

He shakes his head in disbelief. 'This is not happening.'

'Not yet. But that's because you're still standing in the doorway, and the trampolines are over there.'

'Is this an elaborate practical joke?' he asks. 'I won't be upset if you say you've been leading me up the garden path, and you're really taking me to the cute little speakeasy located on the far side of that wall.'

'That sounds fun, but I doubt anyone could obtain planning permission for a speakeasy so close to where children hang out. You can suggest it to the proprietor if you like. He might be interested in the opportunity.'

He pounces on this. 'Exactly! This is a place for children, not for adults.'

I give him a pitying smile. 'You don't escape that easily. There are hundreds of adults here. There's a man sitting at that table, and I see two more standing over there.'

He makes one last, desperate attempt. 'They're only here because their children need someone to keep an eye on them.'

'Short of asking them to produce their ID cards and the birth certificates of any children they may be accompanying, you can't know that for sure. People come here all the time without their children. Lily and Jack spent an evening trampolining here last year. Lily said it was the most fun she'd had for ages. They chose not to invite their own children, which shows this place is for adults too. Besides, it's the place I've chosen to bring you, and I've prepaid, so you'll have to make the most of it. Now, let's join the queue for our wristbands before all the best trampolines have gone.'

Chapter Fourteen

Simon reluctantly stands next to me as I line up to show the QR code I've downloaded onto my phone.

'Trampolining?' he asks in a despairing tone.

'Yes.'

'As in jumping up and down on bouncy mats supported by springs?'

'That's the general idea. I'm delighted how quickly you've understood the concept. It must be your architect training. It sharpens the mind and enables the recipient to understand things the average person would take weeks to assimilate.'

'There was nothing about this in my degree or any of my professional qualifications,' he says.

'How disappointing. You've never had an eccentric millionaire demand you put a trampoline in his bedroom?'

'Never.'

'That seems very odd to me. If I were a multi-millionaire, I'd ask you to design me a huge mansion with trampolines in all of the main bedrooms. And I'd have a swimming pool in the basement, with flumes leading down to it from the rooms on the top floor. I suggested something very similar for the arts centre, but it was vetoed on the grounds of cost.'

'Was that the only reason?' he asks.

'What else could it have been? Mavis said it was a creative difference, which I interpreted as her saying it was an excellent idea, and she wished she'd been the one to suggest it. But economic considerations had to come into play, so we agreed to postpone the idea for now and come back to it later if we had a budget surplus.'

'Which you didn't,' he points out, rather unkindly in my opinion.

'We didn't. But there's no need to rub that in.'

I show my phone to the man behind the counter. 'Two adults for the Big Fun package.'

He scans the barcode. 'It would have been cheaper to buy a family ticket.'

'Cheaper than two adults?' I ask.

'Two adults and two children works out almost five pounds cheaper overall.'

'It would work out more expensive for us,' I say. 'We didn't bring two children, and it's a little late now for us to go out and find any.'

He peers at me suspiciously. 'You don't have children with you?'

'Not to the best of my knowledge.'

'Then you won't need a family ticket.'

'It seems that way,' I agree. 'Although, just to be clear, I'm not the one who raised the subject.'

He hands me my phone. 'Enjoy your evening.'

'We intend to!' I say. 'This is our first date.'

'Good luck, mate,' he says to Simon. 'Next, please!'

'That was nice of him,' I say as we sit down to remove our shoes.

'What was?' asks Simon.

'The man at the desk. He wished us good luck on our date.'

'I think he was talking to me, rather than us. And the good luck part sounded sarcastic to me.'

I hand him a pound coin. 'You'll need that for your locker. And you're wrong about that man. I heard nothing but sincerity in his voice. He was cheering us on. I thought it was very kind of him.'

He pulls me to my feet. 'If you say so. Let's put our things safely into the lockers and get on with it.'

'That's the spirit. I knew you'd come to appreciate the brilliance of this idea.'

'I haven't given up hope of finding that speakeasy,' he warns me.

'And neither should you. Hope is what keeps the human race going. It's aspiration that gets us out of bed each morning. Where would we be without it?'

'What next?' he asks.

'We choose a trampoline, and we bounce! Inside or outside?'

'They have them outside too?'

'Of course. They're very popular on summer evenings such as this one. You leap up and down, feeling the wind in your hair and enjoying the view over' – I peer through the double doors towards the stretch of grass where dozens of children are bouncing and shrieking – 'the car park.'

'That doesn't sound like much of a view.'

'If you bounce high enough, you can catch a glimpse of the factory tower,' I say encouragingly.

He shrugs. 'Your call. I don't really mind.'

'It seems a pity to waste such a lovely evening inside. Race you to the trampolines!'

He lays a hand on my arm. 'Weren't you recently in the hospital with a broken leg? Should you be doing something like this?'

'According to my physiotherapist, I very much should. She said gentle, weight-bearing exercise is essential to restore bone health. She recommended I bought myself a rebounder. I haven't got around to that yet, but I plan to if tonight goes well.'

'I hope you're insured,' he says as we walk across the grass towards a couple of spare trampolines at the far end.

'No need. This place is an insurance broker's dream. They're covered for every eventuality.'

'Is that why we had to sign a waiver?' he asks.

'You worry too much. I'm the one who broke her leg, and I'm not at all worried about this evening. You should take a leaf out of my book and seize life with both hands. Watch me do a double somersault!'

'Isabella!' he says in a warning tone.

I grin at him and give an experimental bounce. 'I'm teasing you. Stop looking so serious and grab that trampoline before someone else does.'

I always loved trampolining as a child. I can't think why I haven't been here before. It's far more fun than spending the evening in a wine bar or watching a movie. My leg begins to ache after about half an hour, and I reluctantly stop and climb off.

Simon stops too. 'Have you had enough?'

'Not even close. But my physiotherapist told me to pace myself, so I will. You'll notice I confined myself to gentle bouncing this evening and didn't attempt my signature triple flip with a reverse double twist.'

'That sounds more like a cocktail than a trampoline move,' he says.

'Are you back on the subject of hidden bars? I hate to disappoint you, but I'm almost sure there's no speakeasy behind those arcade machines. Maybe we can get ourselves something to eat before trying this again. I paid for the all-inclusive ticket.'

He gives me a wary look. 'What's that?'

'A mega-gulp soda and a large hot dog with all the trimmings.'

'A hot dog?' he asks, as though unable to believe his ears.

'A large one,' I reassure him. 'Don't worry. You won't be limited to just one. That's what the ticket includes, but you can order as many as you like. Chips too. It's all on me!'

'Do they serve coffee?'

'I expect so, although it seems a shame to pass up the opportunity of a free mega-gulp.'

'Come on then,' he says. 'Do your worst.'

We join the queue at the hot dog stand. Excited children mill around, shouting to their friends and parents.

'I hope they don't run out of hot dogs before we reach the counter,' I say. 'Children can be so greedy. I'm not sure why. They're only half the size of adults, so by rights they ought only to eat half the amount. But it doesn't seem to work like that. My goddaughter is tiny, but she puts away a terrifying quantity of food. Luckily, her mother remembers to make plenty extra whenever I visit.'

A small boy rushes up and joins the queue behind us. 'Toby! Over here!' he yells.

Another boy runs up to join him. I look at them more carefully. They're scarlet in the face and not as clean as they might be, but I recognise them as Jon's nephews. I hope they're here with friends tonight, or their parents, rather than their uncle.

Simon recognises them too. 'Hi, Toby. Hi, Ollie. I didn't expect to see you here.'

They grin at him. 'Uncle Jon brought us.'

Is there nowhere in the New Forest area I can go to be free of Uncle Jon and his overbearing ways? Maybe he's just dropped them off here and arranged to pick them up later. Or maybe there really is a speakeasy, and he's sitting there right now getting quietly drunk.

No such luck. Before I can ask the question, Simon turns and waves. I recognise the tall figure striding towards us, and my heart sinks. Perhaps my wonderful idea for a date wasn't so wonderful after all.

'This is the last place I expected to see you,' Jon tells Simon as he reaches us.

His gaze falls on me, and his eyebrows shoot up. 'Or you!'

'I might say the same thing to you,' I say. 'Yet here we all are. Life has a habit of surprising us.'

'You're here together?' he asks.

I'm about to tell him that Simon and I were both seized by a sudden, unaccountable urge to spend the evening trampolining. Finding the experience far scarier than either of us had anticipated, we joined forces in the belief it would raise our chances of survival from a mere ten percent to a far more acceptable twenty to thirty percent.

Sadly, Simon pre-empts me. 'Yes, we're on a date.'

'Would I be right in thinking the venue was Isabella's idea?' asks Jon.

'Quite correct,' says Simon. 'What was your first clue?'

Jon looks at the trampolines, then at the hot dog stand. 'Call it intuition.'

'It was a lucky guess,' I say, nettled. 'And isn't it supposed to be females who have intuition?'

'I wouldn't have expected you to subscribe to such out-of-date, last-century thinking,' he says. 'Men can have male intuition nowadays, and I was exercising mine.'

'It's a free country. And you're allowed to make your own decisions.'

'You're very kind,' he says. 'Toby, if you don't stop twisting Ollie's arm, I'm taking you home.'

Toby lets his brother go. A moment later, the pair of them are busy giggling at the sight of a burly man who has climbed onto a nearby trampoline and is struggling to keep his balance as he jumps up and down.

'I know why I'm queueing up to order a hot dog made from ingredients I prefer not to think about,' says Jon 'What I'm less clear about it why you two are doing the same.'

'I love hot dogs!' I say. 'And they're included in the price of our entrance ticket.'

'As is something called a mega-gulp,' says Simon in a resigned tone.

Jon laughs. 'Not your cup of tea?'

'A cup of tea would be a welcome alternative. But it seems as though only old fogies order tea and coffee at a place like this.'

'I promised to buy you as many hot dogs as you could eat,' I remind him.

He winces slightly. 'I remember.'

'Will you buy us as many hot dogs as we can eat, Uncle Jon?' asks Ollie.

'I will not. I don't intend to give you a list of reasons, but I can assure you there are several.'

Ollie shoots me and Simon a resentful look. 'That's not fair. If they're allowed to eat lots of hot dogs, why can't we?'

'Because they're adults, and you aren't,' says his uncle. 'One of life's great unfairnesses is that the things we dream of doing as children – and swear we'll do the moment we're old enough – are often the things we no longer want to do once we're grown up.'

'That can't be true,' argues Toby. 'Isabella just said she's buying lots of hot dogs.'

'I did indeed,' I agree. 'And I'd be happy to buy some for you too. But perhaps we'd better listen to your uncle, who, although horribly strict and grumpy, may have his reasons for behaving as he does.'

'Thank you for recognising that,' says Jon. 'He does.'

'And no one ever grows out of liking hot dogs,' I reassure the boys.

'You can have all mine once you grow up,' Simon tells them.

'Next!' says the woman at the till in an impatient tone.

I hand her our tickets. 'Two, please. And don't stint on the mustard.'

Chapter Fifteen

We sit at a nearby table and watch the boys choose their drinks and order their hotdogs.

'Rather Jon than me,' I say, taking a grateful sip of my soda. Trampolining is thirsty work, and the fizzy lemonade hits the spot.

'I don't know where he finds the energy,' agrees Simon. 'But those boys are lucky to have him.'

I'm tempted to make a flippant comment about tyrannical uncles and the desirability of possessing them, but I restrain myself. I don't know Simon very well, and several of my attempts at humour so far have missed the mark. And it isn't as though Jon is Richard the Third, and his nephews the Princes in the Tower. It's unlikely he's plotting to lock them in a dungeon or pitch them into the Thames any time soon. Not impossible, but unlikely. I should keep my feelings about him to myself and not criticise him to his co-workers. I wouldn't be too impressed if someone came into the bakery to tell Lily she'd made a mistake in choosing to go into partnership with me.

'Can we sit with Isabella and Simon?' asks Ollie. He doesn't wait for a reply, but plonks himself down in the seat opposite me.

'Not tonight,' says Jon. 'They're on a date.'

Toby gives us an incredulous look, and both the boys snort with laughter.

'No, they aren't!' says Ollie. 'People don't go on dates at *Bouncy Benny's Spring'n'Swing.*'

'Not usually,' says Simon. 'But occasionally they do, and this is one of those times.'

He obligingly moves his chair to allow Toby to sit next to Ollie.

'I'd offer to fetch you a chair too,' I tell Jon. 'But I'm afraid I might trip over something if I did. People are so careless, and they leave things lying around in the most unexpected places.'

'I can manage,' he says. 'If you're sure you don't mind us joining you?'

I look at the crowds of yelling, over-excited children, some of whom have abandoned shouting for noisy crying when their parents tell them it's time to leave.

'Not at all,' I say. 'We don't need privacy to eat hot dogs.'

Jon unwraps his greaseproof paper and dubiously inspects the contents. 'So, how's the date going so far?'

'Amazingly!' I say before Simon can speak. 'Simon was telling me how he's never been on one quite like it.'

A muscle quivers at the corner of Jon's mouth, but he doesn't respond.

'I thought it would be fun,' I add. 'And it is. Don't you agree, boys?'

'It's the best place in the world,' says Ollie through a large mouthful of bread.

'Except for Pine Ridge,' says Toby.

'Nowhere is as good as Pine Ridge,' says Ollie, cramming the last of his hot dog into his mouth and swallowing it without feeling the need to chew it first.

'Where and what is Pine Ridge?' asks Simon, handing his hot dog to Ollie, who looks at it as though he's just discovered the lost treasure of the Pharaohs.

'It's the place where Uncle Jon is taking us camping next week,' says Toby. 'It has canoes and a rock climbing wall and ziplining –'

'I've always wanted to do that!' I say. 'I went up in a hot air balloon last year, and it was amazing. Anything involving your feet leaving the ground is fun.'

'Hence the trampolining?' asks Jon.

'Yes, it's nowhere near as good as ziplining, but it's better than going for a walk.'

'Even a romantic one?' he asks, looking from me to Simon as though trying to make sense of something.

'There's nothing romantic about walks,' I say. 'Either they're in a built up area, so you're constantly on the alert for careless drivers and stray joggers. Or you venture into more rural areas, where you have to watch out for bogs and swamps and wild animals.'

'I thought you lived on a farm,' says Simon. 'You must be accustomed to animals.'

'As I told you earlier, I live next to a farm. And my uncle keeps domesticated animals, not wild ones. Most farmers do. The only animals I come into regular contact with are his sheepdogs, who are lovely. And of course, the sheep. They aren't the brightest creatures on the planet, but they're very good-natured and easy-going, much like myself. It may be why we get along so well. That, and the fact they know they can rely on me to turn out at 3 a.m. on a freezing cold February night to mop their fevered brows while they're in labour.'

'I'm sure they appreciate it,' says Jon. 'Do you do anything more useful to help them during their hour of need?'

'Mopping their brows is useful! You must have heard of doulas. People pay them huge amounts of money to turn up and make helpful comments like "Breathe" and "It won't be long now." Whereas I do it all for free.'

'What do you do for free?' asks Ollie, tuning into our conversation in that disconcerting way children have when you think they aren't listening.

'Help the sheep have their babies,' I say. 'They're usually quite happy to have them alone, but sometimes they need a bit of encouragement. So, I pop along and play them whale music and hold essential oils under their noses.'

'What sort of whale music?' he demands. 'Like Baby Shark?'

'Definitely not! I have a goddaughter who was obsessed with that a few years ago. I still have nightmares about it. She demanded to hear it morning, noon and night. Especially night. I had to threaten to stop going over there for sleepovers if she didn't ask Alexa to play something else.'

'Did she?' asks Toby.

'Eventually, but I had to sweeten the deal by promising to bring her favourite cookies to all our sleepovers for a year. I tried to get out of it by secretly telling Alexa she was under no circumstances to play that song again, even if she was ordered to.'

'Did Alexa take any notice of you?' asks Jon.

'Surprisingly, she did for a while. But I think Daisy must have worked out what was happening and unplugged the system before switching it back on. Those electronic so-called helpers have alarmingly short memories. That's when I changed tactics and switched to outright bribery.'

'This is not a story of how you should behave,' Jon warns the boys. 'It's a cautionary tale of an inexperienced godmother getting herself into a mess because she didn't know any better.'

'That isn't the way I'd have put it,' I say. 'But your uncle is right. A year's supply of cookies is too high a price to pay to get something you want. Unless you own a bakery, which I'm fairly sure neither of you do.'

'I wish I did,' says Ollie. 'I'd like to have one just like yours!'

'That's a lovely thing to say. Just for that, you may have another free cookie the next time you come in. Same password as before. Maybe write it on your brother's arm next time so you don't forget it.'

Three hotdogs later, the boys and I are full. I finish my drink and lean back in my chair to catch my breath.

'What next?' asks Simon.

'Everything!' I say with enthusiasm.

'We should leave you to it,' says Jon. 'Enjoy the rest of your evening. Come on, boys. I'm going to take you on at crazy golf and beat you both with one hand tied behind my back.'

'An unconventional way of playing,' I say. 'But who am I to dictate someone else's sporting style?'

'Can't Isabella come with us?' asks Toby.

'I've already told you she and Simon are on a date,' says Jon.

'What do you say?' I ask Simon. 'Would you like to take them on?'

'Me?' he asks, startled.

'I meant together. Look at the three of them! We'll beat them in seconds. Two of them aren't even full-sized.'

I wink at Ollie and Toby, who grin back at me.

'And the other one needs to put his money where his mouth is,' I say. 'He boasted of his amazing golf prowess the first day I met him. Now's the time to make that boast good.'

'I wouldn't call it boasting,' says Jon.

'Well?' I persist. 'Do you accept our challenge?'

The boys high-five each other.

I look at Simon, who grins. 'Why not? This date already feels like Alice Through the Looking Glass. Why not make it even more surreal?'

'That's Alice in Wonderland,' I say. 'Or it is if you're talking about using the flamingos to play croquet.'

'Not particularly. It's been a long time since I read those books.'

'You should try them again. I read them to my lovely goddaughter. She loves them.'

'I can see you getting along well with the Mad Hatter,' says Jon.

'I'll be grinning like the Cheshire Cat when Simon and I wipe the floor with you,' I tell him. 'I confidently predict that by the end of the evening, one of us will be stuck down a rabbit hole – and it won't be me. I'll get the highest score in the history of this place.'

'The aim of this game is to achieve the lowest possible score,' he says.

'Whatever! It doesn't change the fact you're all going down. I expect they'll ring a bell to mark the occasion. And then put your names up on the board of shame.'

'I don't think they have one.'

'They will after tonight,' I say. 'Do you plan to stand around all evening arguing about it or shall we pick up our clubs and begin? I predict we'll have beaten you beyond all hope of recovery by the time you leave.'

Jon pushes back his chair and beckons to the boys to join him. 'Let's find out if you're right.'

Chapter Sixteen

Sadly, we aren't destined to discover whether or not I am. No sooner have we selected our clubs and picked up our score cards than a man appears. He's wearing a red polo shirt with a *Bouncy Benny's Spring'n'Swing* logo on one pocket and a badge saying Justin on the other.

'I'm afraid you can't do that,' he says.

'No need to worry,' I say, swinging my club to assess its balance. 'We aren't amateurs. Except Simon here, and he'll soon pick it up. The rest of us are seasoned professionals.'

He doesn't look reassured by this. Is he about to tell me only amateur players are allowed on this course?

'When I say professional,' I add, 'I'm speaking in the loosest possible sense. None of us has ever won money from playing this sport.'

'That isn't what I mean,' says Justin. He gestures towards my wrist. 'It's the wrong colour.'

I glance down at my wrist, which looks much the same colour as ever. He surely can't be referring to the faint smear of ketchup on my left sleeve. Just in case, I roll up my cuffs.

'Your wristband,' he says with exaggerated patience. 'It's yellow.'

'It is indeed. It's one of my favourite colours.'

He points to the large clock on the wall by the counter. 'Yellow bands finish at eight thirty.'

'Is it that late already?' asks Simon. 'How time flies when you're having fun.'

'No one mentioned a time limit when they gave us our bands,' I say. 'I just saw you opened at six-thirty and made sure we arrived on time.'

'It's written very clearly on our website,' says Justin. 'Yellow bands from six-thirty to eight thirty. After that, it's red bands only.'

'I noticed it at the time I booked,' says Jon. 'But I thought we had another half hour left.'

I look around the hall. Does everything change once the wimpy yellow-banders have disappeared and the macho red-banders have taken their place? Maybe the lights dim at 8.31 p.m. precisely, and the cafe stops serving hot dogs and mega-gulp sodas and switches over to whisky and beef jerky. Why didn't I book us in for a later session?

I know the answer to that one. I was trying to stay away from any time of day that might be construed as romantic, so Simon didn't get any ideas. I'm not entirely sure when the gloaming is, but I believe it happens around 9 p.m. in the summer. I'm equally sure it's a time of day the poets of old considered to be highly sentimental. I wish now I'd taken the risk. It would have been worth it to discover what goes on at *Bouncy Benny's Spring'n'Swing* after the witching hour.

'I don't know how I came to miss that,' I tell Justin. 'I may have been carried away with excitement by the thought of this evening and overlooked it. Could we buy ourselves some red bands now and get over the problem in that way?'

'I'm sorry to say you can't,' says Justin, looking anything but sorry. 'We're booked up. We can't go over capacity or they'll shut us down.'

'We won't stay for the entire two hours,' I say. 'Just long enough for Simon and me to inflict a crushing defeat on these three. After that, we'll make ourselves scarce. We won't even order any more hot dogs. We'll leave them all for the red-banders.'

Not one person in a million could refuse this request. It's reasonable, politely phrased, and makes it clear there's no threat to their sausage and ketchup supplies. If things at the bakery don't work out, I should consider a career at the UN.

Sadly, it appears Justin is that one in a million person everyone dreads meeting.

'I'm afraid I'll have to ask you all to leave,' he says. 'You should have left ten minutes ago. Didn't you hear the announcement?'

'We heard a voice saying something,' I say. 'But it was very crackly. We stopped talking long enough for it to get whatever it wanted to say off its chest, and then we continued with our conversation.'

For some reason, Justin's face now resembles the colour of his shirt.

'I can call the manager if you prefer,' he says in a threatening tone.

I lay down my club. 'That's a kind offer, but there's no need to disturb Benny. I'm sure he has more important things to do with his time than chat with complete strangers. Thank you for a very pleasant evening.'

The boys have been listening to our conversation with interest.

'Aren't we allowed to play golf?' asks Ollie.

'Not this evening,' I say. 'But the challenge still stands, and it gives you time to get in some much-needed practice. Your uncle may even have planned things this way. You'll notice he didn't mention the idea of golf until he knew it was too late for us to finish a game.'

'I didn't mention it earlier because you were eating hot dogs,' Jon tells me. 'I was too busy wondering how many you'd get through. Are you by any chance in training for a speed-eating contest?'

'I am not. But decades of living with my younger sister have taught me never to pause for long while eating. It's the only way to survive in our household.'

'I'm even keener to meet your sister than I was before,' says Simon.

'Your call,' I say. 'But I think you'll be disappointed.'

Justin clears his throat menacingly. 'Am I to take it you're leaving right now?'

Simon takes my arm. 'Definitely. See you next time.'

Justin doesn't look quite as thrilled by the prospect of a second visit as I might have hoped. But perhaps he's had a busy day, or the beer pump at the speakeasy is blocked.

I give him a pleasant smile as we set off towards the lockers. 'Have a good evening!'

'I expect he will once you're safely off the premises,' says Jon.

I don't dignify this as I reach inside my locker for my shoes and socks.

'Uncle Jon bought us socks when we arrived,' says Toby, brandishing one at me. It's bright yellow and says Left.

'Let me guess,' I say. 'The other one says Down?'

'It says Right.' He pulls off his other sock and waves it at me. 'See? Left and Right.'

'Because he's too stupid to know which foot is which,' says Ollie, and Toby flicks him with a sock.

'That's enough,' says Jon.

He doesn't raise his voice, but I recognise the same note of finality as when he told me he had no intention of doing me even the smallest of favours.

'Mine say Flip and Twist!' says Ollie, showing me. 'And Uncle Jon's have trampolining raccoons on them.'

'How sweet,' I say.

'I thought I should get into the spirit of the evening,' says Jon.

'A commendable attitude,' I tell him.

We say goodbye to Jon and the boys and walk back to Simon's car.

'I'm glad to see it's still here,' he says as he opens the door for me.

'Why wouldn't it be?'

'Oh, you know.' He gestures towards the building.

'You think the sort of people who come to *Bouncy Benny's* are likely to vandalise your car?'

He backs out of the space. 'I didn't say likely. Just less unlikely than in some other places.'

'Which other places? Harrods car park?'

'I don't think Harrods has a car park.'

'You're wrong there!' I say, pleased to be able to demonstrate my wide-ranging general knowledge. 'There's one in Brompton Place. But I doubt your car would be any safer there than it is here. What did you expect would happen to it?'

'I have no idea. But there are lots of children running around, so I wouldn't be surprised if it had been scratched.'

'They were just the yellow-banders,' I say. 'Small, but unlikely to be deadly. It sounds as though it's the red-banders you need to worry about. They'll converge on the place any minute now, dead-eyed and full of evil intent, all ready to rumble with their nemeses. I expect the regulars have red jackets with gang logos. I wish I'd thought to book us the eight-thirty tickets,' I finish wistfully.

'The workings of your mind are fascinating,' he says. 'You'd be a dream study for a trainee psychiatrist. They wouldn't know where to start.'

'Many people have said the same thing to me over the years. Yet here I am, still unstudied, and still a valuable member of my local community.'

We arrive in Compton ten minutes later.

'Where shall I drop you?' he asks as we reach the gates.

'Here would be fine. It would be a shame for our gravel drive to chip your car after it's survived such a dangerous evening.'

'If I take you right to your front door, I might meet your sister,' he says.

'I realise that's become your greatest ambition. I'm sorry to disappoint you, but Georgia is out this evening with one of her many admirers. You'd think word of her awfulness would have spread among the local community, but it doesn't seem to have done so. It's all very puzzling.'

'What a shame,' he says, pulling up on the grass verge and switching off the engine. 'Another time, perhaps.'

When I don't answer, he gives me a rueful smile. 'Am I to understand there won't be another time?'

'Probably not. I don't think you and I have a romantic future ahead of us. But now we've got to know each other, I hope you'll drop into The Sugarloaf Bakery whenever you feel in need of a light yet nourishing snack.'

'Of course, I will. Your doughnuts are the best I've ever tasted, exactly as you promised. Can I ask you something?'

'Fire away.'

'What made you agree to a date with me tonight?'

'You took me by surprise.'

'I see.'

'I enjoyed meeting you,' I say, 'but I didn't think we made a particular connection. I wouldn't have said yes if it hadn't been for several conversations I've recently had with Lily about not getting out there enough. She says I don't give people a proper chance, and I should start saying yes to things. I decided to take her advice and give it a go.'

'An admirable policy,' he says. 'Whose idea was it to choose tonight's venue for our date?'

'Mine, of course. Lily suggested dinner theatre.'

He laughs. 'And you still settled on *Bouncy Benny's Spring'n'Swing*. Was that by any chance because it was the most unromantic place you could think of?'

'I can think of far more unromantic locations,' I say. 'A tax-auditing seminar, for instance. But not on a Saturday evening. And believe me, I searched.'

He's still smiling, but there's a faint look of hurt in his eyes.

'I'm so sorry,' I say. 'It wasn't fair of me. The next time someone asks me out and I'm not sure about it, I'll politely refuse and Lily will have to deal with it as best she can. Not that any of this was her fault. She was just trying to help. Maybe I'm someone who can't be helped.'

His face clears. 'Don't worry about it. I appreciate your honesty. I couldn't think why you'd chosen that particular venue when we first arrived. And then we met Jon, and it made more sense.'

'What do you mean by that?'

'It's a place people go to have fun with children. Not for a date. That's why you chose it instead of somewhere more traditional. You didn't want me getting the wrong idea.'

'Dates and fun don't have to be mutually exclusive,' I say.

'But they don't usually include trampolines and mega-gulps.'

'Not at the same time,' I agree. 'That could be catastrophic. I'm sorry, Simon. I didn't mean to hurt your feelings.'

'My feelings will survive, but I'm not sure my ankles will. I'm off home to find myself an ice pack.'

'You were only on that trampoline for half an hour!'

'I'm not as young as I was. And when I'm in your company, I feel one hundred years old.'

'That isn't good. Perhaps it's all for the best that it hasn't worked out for us.'

He gives me a thoughtful look. 'Could I just say one other thing?'

'As many other things as you like.'

'It's about Jon. He's a really good guy.'

'I'm sure he is,' I say. 'If a little too autocratic and keen to get his own way.'

'I'm serious. He hasn't had it easy, and he deserves a bit of a break.'

'Is this because I complained about him refusing us a discount?' I ask. 'Or because I insulted his golf game tonight?'

'I wasn't saying anything specific. Just that he's a nice guy.'

I wait for him to add something else, but he doesn't. Slightly confused, I unbuckle my seat belt and open the car door. 'I'll bear it in mind. Thanks for being such a good sport tonight.'

'Thanks for expanding my horizons,' he says. 'I may not be taking any future dates to *Bouncy Benny's Spring'n'Swing*, but at least I've tried something new and lived to tell the tale.'

'Apologise to your ankles for me,' I say. 'I could call you a taxi if you don't think they'll stand up to the drive home.'

'Both my ankles and I will be just fine,' he says. 'Goodbye, Isabella. See you around.'

I watch him reverse the car and drive away towards Honeywell, before walking thoughtfully up to the house. I want to make myself some dinner before Georgia arrives with whichever unlucky man she's been out with this evening and demands to know who's eaten all the chicken.

Chapter Seventeen

The bakery is only open until lunchtime on Sundays, and Lily and I take it in turns to man the ramparts. She's drawn the short straw this week, so I'm able to sleep in late on Sunday morning. Not because I'm exhausted by an evening of trampolining – I didn't do half as much of that as I would have liked – but because it takes me a long time to get to sleep on Saturday evening.

I lie awake thinking about Lily's theories about my relationships and why they never seem to last for long. But she's always told me to keep an open mind, not to search the local area for the most unromantic possible venue. I remember what Simon said last night about Jon, but I put it out of my mind. Whatever Jon may be going through right now has nothing to do with me. Interfering in other people's lives rarely works out well. I should stay focused on my own problems.

One of my ongoing problems rears its head when I arrive downstairs for a late breakfast at ten o'clock. She's sitting at the dining room table, staring out into the garden while demolishing an enormous stack of toast.

'Enjoying the petunias?' I ask as I take a seat opposite her.

Georgia swivels her eyes away from whichever horticultural wonder she's been admiring and fixes them on me. 'You'll have to make your own toast.'

'Why? There's a huge pile right here.'

I reach out for a piece, and she slaps my hand away. 'I'm warning you, Issy!'

'You'll have to be more specific. You're always warning me about something or other.'

'I'm serious! Make your own toast. This is mine.'

Maybe Lily hasn't drawn the short straw after all. She's probably sitting peacefully in the bakery right now, sipping cappuccinos and chatting with our customers.

I'm about to announce my intention of fighting to the death for my rightful share of any and all bread-based meals in this house when I catch sight of her face. 'Are you crying, Georgie?'

She glares at me. 'No! Why would I cry about some stupid toast?'

'It's difficult to say. But you look more upset about my arrival than I'd expect. I can make my own breakfast if it's that important to you.'

She pushes the plate towards me. 'Eat it all if you want to. I don't care.'

If this is true, things are more serious than I first thought. Georgia cares more about her meals than any person I've ever met.

'What's going on?' I ask, but she only shrugs and resumes glaring at a buddleia bush blooming innocently outside the window.

'Are you feeling ill?' I pursue. It seems the obvious explanation for her being off her food.

'I'm fine.' She bites her lip and stares harder.

It's possible she's concentrating on the flowers and wondering about the life cycle of the common greenfly. But she's never shown the slightest interest in either botany or zoology, so this seems unlikely.

I reach over and take her hand. She doesn't respond, but neither does she slap my hand away.

She blinks away the tears. 'If you must know – I've been fired.'

My first feeling is one of irritation. This is so typical of her. She lands one of the easiest jobs in the world, where all she has to do is stand around all day telling people how lovely they look in the ugly yet expensive clothes she's attempting to sell them. And she can't even do that without annoying the person who pays her salary.

But she looks so miserable that I can't bring myself to say any of this. Either she's already aware of it, in which case there's no point in rubbing salt into the wound, or she won't have a clue what I'm saying, and all it will do is upset her further. Now is not the time to talk about her behaviour in the workplace or the importance of putting in the minimum effort required in order to remain in gainful employment.

Instead, I summon up some sisterly sympathy. 'I'm sorry to hear that. What was it – your time-keeping?'

She gives me one of her usual sulky looks. 'No.'

'I didn't mean to jump to conclusions. What was the problem?'

She shrugs again. 'It was Lucinda.'

'Your co-worker? The one who's having a baby? I thought she'd have left by now to start her maternity leave.'

'She didn't get the chance. Cath made her redundant on Friday.'

'She can't do that!'

'That's what I said, but she did it anyway. And she told me if I didn't stop arguing and get back to work, she'd make me redundant too.'

'You can only make someone redundant when the business is closing down or there's a legitimate reason to reduce staff numbers,' I say. 'It's all in our staff handbook.'

'Cath says the business is going downhill, and she can't afford to keep on two full-time staff. As Lucinda is going off on maternity leave soon, she wanted to let her know there wouldn't be a job for her when that finished.'

'She's on shaky ground there,' I say. 'For one thing, you and Lucinda did exactly the same job. How did she select which of you to let go?'

'There's no mystery about that. She said she couldn't afford to pay someone who was likely to go off and have another baby the moment she came back to work.'

'She definitely can't do that!' I say again. 'A good lawyer will be all over this.'

Georgia looks doubtful. 'Maybe, but it's more difficult with zero-hour contracts.'

My mouth falls open in shock. 'Lucinda is on a zero-hour contract?'

'We both are. We used to be on proper contracts, but those were cancelled when the shop was sold. We were offered the choice between redundancy or staying on under new terms and conditions.'

'And you accepted?' I ask, still unable to believe my ears.

'What alternative did I have? It isn't as though I'm qualified for anything else.'

'That's because you refused to stay on at school and finish your A levels.'

'Don't start, Issy. I've heard your views on my life choices a million times.'

'I've never told you what to do,' I say. 'I wouldn't dare. You've never listened to a word anyone has said, and you probably never will.'

'You may not have told me what to do, but you've always made it very clear you disapprove of every single choice I've ever made.'

'I don't believe that's true. But what I want to know is how things went from Lucinda being made redundant to you being fired? There seems to be a missing link, and I'm interested to hear what it is.'

She takes a moody bite of toast. 'So you can feel even better about yourself and your wonderful life choices?'

'Will you please stop saying that? I've never judged your life choices. I've just wished you'd make some.'

'There you go again.'

'Sorry,' I say, handing her the jam. 'I promise not to say another word. I'll just listen.'

She tips the jam onto her toast, and I heroically refrain from pointing out that half a jar of jam is designed to cover more than one slice of bread. I've never seen her so downcast. Sulky and annoyed, yes. That's been her default mode since her teenage years. But it's a shock to see my usually stroppy and defiant sister look so defeated.

She stares out of the window again, chewing her mouthful of toast. If I didn't know better, I might think she was considering a career in horticulture. But Georgia only goes outside when she's forced to. I've been convinced for quite some time she's part vampire.

'Lucinda was crying,' she says at last. 'Her husband lost his job in February. His investment firm was taken over, and they all had to reapply for their own jobs. He wasn't successful. They've been living off their savings for a while now. But with the baby coming and everything, they've both been worried sick about their future.'

'Poor Lucinda! No wonder she was upset.'

'So, I told Cath to make me redundant instead. She said that wouldn't help. If she let me go, she'd have no one doing any work in the shop for the next twelve months.'

She catches my eye. 'Please don't say it.'

'I'm not saying anything! You've asked me to be quiet and listen, and that's what I'm doing.'

'I told her I could cover Lucinda's maternity leave. Then she could take Lucinda back next year and let me go at that point.'

'That was nice of you,' I say, impressed despite myself.

'I thought you weren't going to talk?'

'I was complimenting you. They're two very different things. What did Cath say to that?'

'She wasn't having any of it. She agreed that Lucinda works far harder than I do, but she said there was no guarantee that would still be true when she came back from maternity leave. She said she'd have a baby keeping her up all night, and her mind wouldn't be on the job.'

'Whereas yours is never on the job?' I ask, forgetting my role as silent listener.

'Would your mind be on a job that consisted of selling some of the ugliest clothes you've ever seen to some of the most unpleasant customers you'll ever meet? Or going out on a coffee run and being sent back several times because the foam wasn't exactly the way Cath liked it?'

'Lily can be surprisingly picky about the foam to caffeine ratio on her morning coffee,' I say. 'But she would never dare send it back.'

Georgia's face has resumed its usual sulky look. 'Cath dared. She once spat in her cappuccino because it didn't have enough chocolate on it. She made me take it all the way back to Cuppa Joe at the far end of the high street, even though it was pouring with rain.'

'What did they say?' I ask, intrigued to hear how other small business owners react to this sort of thing. Maybe I can pick up some tips on how to deal with Wendy Protheroe the next time she comes into the bakery with some ridiculous complaint.

'They didn't say anything.'

'Not even when they heard what Cath had done to their cappuccino?'

'I didn't tell them,' she says. 'They keep their nutmeg and cinnamon and cocoa shakers next to the till. So, I shook a load more chocolate over the top and carried it back to the shop.'

'What did Cath say about that?'

'She said I should tell their barista she'd be sending it back every single time from now on until they learned to get it right. So, unless I wanted an extra walk each the morning, I knew what to do. Lucinda had to pretend she had morning sickness and run out of the shop before Cath saw her laughing.'

'The more I hear about Cath,' I say, 'the more I realise what a wonderful employer I am.'

'I wouldn't go that far. Anyway, you wanted to know about the redundancy thing. I offered to resign once Lucinda got back from her maternity leave. Cath refused. I told her she was a miserable old crone, and she fired me.'

I blink. 'That went from zero to eighty in three seconds. Does that mean Lucinda's job is safe after all?'

'No, she quit too. She said she has her statutory maternity pay for a few months, by which time either she or Mark will have found another job. She told Cath she refused to stay in a place where they treated their employees like that.'

'Good for her! What did Cath to say to that?'

Georgia grins. 'She didn't like it at all. She immediately turned to me and offered me my job back. I asked if that came with a pay increase. She scowled but eventually offered me fifty pence an hour extra and an afternoon coffee break as well as a morning one. After which, I suggested a few things she could do with her job, and we parted company.'

'Didn't you want the extra coffee break?' I ask, confused.

'No, I just wanted her to offer it to me. And the pay rise.'

I can't help laughing. 'That may not have been the wisest course of action, but I don't blame you. She sounds like a monster. But where does that leave you? You can't claim unemployment benefit because you're voluntarily unemployed.'

'I'm aware.' She crams the last piece of toast into her mouth. 'I've just messaged Zac and asked him to take me out to lunch. We've run out of bread, so I can't make myself a sandwich.'

'I could call Lily and ask her to drop you in another bushel of loaves as soon as the bakery closes,' I offer.

'No need. I'd like to get out of the house for a while. But I have ten minutes before he arrives if you want to tell me what a screw-up I am and how badly my life is going.'

Is this really how she sees me, or is she just lashing out because she's worried and upset? I hope it's the latter. I don't like to think of myself as someone she couldn't talk to if she needed to.

'I have nothing to say right now,' I tell her. 'You've taken me by surprise. Maybe I'll have something to suggest when I've had some time to think it over.'

She lays a hand on my arm. 'You won't tell Mum and Dad about this?'

'Not if you don't want me to. But they'll have to know at some point. Otherwise, you'll have to get up early every morning and pretend to go to work. You wouldn't like that at all. You hate getting up before noon, even when someone's paying you.'

'I need a few days to consider my options,' she says. 'I wouldn't have told you if you hadn't gouged it out of me. That's so like you, Issy. You never could mind your own business.'

I'm not sure I can mind it now, but I have no intention of telling her that. What the eye doesn't see, the Georgia doesn't throw a major strop about.

'I promise,' I say. 'I won't be seeing them this morning anyway. I have to go out myself for a couple of hours. You'll be delighted to know my physiotherapist has given me the all-clear to drive, so you and Zac won't have to give me a ride.'

'Are you off to work?' she asks.

'Lily is on the rota today,' I say, carefully evading the question. 'And I have no wish to ride shotgun with Zac. I'm looking forward to driving again. Now I know how Mr Toad must have felt when he finally got behind the wheel. Enjoy your lunch, and I'll see you this afternoon. Don't eat too much. Zac is only a stockbroker, and everyone knows how much they're struggling with the rising cost of living.'

Chapter Eighteen

I find Lily closing up the shop when I arrive.

'Unless the satellite that tells my watch the exact time has slipped out of orbit,' I say, 'you're leaving five minutes early.'

She hands me a cloth. 'Can you wipe down the tables at the far end and put the mugs in the dishwasher while I make us both a drink?'

'Remind me which of us is on duty,' I complain, taking the cloth and wandering over to table eight.

'With great profit sharing comes great responsibility,' she says. 'And when you've done that, someone needs to check the sell-by dates on those cream doughnuts.'

'As you say, we're a partnership!' I say, wiping down the tables as hurriedly as possible and skipping over to the chill cabinet to inspect the cakes.

'Are you planning to eat those now?' she asks as I select three and carry them back to table eight. 'I thought you might like to take them home with you and spread the joy a bit.'

'These doughnuts aren't technically out-of-date,' I say, gesturing for her to join me. 'So, my family wouldn't know what to do with them. I've trained them only to eat cakes that have passed their best-by-date. It would confuse them if I turned up with these.'

'Three?' she asks. 'It's almost time for lunch.'

'Not for another hour, and I didn't get any breakfast. My sister ate the last of the toast. Anyway, one of them is for you.'

'Is that your idea of fifty-fifty?' she asks. 'It's been a while since your accountancy days, but even you –'

I interrupt before she can start on one of her frequent, yet completely unjustified, rants about my number skills. 'You can have two if you like. That's how badly I want to talk to you.'

'Goodness!' she says. 'It really is an emergency. But I'll just have a macaron. Mum's making roast lamb today, and she gets very upset if we don't arrive with good appetites. That's why she likes having you round for lunch. She says she's never seen anyone enjoy her cooking as much as you.'

'That's very flattering,' I say. 'And a sad indictment on the rest of you. Imagine being brought up by someone who cooks like your mother and not appreciating it.'

'Who says we don't appreciate it? Ben, especially. But you have to admit you take culinary appreciation to new heights.'

'It has been remarked upon. But we're getting away from the subject of what I wanted to discuss with you.'

She carries our drinks over to the nearest table and sets one down in front of me. 'It sounds serious.'

'It is serious. It's a three-cake problem. Whenever Sherlock Holmes had a tricky case to solve, he said it was a two-pipe problem or a three-pipe problem. I operate the same way, only with cakes. If I come across a slight discrepancy in the accounts, that would be a one-cake problem. If the freezer packs up, that would be a two-cake problem. I could go on, but I'm sure you get the picture.'

'It all sounds rather worrying,' she says.

I pick up the first doughnut and take a bite. 'I may have been exaggerating when I said this was a three-cake problem. But I am worried about something.'

She takes a sip of her drink. 'Fire away.'

'It's Georgia.'

Her face relaxes. 'When isn't it? What has your awful sister been up to now? Just the facts, please, rather than a long list of every single thing she's done wrong since the day your parents brought her home from the hospital.'

'She's got herself fired,' I say bluntly.

'That isn't great. But she hated that job, didn't she? This may be the push she needs to find something she enjoys more.'

'I wish she'd told me how bad things had got. She grumbled quite a bit while she was driving me here over the past few months, but I assumed that was just her usual allergic reaction to doing any work. But it sounds as though she's been having a pretty tough time of it for a while now. I wish she'd mentioned it to me.'

Lily finishes her macaron. 'I can understand why she didn't. You can be quite hard on her.'

'My sister has been doing exactly as she likes for her entire life. Our parents would never have allowed me to get away with half as much as she does.'

'Is that why you're always on her case?'

'I may have pointed out the error of her ways once or twice, but that's because someone had to. My parents were remarkably lenient with her.'

'They weren't all that hard on you either,' she says.

'That's because they didn't need to be. I worked hard at school. Relatively hard, at least. I didn't step far enough out of line for anyone to report me to my parents, which is more than I can say of Georgia. She was a couple of years below me at school and always getting into trouble. I had to help her out plenty of times.'

'Wasn't that your choice?' asks Lily.

'Possibly, but the honour of the Campbells was at stake. You have no idea how difficult it was to prevent my sister tarnishing our ancient family name.'

'I have to leave in fifteen minutes at the latest,' she says. 'Do you plan to tell me what the problem is or would you prefer to spend the time talking about the history of the Campbells and their illustrious reputation?'

'It's a fascinating subject. But you're right. That isn't what I want to talk about today. When Georgia told me she'd been fired, I was annoyed because this is the first job she's stuck to for more than a year. Before that, she was in and out of work every few months. Martine's didn't sound the most exciting place to work, but it was something to put on her CV, and it showed she had some sticking power. So, I wasn't thrilled to hear she'd finally got herself kicked out.'

'Why are you so worried about Georgia's employment history?' she asks. 'I can't imagine losing a moment's sleep over anything Ben may choose to do now that we're adults.'

'That's just the problem. She's never behaved like an adult, which makes it difficult to treat her as one.'

She smiles. 'You could say that as long as you refuse to treat her as an adult, it makes it difficult for her to behave as one.'

'It's a little early in the day for metaphysical conversations. The main issue is that she's been fired.'

'I'm very sorry,' she says. 'Is there anything we can do to help her?'

'As a matter of fact, there may be. I was wondering about offering her a job here. Not full-time, of course. But we've been saying we could do with another pair of hands. Why not Georgia's? They're usually fairly clean, and I could give her a ride into work to make sure she arrived on time.'

Lily swallows her last mouthful of macaron. 'I don't know what to say. If I'd dared to suggest such a thing, you'd have thrown a plate of doughnuts at me.'

'Out-of-date bread,' I say. 'I never waste good cakes.'

'But you wouldn't have been impressed, and I'd have understood why. Are you sure you want your sister here? You often say this is your haven from the storms of life – the place where you come to get away from it all and spend the day talking to your friends and eating cake.'

'I can still do those things,' I say. 'It may be even more enjoyable to do them while watching Georgia do some work for once.'

'You aren't selling her to me as a new employee.'

'It doesn't have to be for long. And if it doesn't work out, we can boot her out again. Seriously, Lily, I'd like to give her a chance if I can. I know she hasn't been the most industrious little worker bee so far. Very different to her older sister, who's never happier than when toiling away at the coal face.'

I ignore her derisive laugh. 'But this feels different. The reason she was fired was because she was standing up for someone else. That doesn't seem like Georgia. Maybe she's finally growing up. All I know is that I'd like to help her out if I can. But I realise this is a joint decision, and I'd hate to put unfair pressure on you. Why don't you give it some thought and get back to me?'

'There's no need,' she says.

'But you haven't given the idea a chance.'

She picks up our mugs and plates. 'If you think it's a good idea, I'm happy to give it a go. I've never known you to be wrong about our prospective employees. Granted, I didn't expect one of them to be Georgia, but that's irrelevant. If you want her and think we can make it work, go ahead.'

Not for the first time, I'm reminded of why I went into business with her. She's kind and generous and warm-hearted. I couldn't have a better friend or business partner.

'Have I ever told you what a wonderful woman you are?' I ask. 'I'll talk to Georgia the minute she gets back from lunch. Which means very late this afternoon if she's gone for the family dessert-tasting platter.'

'While you're waiting to see her,' she says, 'would you like to have lunch at my parent's house?'

'I haven't been invited.'

'Yes, you have. I texted Mum while you were choosing your cakes. She messaged straight back to say the more, the merrier.'

'Your mother is also a wonderful woman,' I say. 'I wonder if there's any connection?'

She only laughs. 'So, are you coming? I know how much you love her roast lamb.'

'With trifle for pudding?'

'Did you need to ask?'

I run my finger around my plate to pick up the last few crumbs. 'It's always as well to make sure of these things. If you really don't mind me gate-crashing a family occasion, I'd love to join you.'

'You are family,' she says. 'If you don't know that by now, you never will.'

I arrive home mid-afternoon after a large lunch, followed by several strenuous games of tag in the garden with Daisy and Ethan. Lily and Jack, who for some reason made no effort to join in, told me it was the price of one of Angela's lunches. I knew there was a catch. There always is. But it was still worth it.

Georgia is surprisingly reluctant to accept my offer. I expected it would be a case of any port in a storm, but apparently not.

'Unlikely!' she says when I broach the subject.

'What do you mean by unlikely? Have you understood what we're offering, or did you not only make your way through the entire tasting menu but the drinks menu too?'

'I mean it seems like a bad idea.'

'I thought you'd be over the moon,' I say.

'At the idea of working with you? Whatever gave you that idea?'

'Not just me. You'd be working with Lily and Abby too.'

'That might be a little better,' she admits. 'But you'd still be there. Or are you planning to leave and offer me your job?'

I almost choke on my cup of tea. 'Unlikely!'

'See what I mean? Neither of us is thrilled with this idea.'

'But one of us has no choice,' I say. 'Unless you've found yourself alternative employment since I last saw you?'

'How would I have done that?'

'You might have talked Zac into taking you on at his company.'

'I mentioned it, but he says he's seen me trying to calculate a fifteen-percent tip, and he doesn't want me crashing the entire British economy before the end of the week.'

'You could have asked the restaurant whether they needed any casual staff,' I suggest.

'No, I couldn't. I've just had my nails done, and I don't want them getting wet.'

'Which leaves The Sugarloaf Bakery as your only viable option. We provide gloves for any messy work, so your nails should be quite safe.'

'But I don't want to work in your bakery,' she objects.

'How can anyone not want to work in a bakery? Most people would jump at the chance. And that's without taking into consideration the tremendous honour and privilege it would be to work alongside me and learn how all the best businesses are run. People are lining up to work at the Sugarloaf.'

'Is that why you have such a high staff turnover?'

'That's a slight exaggeration,' I say. 'We have, from time to time, needed to take on temporary members of staff to cover various unexpected eventualities.'

'Like Lily's maternity leaves?'

'I can't say for sure how unexpected those were. That's between her and Jack. But yes, we've had to employ people for both of those. And again when we won that contract to provide desserts for the Christmas ball. And most recently when I broke my leg. You do realise I broke it, don't you? I know you don't pay attention to most things, but that surely can't have passed you by?'

'Of course I realise,' she says. 'I was forced to give you all those rides to work.'

'I like to think they were prompted by the goodness of your heart.'

'Forced,' she insists. 'Mum told me if my car failed its next test, she would only pay for it if I drove you to work.'

'I'll pretend I didn't hear that. So, about this job …'

'I don't understand why you'd want me working within ten miles of you,' she complains.

'I thought you'd be pleased. We aren't even asking you to be there full time. Maybe three days a week until you find yourself something more permanent.'

Her shoulders slump. 'I can't say no, can I?'

'Not if I have anything to do with it.'

'This is so typical of you, Issy. You always think you know better than everyone else what they should do. Why do you want me to work for you so badly?'

'I don't want you to work badly. I want you to work well.'

'You know what I mean. Why at your bakery? Is it so you can have me under your eye at all times?'

'The last thing I want is to have you under my eye,' I say. 'Or my feet, for that matter. Is it so difficult to believe I just want what's best for you?'

'Yes.'

'That's fair. We give each other a pretty wide berth these days, don't we? Maybe I'd like to change that.'

'I still think there's something else going on here,' she says. 'But it would get Mum and Dad off my back. Alright, let's give it a try. But no written contract. Let's keep it strictly verbal.'

'That's my favourite type of contract. You'll be our first employee who hasn't refused point blank to accept a verbal contract. The fact you've actually demanded one shows you're shaping up to be the ideal member of staff.'

'And I answer to Lily,' she adds.

'You do indeed. And to me.'

'To Lily,' she repeats stubbornly, and I roll my eyes. This may not be as simple as I envisaged.

'To Lily,' I agree. 'Unless it's an absolute emergency.'

'In which case, I answer to Abby.'

'Again, unless she isn't there. In which case –'

'We close the shop?' she says. 'That works for me.'

There are times in life when it makes sense to argue and times when it doesn't. This is clearly one of the second ones.

I hold out my hand to her. 'Welcome aboard.'

She looks at it. 'What am I supposed to do with that?'

'The traditional thing is to shake it and smile politely. I'll have to give you a copy of our staff handbook before you start working with us. I wrote it myself, and it contains everything you need to know.'

'How long is it?' she asks.

'Just a few hundred pages.'

'Is there an audio version?'

'Not as yet. But that's an excellent idea. One of your first tasks could be to record it for us. You'll have to speak slowly and clearly and do all the accents.'

'What accents?' she asks.

'There are a few quotations in there. Quite a few, now I come to think of it. I like to illustrate my subject headings with short snippets of poetry from appropriate sources. You'll need to adopt a Scottish accent for Robert Burns and an American one for Mark Twain. I'm sure you'll manage.'

'I'll make the coffee and serve the cakes,' she says. 'But I refuse to read any stupid books out loud.'

'I don't usually allow our new employees to make so many demands,' I say. 'But as you insist you won't be answerable to me, I suggest you take it up with Lily. Then Abby, if you're still not satisfied. They'll be more than happy to discuss the matter with you. So, do we have a deal?'

She reluctantly reaches out and takes my hand. 'For now.'

'Your enthusiasm is a lesson to all of us. Let's leave it there for now. I'm frightened of disturbing the delicate balance of our agreement if we discuss it any further.'

I dump my cup into the sink. 'Shall we break the exciting news to our parents? Think what a joyful evening we'll all have when they hear about it. First, we have to shock them with the announcement of your recent unemployment. Before they have time to realise the gravity of the situation, we'll lift their spirits with the glad tidings their little girls are planning to work together. How excited they'll be. I'll bet Mum is on the phone to Aunt Elizabeth within minutes, eager to share the wonderful news!'

Georgia follows me out of the kitchen and down the hall towards the front room. She stops me as I'm about to open the door. 'Thanks, Issy.'

'You have nothing to thank me for.'

'That's very likely true. But thanks, anyway.'

'You're very welcome,' I say. 'In an odd kind of way, I'm looking forward to it.'

Chapter Nineteen

I drive Georgia to the bakery the following morning. I need to talk to Lily about her exact working hours, but I'd prefer not to leave Georgia at home while I make the arrangements. It took me such a long time to persuade her to work with me, even on a temporary basis, that I don't want to give her the chance to change her mind.

Strike while the iron is hot has always been my motto. In Georgia's case, the iron is more of a lukewarm temperature, but that will have to do. No great general in history has ever been handed a perfect set of circumstances with which to work, yet they've all found a way around their difficulties. That's what I intend to do too.

Nelson wouldn't have got very far at the Battle of Trafalgar if he'd allowed his men to sit around in their bedrooms for days, brooding over their wrongs and eating toast. Which is why he didn't offer them the chance. Instead, he sent out his press-gangs, got everyone on board, then removed the gangplank and burned it.

At least, that's what I assume he did. It would have been inconvenient if he'd forgotten his favourite teddy bear or a packet of mints and had to nip off the ship again to collect them. Perhaps he merely hid the plank, although it's difficult to imagine where. A gangplank is a difficult thing to hide – or it is if it's any good at its job. Possibly, he made one of his junior lieutenants swim back to shore instead.

The point is that he didn't allow his merry band of sailors the opportunity to change their minds and wander off to train as shoemakers. And I don't plan to allow Georgia a similar opportunity. I want her where I can keep an eye on her. Her reluctance to accept a once-in-a-lifetime offer to work with one of the bakery business greats is worrying. After a couple of days under my care, she'll be a different woman, and as difficult to dislodge as a barnacle on a ship's hull. But for now, I'm taking no chances.

'It makes a change for me to be driving you to work instead of the other way around,' I say chattily as I drive through the gate and navigate the narrow lane that leads towards Honeywell.

I wait for her to reply, but she only grunts.

'I didn't quite catch that,' I say. 'It may be my hearing to blame rather than your pronunciation, but you'll have to speak up once you get to work. Some of our customers are elderly, and their hearing isn't quite what it was.'

'All the customers in Martine's were elderly,' she says. 'They'd have to be. No one of our age would be seen dead wearing any of the clothes Cath sells.'

'They are a bit moth-eaten,' I agree. 'No, that's the wrong word. I doubt any self-respecting moth would go near them. I only popped into Martine's a couple of times, but I remember wondering how anything so awful could have made it onto the production line, let alone into an actual shop. Who designs them?'

'Lucinda and I had a theory it was the work-experience kids.'

'Fresh out of design school? You may be right.'

'I'm talking about the work-experience they make you do in year eleven after your exams,' she says. 'When you have to spend five days working for a local business.'

'I enjoyed my work experience. Uncle Henry let me shadow Ben Hibbert for a week. I helped him stack the hay-bales and look after the sheep. I was supposed to do some work in the farm office, but I was so absorbed in learning how to drive a tractor that I never got around to it. I almost applied for farm management instead of accountancy when I went to university. How different my life would have been now if I had. You didn't ask Uncle Henry when it was your turn, did you?'

She shakes her head. 'He was away for six months doing that farm swap thing with the guy from Canada.'

'I'd almost forgotten that!'

'Dad told me I wasn't to ask the new family for work experience,' she says. 'He said they had quite enough on their plates without adding me into the equation.'

'I'm sure he didn't mean it personally.'

'Yes, he did. I told him you'd done your work experience there, but he said that was different.'

'Did you find yourself anything more interesting to do?' I ask.

'No. Most people had a family member who could offer them something. The rest of us had to sign a list, and Miss Marshall allocated us random jobs.'

'That sounds quite exciting,' I say. 'I might have signed up for that programme too if I'd known. Think of all the possibilities. You could have worked at the zoo for the week, riding all the elephants and feeding the baby pandas. Or got yourself a job at the circus tightening all the guy ropes on the Big Top.'

'I ended up working at the skating rink,' she says bitterly.

'That doesn't sound too bad. I love ice skating.'

'Handing out the skates and checking the returned ones for damage,' she adds.

'How much damage can someone do to a pair of skates during a two-hour session?'

'You'd be surprised. I had to spray them with some sort of fabric spray when they smelled really bad. My manager made me sniff them all to check.'

'For unpaid work experience?' I ask. 'I'd have charged danger money.'

She gives me one of her rare smiles. 'Don't think I didn't try. But she said she was writing a report on me at the end of the week, so I should do as I was told. I just held all the skates at arm's length, closed my eyes, and sprayed in their general direction. It worked for a while until my manager came into the booth while I had my eyes closed and got a face full of fabric spray.'

'Serves her right,' I say. 'Did she fire you?'

'I wish. She told me if I didn't shape up and start doing my job properly, she'd put me on toilet cleaning duty.'

'What an unpleasant person! Your duties at The Sugarloaf Bakery will be very different. And the worst we'll do is issue you with a written warning.'

'Cath gave me one of those at Martine's,' she says. 'I didn't read it, but it came in useful for wedging under a wobbly table leg in the break room.'

'It sounds as though you'll fit right in at your new place of work,' I say. 'Sadly, neither of my colleagues has the slightest respect for my written warnings, and nor do most of our temporary staff. But I live in hope. Here we are, safe and sound. Happily, my superb driving skills have survived my time off the road. Be careful with your door as you climb out. I may have parked a little too close to the lamp post.'

Lily is waiting for us when we arrive.

'It's lovely to see you,' she tells Georgia. 'I was delighted when Isabella told me you'd be joining us for a while.'

I scan her face for signs of sarcasm, but she seems genuinely pleased to see Georgia.

To my surprise, Georgia smiles back at her. 'Thanks for offering me the job.'

She catches my eye. 'Temporary job.'

'No problem,' says Lily. 'Who knows – it may turn into a permanent job after all? Stranger things have happened.'

I'd like to ask what stranger things have happened, but this isn't the right time. To my surprise, I find myself feeling protective of Georgia now she's here, whereas I was expecting to feel protective about Lily and Abby. They're the ones who are woefully unprepared for what I've unleashed upon them.

Is this how parents feel the day their little darlings finally start school? I imagine them waiting anxiously at the school gate, hoping their child gets through the day without burning the place down – and maybe even earns a gold star into the bargain. We don't hand out gold stars at The Sugarloaf Bakery, but I do use cookies as a reward. I find them more motivating than threats of instant dismissal or complicated performance management plans.

'You can hang your jacket here,' Lily tells Georgia, indicating the row of pegs.

Georgia stares at the sticker on the nearest peg. 'New Girl?'

'That was Isabella's idea,' says Lily. 'We used to hang our coats wherever we liked until she was off sick one day. Apparently, she spent the time watching back-to-back re-runs of some home organisation show. She returned the following day, all fired up with ideas about reorganising the bakery in line with modern thinking.'

'Lily likes to exaggerate,' I tell Georgia. 'Anyway, you can use that peg as long as you're here.'

'She tried to make us throw everything out,' says Lily as though I haven't spoken. 'Except for the cakes, of course. She came up with hundreds of reasons why just about everything at the bakery was interfering with our creative flow. I finally got fed up when she waved the cake tongs at me, demanding to know whether they sparked joy. I told her she was welcome to reorganise her office in any way she saw fit, but if she tried to mess with anything else in the shop or the cafe, I would take immediate steps to dissolve our partnership forthwith. Even that didn't do the trick. It wasn't until she ventured into the kitchen and was chased out by Abby two minutes later that the message sank in.'

'I don't blame Abby,' says Georgia. 'I'd hate it if anyone came into my workspace telling me how I should organise things.'

'Abby rarely loses her temper,' says Lily. 'But Isabella almost lost a member of staff that day. Things quickly went back to normal, but she'd already bought herself a label maker and marked the row of pegs with our names, so we've stuck to that ever since.'

'We don't need to go into all that right now,' I say in my most pleasant yet professional tone. 'Georgia is here to work, not listen to irrelevant stories about our work history.'

'Can't I do both?' asks Georgia, taking the apron Lily hands her.

'Probably not. You've never shown much aptitude for multi-tasking. It would be better for us to concentrate on bringing you up to speed as quickly as possible, rather than wasting time arguing about things that definitely didn't happen.'

'Why don't I show you how to use the till,' Lily asks Georgia, 'while I tell you what happened when Isabella almost flooded the storeroom?'

I stomp off to the kitchen, wondering what happened to the concept of loyalty. Lily and I will be having words later – followed by, but not limited to, a possible written warning.

I spend a few minutes talking to Abby about next week's order and return to the shop in time to hear Lily and Georgia break into a gale of laughter.

'I was telling her about the time you sent a cake saying Eighty and Fabulous to that children's birthday party,' says Lily. 'And poor Mrs Fenton received one in the shape of a train saying All Aboard for the Birthday Boy!'

I fix her with a gimlet stare. 'Were you indeed? How would you like it if I told her about –'

I break off, unable to come up with something suitably awful. I'm sure Lily makes huge mistakes all the time. I just can't think of any offhand.

'I'll leave you to think about that,' says Lily, grinning at me in a most unprofessional manner. 'While you're doing so, I'll give Georgia her first lesson in using the coffee machine.'

'It takes a while to learn all its quirks,' I warn Georgia. 'Don't despair if you can't get the hang of it for a few days. We've all been through it.'

'Is that Jon?' asks Lily, peering through the shop window and down the high street. 'It must be. He has his boys with him. I wonder if he's coming in our direction.'

'Who's Jon?' asks Georgia.

'The project manager for the arts centre. I daresay you've heard all about it.'

'Isabella mentioned something about fund-raising, but she didn't say what it was for.'

'I didn't think you'd be interested,' I say. 'But you knew about the ball. You refused to come on the grounds that you hated people, and you went away for the weekend to avoid it.'

'I remember that,' Georgia says vaguely. 'Was that to raise money for your arts centre?'

This is her first day here, and I need to cut her some slack. But if there's anyone more frustrating living in the whole of the New Forest area, I've yet to meet them.

The bell jangles as the bakery door opens. It is Jon. And, as Lily said, he's brought Ollie and Toby with him.

'Good morning,' he says, gesturing to the boys to come in.

They're carrying what looks like a set of blueprints. Looking at it more closely, I see it's a sort of scroll. It has torn edges and smells of smoke. Have they been setting Simon's carefully drawn-up plans on fire? He won't be happy about that.

Apparently, they haven't. Ollie thrusts the roll of paper at me, beaming with pride. 'Toby and I made this specially for you!'

Chapter Twenty

I put my hands behind my back. 'I'm not falling for that. The moment my fingerprints are on it, you'll take it to the police and claim I've committed some dreadful crime.'

Toby giggles. 'No, we won't. Go on – take it!'

I glance suspiciously at Jon, whose face is as impassive as ever.

'Fine,' I say, reaching out and taking the scroll. 'What is it?'

'It's a challenge!' says Ollie. 'From all three of us.'

'It's only signed by the two of you,' says Jon.

'Uncle Jon thought it was a brilliant idea too,' says Ollie. 'He was the one who helped us singe the edges of the paper.'

'Only because I was worried you might burn down the entire house,' says Jon.

'And he helped us with the spelling,' says Toby.

'It looks to me as though you're trying to evade responsibility,' I tell Jon. 'I'm not yet sure for what, but I can tell you now it won't work. If you were a part of whatever this is, stand up like a man and take the consequences.'

'This isn't how we usually talk to our customers,' Lily tells Georgia. 'But Isabella sometimes forgets to consult the staff handbook before speaking. It's confusing because she's the one who wrote it, as she never tires of reminding us.'

I lay the scroll on the nearest table and unroll it. 'So, what's this challenge?'

'Read it!' says Toby.

'I'll do my best, but I don't want to tear it. Are you sure you two made this? It appears to have been written by pirates. Bloodthirsty ones, at that!'

'We used lots of blood!' says Ollie in what I can only think of as an inappropriately cheerful voice.

'Your uncle's?' I ask, and Jon grins.

I bend closer and sniff. 'I'm picking up notes of tomato, with a faint hint of vinegar.'

'Uncle Jon wouldn't let us use actual blood,' says Toby. 'It's a shame because we were planning to use Ollie's.'

'Did he volunteer?' I ask.

'Kind of.'

I clear my throat and read aloud.

'*We the undersigned challenge you to a game of crazy golf on Saturday next.*'

'Undersigned means we wrote our names on it,' Ollie tells me. 'Uncle Jon added that bit.'

I glance at Jon, who gives me a smug smile in return. 'I'm very good with the legal stuff.'

'Quite right,' I say. 'Our family solicitor insists on splashing blood over all our legal documents. He says they aren't valid without it. It caused all kinds of problems when my uncle transferred the deeds of our house to my father. There was so much blood splattered around, it almost created a boundary dispute.'

I squint at the document again.

'*The game to be fought fair and square at nearly seven bells on the dread course known as Bouncy Benny's Spring'n'Swing. Let it be known across land and sea that we play not for gold, nor glory, but for pride, honour, and the joy of watching someone fall into the water feature. The rules be these. No quarter shall be given. Cheating be allowed, but only if none shall catch ye. No wooden legs permitted, even if the participant's leg be previously broken. To the Death!*

'That all seems clear and legally acceptable,' I say. 'To sum up – we sail over to Cap'n Benny's Island on Saturday evening, where we receive the correct colour bands. We hope to goodness Justin isn't on duty, then proceed to the crazy golf course via the hot dog stand, after which I make you all wish you'd never heard of the words *crazy* or *golf*.'

'Very good,' says Jon. 'It's obvious you've had plenty of experience with professional legal documents. I won't embarrass you by asking how. The only thing I'm not sure about is where you saw a reference to the hot dog stand. Neither I nor the boys mentioned that when we were writing the challenge.'

'It was part of the subtext,' I explain. 'Uncle Harry, our family solicitor, is always talking about implied agreements. You obviously don't understand legal terms as well as you think you do.'

'Do you accept?' asks Toby.

'My blood is up!' I tell him. 'I not only accept but intend to make the pair of you regret having ever issued me this challenge. By the end of the evening, my name will have gone up on the board of honour. And your names will be inscribed on the permanently banned list for being so terrible at crazy golf that no one should be forced to watch you, let alone play against you, ever again.'

'That's a yes, boys,' says Jon. 'Isabella appears to be someone for whom one word won't do if there's an opportunity for her to use fifty.'

Georgia gives a snort of laughter. 'She is! I've known her ever since I was born, and she's never stopped talking, not even when she had her tonsils out when she was ten. I remember her croaking for ice-cream every few minutes. She went on for ages about the different flavours that were best for healing a sore throat.'

'I don't remember that,' I say. 'Although I do remember you trying to sneak mine when you thought I wasn't looking. Jon, this is Georgia, my younger and far less charming and talented sister.'

'Nice to meet you,' says Jon. 'I've heard so much about you.'

'Really?' asks Georgia. 'I didn't think I was one of Isabella's favourite topics of conversation. She usually pretends she doesn't have a sister. When I first started high school, she told everyone she was an only child, and the girl two years below who looked so much like her was possibly a distant cousin. But she said it was more than likely just a coincidence.'

Now she finds her voice? This is so typical of my sister. She spends decades communicating with me and the rest of our family in little more than grunts. But when she's finally in a position to do a considerable amount of damage to my hard-earned reputation, she discovers the power of speech.

'That isn't quite how I remember it,' I say. 'But we can talk about it another time. Right now, we're discussing this challenge. How should I answer it? Do I book a herald and ask him to parade up the street, blowing his trumpet and shouting my acceptance? Or is this the sort of occasion where I send my second over to meet yours?'

'The boys have challenged you to a game of golf, not a duel,' says Jon.

'I'm not sure I understand the difference.'

'No one will be waving pistols around or stabbing each other with fencing swords.'

'Those are sadly outdated methods of settling disagreements,' I agree. 'But I expect I could do some damage with a golf club if the situation demanded it.'

'Which it very much won't,' he says. 'Will you give us your formal answer now, or do you need time to consider? The boys and I will understand if, upon mature consideration, you decide you aren't up for it.'

'I don't need to give it any consideration, mature or otherwise.'

'That's lucky,' comments Georgia, and I freeze her with a look.

'Challenge accepted!' I tell the boys, who high-five each other.

'Now that's sorted out, we'd like some cookies, if you have any left,' says Jon.

'It's barely ten o'clock in the morning. Why would we have run out of cookies? Unless you're referring to my sister's presence here. That might explain your doubts.'

'Not at all,' he says. 'But my admittedly limited experience of you has led me to wonder. That's all.'

'Which flavour would you like?' Lily asks the boys before I can answer.

No sooner has this question been settled than the shop door opens again, and several of the Silver Surfers walk in, accompanied by Bernie.

'Good morning!' booms Mabel in a voice calculated to shake the last of the tiles off the arts centre roof. I suppose it might save the village a few pounds in labour costs.

'How are you all today?' asks Lily, bending down to say hello to Bernie, who gives her hand a lavish lick and rolls over to have his stomach rubbed.

'Can't complain,' says Mabel. 'I mean, obviously I could, and with good cause. But there's no point. Anything I say just rolls off Edie like water off the mutt's waxed jacket. So, I've learned to suffer in silence. People say it's character building.'

'You misplaced that shoe all by yourself!' Mrs Ogilvie tells her crossly. 'It's no use saying Bernie hid it. You're always leaving things around the house and blaming it on him.'

'I know what I know,' says Mabel. 'And what I know is that I had that loafer yesterday evening, and it had disappeared by this morning. I didn't have time to search under all the beds, but I'll do so the moment I arrive home. And we shall see.'

'Those brogues you're wearing are very smart,' I tell her. 'Bernie may have done you a favour without you realising.'

She glances down at her feet. 'They're well enough, but they pinch my toes. I'll have terrible blisters by the time I get home, and it will be all his fault.'

'I'm sure you'll be fine,' says Lily soothingly. 'Why don't I get you a nice cup of tea? You can drink it while you rest your feet.'

'And a plum slice?' asks Mabel. 'Or has Isabella eaten them all?'

The way our customers carry on, you'd think there was something abnormal about my cake-eating habits. It's particularly annoying that Mabel has chosen to make this ridiculous joke while Jon is there to hear it. He may misinterpret the situation and take it as confirmation of some of the strange conclusions he seems to have drawn about me.

'I haven't had a plum slice for weeks,' I say with dignity. 'There are plenty left for you and anyone else who wants one. Find yourself a table, and we'll take your orders. What would everyone like to drink?'

Ivy settles herself into a chair opposite Mabel. 'Cappuccino for me and Edie, please. And Barb and Mary usually have a flat white. How about you, Phyllis?'

'I'll have a latte,' says Phyllis. 'With extra foam.'

'Can you make Mabel's tea?' I ask Georgia. 'She has Earl Grey with lemon. I'll do the coffees. It will be a while before we let you loose on those.'

'No need,' she says. 'I've got it.'

'What have you got?' I ask, surprised. Knowing Georgia, it could be anything – an itchy foot, the Bubonic Plague, a sudden urge to run screaming from the room at the prospect of having to do some work.

She walks over to the coffee machine. 'The drinks, of course. I'm offering to make them. Two flat whites, two cappuccinos, and a latte with extra foam coming right up.'

I'm too taken aback to speak. By rights, I ought to fling myself in front of the machine and forbid her from going anywhere near it until she's been trained. But she's already switched it on and picked up the bag of coffee beans.

I cast a helpless look at Lily, who shrugs. I debate pre-emptively calling an ambulance so it will be waiting outside the bakery by the time our customers have finished their drinks. But my phone is by the counter, and I don't want to startle Georgia by making any sudden movements. No one knows what could happen, and we may not be insured for whatever it is she has in mind.

Mabel looks from me to Georgia and back again. 'Your sister, I presume?'

'How did you know?' I ask, not taking my eyes off Georgia in case an opportunity arises for me to dive across the shop and rugby tackle her to the ground.

'She's the image of you. I doubt there are two unrelated people running around Honeywell who look like that. You could almost be twins.'

Ollie looks up from his cookie. 'Me and Toby are twins.'

'Toby and I,' says Ivy.

He stares at her in blank incomprehension. 'No, you aren't. Me and him are.'

I give a choke of laughter, which I swiftly turn into a cough as he turns to stare at me.

'How interesting,' says Mabel. 'You don't look much like each other.'

'That's because we aren't identical twins,' says Toby in the tone of someone who has to explain this rather more often than he'd like.

'I can see that.' She gestures to Mrs Ogilvie. 'Edie and I are twins too. But we're identical twins.'

'Are you sure?' he asks.

'Of course, I'm sure, you daft child! That's why we look exactly like each other.'

'Your faces are the same,' says Ollie. 'But not the rest of you.'

'I'll take that as a compliment,' she says.

'So will I,' says Mrs Ogilvie with a small smile.

'That's told you!' I say to Mabel, who grins.

'Edie is capable of giving as good as she gets when she wants to.'

I've been so busy following this conversation that I've allowed myself to become distracted. I swivel around to face Georgia and see she's wiping her hands on her apron. Under my astonished gaze, she picks up a tray, loads the drinks onto it, and carries it over to the table.

'Latte for you,' she says, handing Phyllis her drink. 'You two were both flat whites, I think. And here are your cappuccinos.'

She places the final mug in front of Ivy. 'I hope you enjoy them.'

I nudge Lily and lower my voice. 'What just happened?'

'Your sister made hot drinks for our customers. And, by the looks of things, she's done an excellent job.'

I look at the women, happily sipping their drinks and chatting to each other, displaying no signs of incipient gastric poisoning.

I turn to Georgia. 'Explain!'

She smirks at me. 'I don't understand what you mean.'

'You know perfectly well what I'm talking about. What's going on?'

She shrugs and starts ladling Earl Grey tea leaves into a pot. 'Your customers ordered drinks, and I made them. I don't understand why you're making such a fuss about it. Where do you keep your lemon slices?'

'In the fridge under the counter,' says Lily.

'Thanks.' She pours boiling water into the pot and hands it to Mabel.

'Where did you learn to do that?' I demand.

She shrugs again. 'I was a barista for a few months while you were in your first year at university.'

'Why didn't I know that?'

'Because you were too busy nagging me about getting better grades so I could take more meaningful A levels than Art and History.'

I wonder where else she's worked without my knowledge. Has she been employed at a Parisian atelier, interned at a vineyard, or helped out on a llama farm? Maybe she's enjoyed a month's work experience on the International Space Station. How is it possible the pair of us have lived together for all these years and still know almost nothing about each other?

'You always tell me you and Georgia are completely unlike each other,' Lily tells me. 'I'm starting to think that isn't true.'

'It is!' Georgia and I say in unison, the same shocked look mirrored on both our faces.

Mabel looks amused. 'I used to hate it when people said Edie and I were alike. I couldn't deny our physical resemblance, but I hated anyone saying we had similar personalities. I've changed my mind over the years. It's possible to have similarities with other people without losing your individuality. Take the mutt, for instance. I merely tolerate him, while Edie's entire life revolves around him. But that doesn't mean she and I have nothing else in common. We both like watching detective films, and we both enjoy gardening. And if either of us were in trouble, the other one would move heaven and earth to rescue us. I don't know what you're so bothered about, Isabella.'

'I've never thought of having anything in common my sister,' I say. 'It's all a bit of a shock.'

Mabel takes a bite of her plum slice and chews it thoughtfully.

'The way I see it,' she says when she's swallowed her mouthful, 'we all overlap with everyone else, even if only a little. What did that poet fellow say about islands?'

'No man is one,' says Jon.

'That's it! Daft way of putting it, if you ask me. Whoever thought we were? None of us is entirely surrounded by sea or covered in penguins. But he was onto something all the same. If he'd been a bit smarter, he'd have said we're all Venn diagrams.'

'Venn diagrams?' I ask, fascinated.

'Those things we used to learn about in our mathematics lessons. I'm not sure why the poet didn't use those as an example instead. Maybe he couldn't find a decent rhyme for them. The point I'm trying to make is that people are like that too. We're all made up of a set of overlapping circles. Sometimes, our circles overlap with other people's only the tiniest bit. Sometimes, they overlap rather more. The part in the middle that we shade in coloured pencil shows how similar we are to the people we meet.

But the parts around the edge of each circle are what make us all individuals.'

She takes another bite of her cake. 'I doubt I'm making much sense to you, but that's the way I've always seen it in my head.'

I glance at Lily, then at Georgia, who's watching me with a curious expression.

'Actually,' I tell Mabel. 'That makes a lot of sense. I've never thought of it like that before.'

'That's because they don't teach mathematics properly these days. It's all calculators and computers now. No one understands basic principles anymore. Speaking of maths, I'm sure that plum slice was about fifteen percent smaller than the ones in Abby's last batch. I'd like another one, please. And make sure it's the proper size this time.'

Chapter Twenty-One

I spend the next few days practising my golf swing at every available opportunity. After the first morning, Lily insists I do this outside during my breaks.

'I don't care!' she says when I protest. 'You've already broken one vase. I'm not having you smashing up the furniture too.'

'In my defence, the vase was sitting nearer the edge of the table than usual. Possibly, Georgia hasn't yet read the part of my training manual where I make it clear that all vases should be placed in a central position, rather than balanced right on the very edge. I'm not blaming her. Staff training is very much my purview. I dropped the ball there.'

'Almost literally,' says Lily. 'If I don't put a stop to it now, you'll be bringing in a box of golf balls in order to practise your short game, and we'll have no glasses left in the place.'

'Also, I'm standing right here,' says Georgia. 'If you want to talk about how badly trained I am, I suggest you wait until I'm not around.'

'If you'd been listening properly,' I tell her, 'you would have heard me explain to Lily that the fault was mine for neglecting such a vital area of your training. No one blames you for being less than professional so early in your time here. Speaking of training, perhaps you could make me and Lily a cappuccino for our morning break? I was concerned yesterday that your chocolate sprinkling might need a little work. It wasn't as consistently applied as our customers have grown to expect.'

Ivy and Mabel are sitting nearby, listening to our conversation.

'Her chocolate sprinkling seems great to me,' says Ivy, lifting her mug to show me. 'A fine, light dusting, evenly spread across the foam, with no lumps or empty patches. All in all, some of the best powder work I've seen in a long time.'

'Thanks, Ivy,' says Georgia. 'It's a pleasure to prepare hot drinks for such appreciative customers.'

She shoots me a challenging look, and Mabel laughs.

'I'm not criticising,' I tell her. 'Just pointing out a few areas that could use some improvement. And suggesting you prepare your employers a hot drink while they enjoy a temporary break from their labours.'

'Not unless you ask properly,' she says.

'Please,' I add with my sweetest smile.

'And tell everyone the reason you want me to prepare your drink instead of doing it yourself is because I make the best cappuccino you've ever tasted.'

Three faces turn towards me. Lily seems as interested in our conversation as Mabel and Ivy. So much for staff solidarity and the collegiate spirit.

'The best?' I ask, playing for time. 'As in the absolute ultimate?'

'As in the best,' says Georgia, fixing me with a beady eye.

'Not just a good cappuccino?'

'Only if you're happy to describe Roger Federer as a good tennis player.'

'But coffee isn't of Swiss origin,' I argue.

It's no use. When Georgia decides she wants something, she'll go to any lengths to achieve her aim.

'I'm waiting,' she says, clutching the bag of coffee beans like a battleaxe.

'Your coffee is surprisingly good,' I say.

'Try again.'

'Fully adequate. Of a saleable standard.'

'You had your chance, and you've blown it,' she says. 'Lily, would you like a cappuccino?'

Now is the chance for my friend and business partner to step up and do the right thing. And for her to give Georgia a much-needed lesson in respecting your elders and betters into the bargain.

'I'd love one,' says Lily. 'Thank you so much.'

Georgia turns and walks back to the coffee machine.

'It's more than drinkable!' I call after her.

She picks up the coffee beans and measures them into the grinder.

'Most enjoyable,' I add.

She makes a big deal of reaching for just one mug.

'Fine,' I say. 'It's the best coffee I've drunk for a long time.'

She pauses and casts a glance at me over her shoulder.

'Possibly ever,' I concede, and she smiles.

'Was that so difficult?'

I'd like to tell her it's the most difficult thing I've ever done in my life, but I'm wary of getting into another argument with her and causing further offence. I really want that coffee. It's been at least an hour since my last one, and I can feel my red blood cells congealing as they limp slowly around my veins.

Ivy nudges Mabel and says something I can't hear. The pair of them burst out laughing.

'Would you care to share the joke with the rest of the class?' I enquire coldly, and they break into fresh gales of laughter.

'Ivy was saying it looks as though you've met your match at last,' says Lily.

'Is that so? And do you agree with her?'

She raises her mug to me in a silent toast. 'You know me. I don't like to get involved in other people's family squabbles.'

'Ivy and Mabel have no idea what they're talking about,' I say. 'Just because I've decided to cut the new girl some slack doesn't mean I approve of her behaviour or intend to allow her to take too many liberties.'

Georgia half turns and raises an eyebrow.

'Although I must admit she's doing very well so far,' I add hastily.

The shop door opens before she can do anything too drastic, and Jon walks in.

'I didn't expect to see you here today,' I say. 'Where are the minions?'

'At their holiday club. I'm not picking them up until four thirty.'

'So, you popped in for a reviving drink and something to eat? Good choice. Although this isn't the standard time for a work break. Are you bunking off during working hours?'

'Not at all,' he says. 'You'd be hard pushed to find a more exemplary employee than myself. I came in to tell you I'm afraid we need to postpone our game of golf.'

'You're withdrawing the challenge?' I ask. 'Having thought the matter over in the cold light of day, you've realised how rash you were to issue it? I think you're wise. There's no shame in realising you've bitten off more than you can chew and backing away before someone gets hurt.'

'You have an extremely vivid imagination,' he says.

'You don't know the half of it,' says Lily, then buries her face in her mug as I give her a hard stare. I make a mental note to sit down with her later for a good, long chat about the attitude I expect from my fellow professionals.

'There's been a change of plans,' says Jon. 'The boys are no longer free on Saturday evening. They were very disappointed, but I promised I'd reschedule with you for a mutually convenient time.'

I pull out my phone and open my calendar. 'When did you have in mind?'

'How about Sunday afternoon? The boys have a soccer game in the morning, but they'll be free from about three o'clock onwards.'

'I can't. I promised my mother I'd go out to dinner with my great aunt and uncle. It's a long drive, so we're leaving around four thirty.'

'I didn't know you were coming too,' says Georgia, sounding less enthusiastic than one might have hoped.

'Likewise,' I say. 'I only agreed because Mum said she needed someone with her for moral support.'

'She told me the same thing.'

'Your mother sounds as sneaky as you, Isabella,' says Lily in her new role as critic in chief. I make a note to have that talk with her sooner rather than later.

'I can do Tuesday or Thursday evening next week,' I say.

'I'm booked up for both of those,' says Jon. 'How about Saturday? No, I forgot! I'm taking the boys camping next weekend. That pushes us towards the middle of August.'

'Or you two could go by yourselves,' says Mabel.

'Excuse me?' asks Jon.

She beams at him. 'You and Isabella want to play a game of golf together.'

'Crazy golf,' I murmur before she can run away with the idea of me being the new Jack Nicklaus.

'And you're both free this Saturday evening,' she adds. 'So, why not stick to your plan?'

To my annoyance, I feel my cheeks turn pink. 'Because the entire point of this game is that it's a challenge from the boys to me.'

'I doubt it's the entire point,' chips in Ivy, grinning at Jon. 'I could be wrong, of course.'

I can't think what's happening to this place. First, my junior employee makes quite unnecessary difficulties about preparing me a simple cup of coffee. Then my so-called business partner forgets where her loyalties are supposed to lie and sides with the enemy. Now our customers are getting involved in things that are none of their business. No wonder the newspapers are always saying the country is going downhill. No one seems to have any standards at all these days.

I wait for Jon to put Ivy in her place. I don't even feel sorry for her. I allow my customers a great deal of latitude, but someone needs to draw the line.

To my surprise, he hesitates. 'The boys would be very disappointed to miss out on seeing Isabella –'

'Of course, they would,' I say. 'I'm sure we can find a date that suits us all if we keep looking.'

'On the other hand,' says Jon. 'I've booked the tickets now, and I'm not sure whether they offer refunds.'

'If Justin has anything to do with it, they won't,' I say. 'I hope you had the sense not to book the tickets under your own name.'

'That never occurred to me. But we should be fine. You're the one who had the run-in with him, not me.'

Georgia's eyes light up. 'Issy didn't mention that. What happened?'

'Nothing at all!' I say quickly. 'And it's no use your asking Jon because he doesn't remember either.'

'I'll bet he does. Why don't you tell us all about it, Jon? I'm sure Ivy and Mabel want to hear too.'

I frown at Jon, who grins. 'Just for now, it's slipped my mind. So, what do you say, Isabella? Shall we use half the tickets?'

'Are you blackmailing me into going with you? If I say no, you'll misrepresent what happened last week to my awful sister and the customers who respect me so deeply?'

'Not at all. I'm suggesting we use the tickets I've already bought and buy ourselves some more for a time when the boys are available.'

He sees my hesitation and adds temptingly. 'If we can't get the boy's tickets refunded, we can at least use the snack part of them. Two extra hot dogs and two extra mega-gulps.'

'Crazy golf can be thirsty work,' I admit. 'Or it is the way I play it. Very well. Let's do it.'

'Good for you!' says Mabel. 'I've never heard so much fuss about accepting an invitation from a good-looking young man.'

I glance at Jon, who's clearly trying not to laugh.

'I don't know about the young bit,' I say. 'He must be at least forty years old.'

'Thirty-eight,' says Jon. 'But thank you for not contradicting the good-looking part.'

'Anyone under seventy seems young to me,' says Mabel. 'And if he doesn't know by now he's a nice-looking man, his mirror must be broken.'

'It will be by the time he's played golf with my sister,' says Georgia. 'She isn't known as Cyclone Isabella in our family for nothing.'

'Thank you for your input,' I say. 'Isn't it time for you to help Abby with tomorrow's dough?'

Jon looks at his watch. 'I have to go. Contrary to popular belief, I have plenty of work to do. Shall I pick you up on Saturday?'

'I have some shopping to do in Christchurch in the afternoon, so I'll go straight to *Bouncy Benny's* afterwards and meet you there.'

'No problem,' he says. 'But I should warn you that as well as being incredibly young and good-looking, I'm extremely punctual! I'll see you on Saturday evening. Don't be late or I'll assume you've lost your nerve at the last moment and decided to forfeit.'

Chapter Twenty-Two

True to his word, Jon is waiting for me when I arrive at the trampoline park on Saturday evening. I check my watch, which says I'm right on time. This is a relief because my timekeeping skills are not always the strongest. Last year, I forgot the clocks had gone forward and arrived at work an hour late on a day neither Lily nor Abby was rostered to come in.

The look on our customers' faces as they waited outside the bakery is one of my most painful memories. I would never voluntarily deprive a fellow human being of cake, and I still feel guilty about it. To add insult to injury, it was pouring with rain. It was nice to think they were so determined to get in that they were prepared to wait outside in the damp and cold. It was less nice when they told me they'd realised at once what must have happened and passed the time by laughing at me. Mabel even had the cheek to suggest I give myself a written warning.

'You made it on time!' says Jon when I walk in. 'Just.'

'I have two minutes to spare,' I tell him. 'I never understand people who arrive earlier than necessary, then waste that time thinking about how virtuous and wonderful they are when they could have been doing something useful.'

'I have been doing something useful!' he says. 'I've been to the hot dog stand to make sure they have a good supply of sausages, and that the mustard and ketchup delivery vans have been this week. I noticed last time we were here that you employ a different sausage-to-sauce ratio to most people.'

'I employ the correct ratios in everything I do. My other reason for arriving exactly on time is that if I'd got here any earlier, Justin might have spotted me and thrown me out.'

'You could have worn a disguise.'

'I considered it. But I don't have the bone structure for a false moustache, so I decided to risk it.'

'You have very nice bone structure,' he says.

He notices my surprised expression and looks faintly embarrassed.

'I appreciate the compliment,' I say. 'But facial symmetry won't get me far in our upcoming tournament. I'd rather have excellent biceps and forearms.'

'It's a game of crazy golf,' he says. 'Not a duel to the death on St Andrew's Golf Course.'

'Nevertheless, I'm here to win. Aren't you?'

'Always. That's the problem with spending time with young children. You have to master the skill of allowing them to win instead of you. What's more, you have to do it without them realising you've thrown the game deliberately, or else you end up hurting their pride.'

'That's why I don't plan on having children,' I say.

'Never?'

'Not in this lifetime. I can't say how I'll feel the next time around. Knowing my luck, I'll end up being reincarnated as the governess to a family of ten.'

He looks amused. 'You believe in reincarnation?'

'No, but it's fun to think of the different sort of lives you could have had.'

'What's wrong with making the best of this one?'

'Nothing at all. And I try very hard to do that, which is why I'm choosing not to have children of my own. Everyone has the chance to shape their lives as they wish, and that's the way I plan to shape mine. But I realise I'm in the minority here.'

'Not necessarily,' he says. 'I've never been that fussed about having them either.'

'But you seem to spend most of your time with your nephews. And they clearly adore you.'

'I've seen a lot of them recently. I'm not so convinced about the adoration part, although it's always nice to be revered.'

'Don't look at me!' I say. 'You'll have to organise your own fan club if that's what you want. I'm far too busy perfecting my role as the local Honeywell child catcher.'

'Do you dislike children on principle?'

I fasten my yellow wristband more securely. 'I don't dislike them at all. I have a goddaughter who's the most adorable child ever to walk the face of this earth. Her younger brother comes a close second. And your two seem delightful. But there's a difference between spending time with children before handing them back, and wanting to produce a batch of your own. I plan to leave all that sort of thing to my younger sister. Although she'll have to persuade some deluded man to take her on first.'

'I knew who she must be the first moment I saw her,' he says. 'The pair of you bear a striking resemblance to one another.'

'I wish people wouldn't keep saying that. It isn't remotely true. We may have similar colouring, but that's where the resemblance ends. When it comes to our personalities, we're as different as –'

'Peas in a pod?' he suggests.

'Project managers and bakery owners,' I finish.

He laughs. 'I stand corrected. Shall we get on with our game of golf, or would you prefer to cash in one of your snack tickets first? I'd hate to be accused of winning by default because I'd allowed your blood to mega-gulp ratio to fall too low.'

'That would be tempting if I didn't realise you were trying to put me off my game. You want to fill me with so many hot dogs that I'm thrown off balance and miss a vital stroke. That won't happen, so you'll have to come up with some other ingenious plan.'

'The thought never crossed my mind!' he says. 'I'll have you know I pride myself on being the perfect date.'

'This isn't a date.'

He recovers quickly. 'Just a figure of speech. An assignment – a chance meeting. Call it what you will.'

'A fight to the death, which is the very opposite of a date. Most of them, at least,' I add, remembering a few of my less successful past dates. Jon doesn't need to hear about those.

He hands me a golf club, then raises his own in a gesture of salute. '*Ave Caesar, morituri te salutamus.*'

'It's highly unlikely either of us will die during this game,' I say. 'Who's supposed to be playing the part of Caesar in this scenario – Justin?'

'I'm sure he'd play it with great enthusiasm. He would definitely give you the thumbs down if you asked him for mercy.'

'I could offer to trade my life for a mega-gulp and half a hotdog,' I say. 'It's a pity they don't sell anything more interesting that I could use to barter with. Simon thought there might be a speakeasy behind the wall. He was quite disappointed when I told him I thought it was unlikely.'

'Wishful thinking on his part,' says Jon. 'I imagine many of your dates are keen to locate the nearest supply of alcohol after the first half hour. Or was that not really a date either?'

I run my thumb over the head of the club to test its sharpness. 'Yes, and no. Simon asked me out when I wasn't expecting it. I agreed on the condition that I got to choose where we went.'

He glances around the hall. 'And this was your idea of a romantic evening?'

'Quite the opposite.'

He thinks about this for a moment, then nods. 'So, you and he …?'

'Are not destined to become Honeywell's version of Romeo and Juliet? That's correct. I think he's regretting now that he didn't meet my sister first.'

'I doubt it. Although I'm sure she's very nice too.'

'Have you paid the slightest attention to anything I've said to you since we met?'

'To the best of my recollection, you've mainly talked about cake. With the odd digression into the subject of ducks and ballet.'

'I've also mentioned Georgia once or twice. And I've left you in no doubt of my feelings towards her. I consider it my civic duty never to hide the truth from those who would benefit from hearing it.'

'I can see you do. Which doesn't explain why she appears to be working alongside you. Did she suggest she might burn down the bakery if you refused to offer her a job, or did she threaten you with some form of blackmail?'

'Not exactly,' I admit.

'Then why is she there?'

'I may have suggested it in a moment of intense weakness. In my defence, it's only a temporary job. She doesn't have a proper contract. I can throw her out into the snow any time I choose.'

'In August?' he asks.

'The rain, then. Do you have to be so nit-picky about everything? The thing to remember is that it's a short-term situation. Everyone concerned is very clear about that.'

'I'm glad you're all on the same page,' he says. 'Time's getting on. Should we start our game?'

'Good idea. I don't want to put off the moment of victory for a second longer. I suggest we play through the course once, just to get the lie of the land and assess our golf equipment and our opponent's strengths and weaknesses. Then we pause to enjoy the first round of our well-deserved refreshments. After that, we play the real thing. Sudden death, winner takes all.'

'That sounds good to me,' he says. 'What's the prize?'

'I haven't thought about it. What do you suggest?'

'If I lose, I buy you a pair of those trampolining socks they sell here. Any design you like.'

'And if I lose?' I ask. 'I realise it's a hypothetical question, but we may as well get the rules straight up front. That way, if there's a disputed call and we have to go before the judging panel, no one can disrupt the process with minor legal quibbles.'

He considers this. 'Who's on the panel?'

'Lily will be my legal advocate. Yours is up to you. But not Justin. Something tells me he wouldn't be an impartial arbitrator.'

'How about your sister?' he asks.

I give my club a menacing swing. 'On second thoughts, you can represent yourself. My solicitor always says the person who represents themself in court has a fool for a client. But that shouldn't be too much of a problem for you.'

'Thank you. You still haven't told me what I get if I win.'

'What do you want?'

A faint smile crosses his face. 'I can't say another date with you because you've made it clear this isn't a date. You'll just have to give me your marker, and I'll ask you to make it good at a time of my choosing.'

'It will be an extremely small marker,' I warn him. 'Only enough for half a tiny cookie that's about to pass its sell-by date.'

'That works for me.'

He gestures for me to approach the first hole – a brightly painted windmill. 'Let the games begin!'

Chapter Twenty-Three

It doesn't take us long to complete the course. None of the holes is particularly difficult. By the time we reach the final one – a terrifying clown with a wide open mouth – we're neck and neck on the scoring.

'You said this round doesn't count?' asks Jon as he tees up his ball.

'Are you having second thoughts about playing with a golf master such as myself?'

'We both have the same score,' he says, eyeing the clown with distaste. 'Do you think they gave it a malevolent leer to scare away the younger children?'

'My father always told me a bad workman blames his tools. Stop complaining and get on with it. I've heard nothing but grumbles from you so far. Your club handle isn't straight, the water feature is in the wrong place, and now it's the clown's appearance. Be a man and knock out what's left of its teeth before the people behind us complain to Justin that you're holding up the queue.'

He takes a deep breath and hits the ball. It bounces off the clown's left eye and rolls back towards us.

'I said its teeth, not its eye,' I tell him. 'Didn't they teach you basic anatomy at Project Manager school?'

'Oddly enough, they didn't. Please stop talking and let me concentrate.'

The second ball hits the clown's lower lip and rolls away again. He makes the shot on his third try.

'Your turn,' he says, retrieving his ball. 'You'll find it's more difficult than you think once you're face to face with the thing and able to appreciate its true horror. Even Stephen King would have second thoughts about putting this clown into one of his novels.'

'Don't be ridiculous. It's one of the nicest clowns I've ever had the privilege of meeting. Your mistake was hitting the ball too hard. You need to tap it gently – like this.'

I tap the ball, which rolls a few inches, hits a slight bump in the green baize, and comes to a standstill.

I sigh. 'That's a design fault on the part of the course engineer. It doesn't count.'

'I'm counting our strokes very carefully,' he assures me.

'Has the concept of sportsmanship completely passed you by? Please stand back. You're blocking my light. I have to perform a complex mathematical calculation involving angles of trajectory and the frictional properties of green baize. It's impossible to do that if I can't see what I'm supposed to be hitting.'

I take a deep breath, send up a prayer to the patron saint of golfers, and hit the ball.

Apparently, the golfing saint is away on his annual holiday this week because the ball skids sideways, hits the wooden edge, and rolls to a stop about a metre away from the clown's mouth, at an annoyingly difficult angle.

'Bad luck,' says Jon in a sympathetic tone that doesn't fool anyone.

'You were casting a shadow. I don't need to take this one. It's obvious it will go in on my next try, and we wouldn't want to wear out their equipment.'

'Take the shot,' he says.

'Fine!' I wiggle my hips in what I'd like to think is a professional manner and squint at the ball. I'm about to hit it and hope for the best when a small boy standing watching us breaks free from his sister's grip and runs over to the clown.

'Cwown!' he shouts gleefully.

'It's a beautiful clown,' I tell him. 'Some people don't appreciate it, but I'm glad to see you do.'

Before anyone can move, he bends down and picks up the ball, waving it above his head. 'Bawl!'

'Put that down, Eddie!' shouts his sister, but he's not listening. He waves it triumphantly before dodging past her and disappearing towards the trampolines, with the little girl in hot pursuit.

'What a shame,' I say. 'Still, it isn't as though that hole was in question. It was a simple matter of trigonometry. A trivial calculation for a mathematician such as myself.'

'If you hadn't been with me all this time, I'd have suspected you of paying him,' he says.

'Are you suggesting I don't respect the golfer's code?' I ask, shocked. 'I'm lost for words.'

'Why do I think that may not be true?'

He takes my arm and steers me away from the line of people waiting to tackle the final hole. 'Let's get you something to eat while you tell me more about this golfer's code of yours.'

Two hot dogs and a large drink of raspberry soda later, I'm refreshed and ready to face the idea of our next game.

'How are you feeling?' asks Jon. 'Are your hands steady and your eyesight keen? I'm glad we had that preliminary run through. The windmill is trickier than it seems. And we now know what to look out for when we reach Clubber the Clown.'

'He was cute and lovable!'

'A clown only his mother could love,' he insists.

'Not at all. If he were mine, I'd have loved him dearly and named him Caddyhack.'

'If he were mine, I'd lie awake half the night worrying whether the lock on my bedroom door would hold.'

'I know that feeling,' I agree. 'I always keep my door locked when my sister is in the house in case she takes it into her head to start sleepwalking. It's terrifying enough encountering her during the day. I can't face the thought of dealing with her in a somnolent state.'

'Ollie is prone to sleepwalking. I once found him at the bottom of my stairs searching for the cat. He didn't remember a thing about it the next morning.'

'Did he find it?' I ask.

'I don't have a cat. He must have dreamed the whole thing and somehow got himself out of bed and gone looking for it without waking up.'

'Do the boys live with you?'

I hadn't meant to ask this so bluntly, but I've been curious about their setup ever since Jon told me he was their uncle, not their father.

'Sorry,' I say as I see his expression. 'It's nothing to do with me. Forget I asked.'

'No, I'm glad you brought it up. I've wanted to tell you about it, but I've never had the chance because the boys are usually with me when I meet you.'

'You don't need to. Lily and my customers will tell you I'm the world's nosiest woman, but it isn't true. I can mind my own business when the situation demands.'

'They're my sister's children,' he says. 'Their father died last year.'

'I'm so sorry! How awful for those poor boys. And their mother too.'

'As you say. David died in a car crash coming home from work one evening. One moment he was there, and the next he just wasn't. It was all so sudden and shocking. I was on holiday in Greece that week, so Ali was on her own until I could fly back home. Our parents moved to Cornwall a while back and aren't in the best of health. And David's parents both died a few years ago. So, poor Ali has had to cope with most of it by herself.'

'She has you,' I say. 'It sounds as though the pair of you are close.'

'We are now. She and I always got on well, but she's five years older than me, so we didn't see all that much of each other after she left home. I went off to university a few years later and got my first job, and we drifted apart a bit. But David's death changed everything. I left my job in London and moved down here to be closer to her and the boys.'

'That was nice of you,' I say. 'Not everyone would be that supportive.'

'It was lucky I did. She was doing ok for a while – at least, we all thought she was. There was so much to do when it first happened that the adrenaline kept her going. Ali's a wonderful mother, and she always puts the boys first. She concentrated all her energies on making sure they were alright.'

'Which they couldn't have been,' I say. 'No one could after something like that.'

'You're right. It was pretty tough there for a while. But children are surprisingly resilient. I don't mean they forgot about their father. They'll never do that. But we all tried to hold it together for them and make sure they had a routine and as much stability as possible, and things started to improve.'

'That isn't the whole story, is it?' I ask.

'No. I was so busy concentrating on the boys that I overlooked Ali. She started going downhill after the first few months. The boys were her priority, and they gave her a reason to keep going and something to focus on. But she'd suffered a huge loss too, and she never stopped to deal with it. I blame myself for that. It was natural she shouldn't have thought much about herself, but I ought to have realised.'

'It isn't always that simple,' I say. 'I imagine you had your hands full helping out with the boys. It was a good thing you were there. I've seen the way they interact with you. The three of you have a very strong bond.'

'We've become very close,' he agrees. 'They're great kids, and it's a privilege to be in their lives. But I should have noticed what was happening with Ali much earlier. It all happened gradually, which made it more difficult for people to notice. It wasn't as though she was fine one day and not the next.'

'I didn't mean to pry into your family's personal business,' I say.

'I'd like you to know. To cut a long story short, Ali stopped being able to cope. She'd held everything together for the boys for as long as she could – far longer than many people would have done in her situation without asking for help. And because she didn't ask for it, and my parents and I were so busy keeping an eye on the boys, none of us realised she was in such a bad way until she collapsed. The boys called me one morning to say their mum couldn't stop crying. I rushed over there at once and found her in quite a state. I got the boys to school and took Ali to the doctor. He said she was suffering from clinical depression and needed a complete break.'

'Poor Ali,' I say. 'I can't imagine how awful that must have been for her. For all of you.'

'It was rough,' he agrees. 'My parents took her back to their house for a couple of weeks, and I moved in with the boys until she came home. I think the break did her good. She came back in a much better state, and we arranged a therapist for her, which has helped a lot. But none of us wants to see that happen again. So, I've been looking after the boys as often as possible while she recovers.'

'She's lucky to have you,' I say. 'They all are.'

He shrugs. 'It's what anyone would have done.'

'I think you know that isn't true. How is she now?'

'Much better. She and the boys are finding a new way of doing things. She thought about moving somewhere different. They could use an extra bedroom and possibly a larger garden. But her therapist told her not to make any major changes for at least a year, so they're staying put for now. I take the boys out as often as I can to tire them out. It's amazing how much energy two nine-year-olds can produce. If only we could find a way of harnessing it, we could power a small town off its local pre-teen population.'

'It's a great idea,' I agree. 'My goddaughter could power half of Honeywell by herself. And her brother could take care of the other half.'

I look at him more closely. 'You're looking quite tired. I assume that isn't entirely the result of our recent golf game?'

He smiles. 'Keen as the competition was, you're right. I stayed up late last night helping put up a swing set for the boys, and I was up again early this morning to take them to football.'

'I hope they were grateful.'

'I imagine they were. Ali told me off when she found out about the swing set. She said she's capable of doing that sort of thing herself.'

'Maybe she is,' I say. 'She ought to know.'

He doesn't look convinced. 'I'd like to give her a little more time to recover. And it's no trouble.'

'Except that you're exhausted. But that works out well for me. I came here this evening intending to win by a minimum of eight strokes. But now I'm thinking it may be double digits.'

'Are you forgetting we've already played one round, and it was a dead heat?' he asks.

I give him my most enigmatic smile. 'You're overlooking one fact.'

'Which is?'

'I'm not right-handed.'

'Congratulations?' he hazards.

'You're missing the point! I played right-handed during that round just to throw you off the scent. I won't be doing so during our next round.'

'A sneaky move.'

'Sneaky yet brilliant.'

'You're also overlooking something,' he says.

'I very much doubt it, but go on.'

'I'm not right-handed either.'

'Really?'

He sighs. 'Not really. But I've always wanted to say that. I also wanted to wipe the smug expression off your face.'

'Many have wished to do exactly that, yet here it still is.'

He pushes back his chair. 'Let's get this over with, unless you'd like something else to eat first? I notice they're selling some delicious-looking rainbow-coloured candies.'

'A good golfer knows when to practise moderation,' I tell him. 'You can buy me a packet after we've finished.'

We each select ourselves a golf club and prepare for action.

'Shall we toss a coin to see who goes first?' he asks.

'You'd be better off keeping your money safe for when I annihilate you and demand my prize socks.'

'I don't appear to have a coin,' he says. 'How about you?'

'I've left my bag in the locker, and I have more sense than to wander around spoiling the line of my jeans by stuffing my pockets full of coins. How will we decide who goes first?'

'I could toss my debit card instead,' he offers. 'Metal chip, you win. Signature strip, I win.'

'Could you hurry up, please?' asks the man behind us. 'Or else stand aside and let other people have a turn.'

'You start!' I tell Jon. 'It's always more satisfying to see how badly someone else performs so you can show them how it ought to be done.'

He measures up the distance to the water feature and flexes his shoulders. 'Prepare to learn some humility!'

He draws back his golf club, and every alarm in the building goes off.

Chapter Twenty-Four

'So, what happened after that?' asks Lily when I arrive at work the following morning and fill her in with all the details.

'We went home. There was no sense in hanging around the carpark for hours, waiting to find out what was going on. We only had twenty minutes left on our tickets, and all the horrible red-banders were arriving. They didn't look as terrifying as I'd imagined. Rather fewer Hell's Angels and rather more spotty teenagers than Justin had led me to believe. Do you realise you're wearing your cardigan inside out?'

She sighs and unbuttons it. 'I dressed in a hurry this morning. We were late for the school run.'

'Please don't change it on my account. I thought it was some new fashion the local teens had adopted, and you were trying to reclaim your lost youth by becoming one of the gang.'

'Wrong on both counts,' she says, turning her cardigan the right way around and refastening the buttons. 'I wasn't doing it on purpose, but neither is my youth lost. Or yours either, for that matter.'

'That's kind of you to say, but not entirely accurate. Why don't we take a moment's silence so we can gather the final remnants of our earlier youth and beauty around us and think wistfully of what used to be, and never will be again?'

She laughs. 'Most people would struggle to believe you're even in your twenties, let alone your thirties.'

'It's nice of you to console me. It must be my mother's anti-wrinkle cream. She pressed a pot into my hands on the morning of my thirtieth birthday and encouraged me never to leave the house without it. And I don't.'

'You use anti-wrinkle cream?' she asks disbelievingly.

'I said I never leave the house without it. It comes in very useful as a paperweight or for throwing at difficult customers.'

'So, did you discover what set off the alarms?' she asks. 'Presumably, it had nothing to do with you and Jon?'

'I hope not. Although they may have discovered we were holding a competition for gain and decided it was against the spirit of *Bouncy Benny's Swing'n'Spring*.'

'What gain? Were the Silver Surfers running a book on the outcome?'

'It's always possible,' I say. 'Although if they were, I'm a little hurt no one offered to cut me in on it. But Jon promised to buy me some socks if I won – by which I mean when I won.'

'And what were you going to buy him?'

'I would have given him my marker.'

'What sort of marker?' she asks. 'Do you mean a highlighter?'

'Don't you watch any gangster movies? People are always handing them out. No one can leave their cell without tripping over the increasing piles of markers the other inmates have left lying around. And possibly several of the guards too.'

'I'll make a note to watch one,' she says. 'What would your marker have said?'

'I'm not sure. There are various types of markers – gambling, business loans, fake alibis, promises to bump off someone of your choice in return for you removing the person standing in their way. You know the sort of thing.'

'Thankfully, I don't,' she says. 'So, yours would have been a non-specific marker?'

'Exactly! An abstract marker for a future favour of an unspecified type.'

'That seems rather risky. It feels like signing a legal document without reading it.'

'I see what you mean. But in this case, there was no risk. I've seen Jon's golf swing, and he won't be appearing in a *How to Play Crazy Golf in Six Easy Steps* video any time soon.'

'It doesn't matter, anyway,' she says. 'You didn't play the game, so neither of you won or lost.'

'True,' I say sadly. 'And I'd set my heart on a pair of socks with cupcakes on them.'

'You could always have bought them for yourself.'

'I only purchase items that are tax deductible. And those socks wouldn't be half as much fun to wear if I had to buy them myself. If Jon had been forced to buy them for me, I could have worn them every time I saw him and really rubbed it in.'

She raises an eyebrow. 'Do you expect to see him often?'

'I mean I could have worn them each day just in case I bumped into him.'

'And are you planning to bump into him again in the near future?' she pursues.

'You know me – I never plan more than five seconds ahead. Less, if I can get away with it.'

She hands me a cloth. 'It's your turn to clean the coffee machine. You have ten minutes before we open the shop.'

'That would make a good crazy golf hole,' I say. 'A giant coffee machine where you have to get the ball inside the nozzle without hitting the On switch.'

Mabel arrives half an hour later, accompanied by Phyllis and Bernie.

'Edie has a cold today,' she explains. 'So, I offered to take the mutt for a walk.'

'Doesn't he usually have his morning walk down by the water meadows?' asks Lily.

Mabel sighs. 'My sister won't allow me to take him there alone since he fell into that ditch. She seems to think her presence will protect against it happening again. I don't know why because we were both with him the last time he did it. But you know me –

I always do as I'm told. Anyway, Bernie seemed to want to come up here to watch me eat a plum slice. And we bumped into Phyllis on the way and joined forces.'

'What does he want to watch Phyllis eat?' I ask.

'A lemon meringue tart,' says Phyllis. 'He was also hoping to enjoy the spectacle of me drinking a nice foamy latte. Is Georgia around this morning?'

'My sister's presence isn't necessary in order for our customers to experience a fine cup of coffee,' I tell her. 'Lily and I were here long before she was, and we're both highly skilled operatives.'

'But you must admit she has a wonderful touch,' says Mabel. 'Edie commented on what a lovely cappuccino Georgia made for her last week.'

'Beginner's luck,' I say. 'The true measure of a barista is consistency. And my sister is an unknown quantity as far as that goes.'

I'm annoyed to hear them laughing as they sit down at their regular table.

'Will you make Phyllis' latte or shall I?' asks Lily.

'You'd better do it. She'll only find something to criticise if I make the attempt. I can't imagine why all our customers are falling over themselves to encourage Georgia. You'd think they'd never heard of the word loyalty.'

'I think it's lovely,' says Lily, picking up the bag of coffee beans. 'They're supporting us just as much as Georgia. You weren't hoping she'd do a terrible job and have to leave, were you?'

'No, because that would reflect poorly on us. But it would be nice if they occasionally acknowledged the real professionals around here.'

'You do that for them several times a day. You'd better check those plum slices before Mabel brings out her ruler and protractor to compare their size with last week's batch.'

'How did your date go with Jon?' Phyllis asks as I set their cakes in front of them.

'It wasn't a date.'

'It looked like one to me,' says Mabel.

'I agree,' says Phyllis. 'If it walks like a date and quacks like a date, it's a –'

'Free trial of possible future disappointment?' I suggest.

'Jon seemed pretty keen to me,' says Phyllis, taking a bite of her tart.

'He wasn't keen. He just didn't want to waste the pre-bought tickets.'

'So, why didn't he change them for another day?' she asks.

'Because they were non-transferable.'

'They must have been special tickets,' says Mabel. 'Because the normal ones can be exchanged. Edie and I checked the website. You can switch the date of your booking as long as you give them more than twenty-four hours' notice.'

'You looked it up?' I ask incredulously.

'The moment we got home. Mavis is always telling us we should incorporate technology into our everyday lives. She says the more we do it, the less scary we'll find it. So, that's what Edie and I did. It took us a while because the first one she found was *Benny's Play Place*. The directions didn't seem quite right, and when we looked at it more closely, we realised it was in Cumbria. So, we tried again and found the one in Christchurch. And there was the exchange policy – right at the top of the home page.'

Our customers are unbelievable. Particularly the Silver Surfers. None of us can make a move without one of them knowing about it and putting an electronic trace on us.

'Maybe Jon didn't realise the tickets were transferable,' I say at last. 'Or maybe he realised it might be months before we could find a mutually agreeable date.'

'Or he didn't want those boys of his hanging around watching you,' says Mabel.

'Little pitchers have big ears,' agrees Phyllis.

'It wasn't like that at all!' I say. 'Jon would never leave the boys out on purpose. He –'

I break off before I can say too much. Jon didn't authorise me to discuss his family situation with anyone. I'm touched he trusted me with as much information as he did, and I have no intention of betraying that trust.

'That isn't what happened,' I say more calmly. 'Jon had the tickets, the boys were busy, and it seemed a shame not to use them. Let's talk about something else. How's Mavis getting on with the funding shortfall? Has she decided what to do about it?'

'I expect something will turn up,' says Mabel. 'It always does. Have you finished your biscuit, Bernie? We must be getting home to see how your poor mistress is doing. I promised to bring her a packet of throat sweets from the chemist.'

She clips Bernie's lead onto his collar and slips on her jacket.

'I'll come with you,' says Phyllis. 'Then we can walk back together.'

'Good idea,' says Mabel. 'Two pairs of eyes are better than one if we pass any uncharted ditches. The mutt isn't one to learn from experience.'

'They didn't mean to annoy you,' says Lily when they've left.

'I wasn't annoyed,' I say. 'Or not about them teasing me. I'm used to that. Our customers rarely treat me with the respect I deserve. But it didn't seem fair on Jon. He would never dump Ollie and Toby for a date.'

'But Mabel and Phyllis weren't to know that, and I'm sure neither of us grudges them a bit of fun.'

'Of course not. And they had the sense not to do it when Georgia was here, so I'll let them off this once.'

She picks up a tray and starts to clear their table. 'So, you went home last night without looking for something else to do?'

'The session was almost over. Even if the alarms had been switched off, we would barely have had time to pick up our clubs before Justin appeared to say he'd call the police if we weren't out of there in the next five minutes.'

'You could have gone on somewhere for dinner or a drink.'

'We went out last night with one purpose only,' I say. 'Which was for me to teach Jon once and for all who is the undisputed

Hampshire crazy golf champion. Due to circumstances beyond our control, we weren't able to complete that mission. But we managed a test game, and I let him see what he'd be up against in the final round. I wouldn't be surprised if he set those alarms off himself.'

'While he was with you?' she asks.

'It could easily be done. I can think of five ways off the top of my head. I'm sure I could come up with lots more if I really thought about it. The simplest thing would be to have a friend on site keeping an eye on the pair of us. If things weren't going well, and it became clear Jon wasn't going to win, he could have given the pre-arranged signal, and the friend would have set off the fire alarms.'

'It seems unnecessarily complicated for something as trivial as a game of golf,' she says.

'I've had to speak to you several times about your lack of competitive spirit. Last night wasn't trivial, but neither was it a date!'

'So, it was a one-off?'

'Exactly,' I agree.

'A something and nothing?'

'It was just below a something and just above a nothing.'

'No plans for a replay?' she asks.

'None whatsoever. If you ask me, it's unlikely either of us will see Jon again for quite a while.'

'Interesting,' she says, peering past the display of macarons in the window. 'But I'm not sure you're right. Unless those boys have escaped from their uncle's eagle eye and set off for the bakery by themselves, which doesn't seem likely, it looks to me as though you'll be seeing him again in the very near future.'

Chapter Twenty-Five

A minute later, the door opens, and the boys appear.

'Good morning,' I say. 'Did you lose your uncle on your way over here?'

'He isn't lost,' says Ollie. 'He stopped to talk to Simon about something to do with work. He told us to go on ahead.'

'Are you sure he hasn't fallen into a ditch? That happened recently to one of our village's most popular residents. It took several people to rescue him.'

'If you're talking about Bernie,' says Lily. 'He climbed out all by himself before the rescuers arrived.'

'Let's hope Uncle Jon manages to do the same,' I say. 'If not, we can send our customers out with head torches and coils of rope. Why don't you two sit down while you're waiting for him and tell me what you'd like him to buy for you?'

Ollie doesn't seem his usual cheerful self, but that may be because I don't know him very well.

'Uncle Jon said we could have anything we wanted,' he tells me.

'Why am I not convinced that's true?'

'It is!' says Toby. 'He told us to order anything we liked.'

'To make up for our disappointment,' adds Ollie.

'I'm sorry to hear you're disappointed,' says Lily. 'May I ask why?'

'Because of our camping trip,' says Ollie, relapsing into gloom.

'Jon mentioned he was taking you camping next week,' I say. 'Is there a problem with your tent?'

'It's Grandpa,' he says. 'He has to stay in Cornwall because he and Grandma have the flu.'

'Poor thing,' says Lily. 'Was he going camping with you?'

Toby nods. 'Grandpa was coming to stay with us, and he and Uncle Jon were taking us to Pine Ridge for three nights. We've been looking forward to it for ages.'

'Can someone else go with you instead?' asks Lily.

'Mum wanted to,' says Ollie. 'But now she has to drive down to Cornwall to look after Grandma and Grandpa.'

'What a shame,' says Lily. 'I hope they both get better soon. And you'll be able to go camping with her once she gets back.'

'But not at Pine Ridge,' says Toby. 'They're booked up for the whole of the summer holidays. Uncle Jon only got these nights for us because someone cancelled at the last minute.'

'Can't Uncle Jon take you by himself?' I ask. 'I don't know you very well, but neither of you seems that badly behaved.'

'He can still take us,' says Toby. 'But he says we won't be able to do all the things we wanted to do. Ollie was going ziplining, and I was going whitewater rafting.'

'Couldn't you take it in turns to do those things with him?'

'Ollie is frightened of whitewater rafting,' says Toby. 'And Uncle Jon can't leave him alone all afternoon. And I don't like heights, so I can't go on the zipline. Uncle Jon says we can do both those things next year, and there are lots of other things to do instead. But it won't be the same.'

'We have some extra-large cookies today if that helps,' says Lily.

They thank her politely and tell her which flavours they'd like, but it's obvious it would take more than a giant cookie to cheer them up right now.

'How far away is the campsite?' I ask.

'It's in Wales,' says Ollie. 'Uncle Jon says it's a long drive, but it's worth it.'

Toby gives me a speculative look. 'Do you like whitewater rafting?'

'I've never tried it,' I say. 'But I have been up in a hot air balloon. That was great fun.'

I realise too late that wasn't the most tactful remark to make. A nine-year-old who's had their whitewater adventure taken away from them is unlikely to be cheered by the thought of someone else having a wonderful time floating through the skies.

'Would you like to try ziplining?' Ollie asks me.

'Maybe one day. And hopefully you will soon. Whitewater rafting too.'

'Not if we have to go camping without Grandpa,' says Toby.

'There must be someone else your uncle could ask,' says Lily.

'He's asked everyone he knows. But all our friends are away on holiday at the moment.'

He gives me a speculative look. 'Would you like to come with us?'

I'm taken aback by this direct request. 'Did your uncle tell you to ask me?'

'No. I just had the idea right now. We didn't get to play golf with you on Saturday. There's a crazy golf course at Pine Ridge and a heated swimming pool with flumes.'

'You love flumes!' Lily tells me.

'Everyone loves flumes. But that doesn't mean they can drop everything and take off for days.'

'We aren't too busy now we have Georgia working here. We could ask her to cover those days if you want to go.'

'How did we go from "What a shame" to "Isabella can do it" in the course of twenty seconds?' I ask. 'You're also overlooking the fact I haven't been officially invited. I'm sorry, Lily, but this one isn't going to fly.'

'Not unless you go ziplining,' says Toby, and he and Ollie grin at each other.

The bakery door opens, and Jon walks in.

'You found it!' he says. 'I was a little worried you might not remember the way. I should have remembered that nine-year-old boys are like homing pigeons when it comes to cake.'

'The boys have been telling us about their upcoming camping trip,' I say.

He nods. 'It's a shame their grandfather can't come along. But we'll have lots of fun even if we can't do everything we had in mind.'

'Of course, you will,' says Lily. 'But it's a shame Toby can't go rafting.'

'That's only a tiny part of the trip,' he says. 'I have all sorts of exciting things planned. We can build our own campfire and cook all our meals over it. We can swim every day too. The boys love waterslides.'

'But we wanted to do the whitewater rafting and the ziplining,' says Toby stubbornly. 'That's why we thought Isabella could come with us.'

Either the startled look on Jon's face is genuine or he's one of the best actors in the world. Given the fact he doesn't appear to have starred in any recent blockbusters, I'm inclined to think it's the first one.

'Can we take her?' asks Ollie.

I interrupt before he can say anything else. 'I'd like to make it clear to everyone concerned this wasn't my suggestion. Of course, I can't go camping with you.'

'That lady said you weren't busy,' says Toby, pointing at Lily, who grins at me.

'That lady isn't in charge of my timetable,' I tell him. 'I understand you're disappointed, but you can't go around inviting random strangers to join in your camping trips. Ask your uncle if you don't believe me.'

I look at Jon for confirmation and see he's smiling. 'As a general rule, you're right. But although in many respects you're one of the most random people I've ever met, I wouldn't say you're totally strange.'

'I said a stranger,' I correct him. 'I seem to remember lots of lessons in primary school about stranger danger.'

'You aren't a stranger!' says Ollie. 'You've given us loads of free cookies.'

Jon sighs. 'We may need to circle back to that topic at some point. I agree Isabella isn't a stranger, but that doesn't mean she wants to come along on our trip. Who would? I'm your uncle, so I have to pretend to like you. But there's no obligation on anyone else to be anything more than polite to the pair of you.'

'So, will you come?' Ollie asks me.

I catch Jon's eye. 'Help me out here!'

'Certainly. You'd be most welcome to join us next weekend. More than welcome, in fact. It's obvious the boys would love it. But please don't feel you have to agree if you don't like the idea.'

'That isn't helping me out,' I say. 'It's behaving most unfairly.'

'We'll share our marshmallows with you,' promises Ollie.

'And help you put up your tent,' says Toby.

'It isn't fair to pressure her,' says Jon. 'I'm sorry, Isabella. Let's change the subject. What do you recommend I order today? Anything with whipped cream would hit the spot. I skipped lunch, and I'm ravenous.'

I'm about to launch into an enthusiastic recital of every cake we sell that contains even the smallest amount of whipped cream when I notice the boys' faces. They're still concentrating on their cookies. Like me, it obviously takes a lot to distract them from whatever is on their plates. But the sight of their disconsolate faces gives me a sudden pang. They've been through so much this year. First, they lost their father. Then their mother was diagnosed with clinical depression. Would it be the worst thing in the world to give up a few days to make sure they get the holiday they deserve?

'Alright, I'll come with you,' I tell them. 'As long as that was a genuine invitation and your uncle wasn't winding me up.'

The change in their demeanour would be comical if it weren't so touching. Ollie drops his cookie and beams at me. Toby goes one better and tosses his cookie towards the ceiling in the manner of a recent graduate flinging his cap into the air. It hits the lightshade and falls to the floor in a shower of crumbs.

'Don't worry,' says Lily, seeing his panicked expression. 'I'll fetch a dustpan and brush, and you can sweep up the crumbs while I replace it.'

'I can't help feeling as though we've unfairly pressured you,' Jon tells me.

'You have. But Lily will tell you I'm a woman of my word. Once I've given it, there's no going back.'

'Thank you,' he says quietly.

I remember our conversation from yesterday evening. 'Does this have anything to do with the marker I was supposed to give you? Because if so, I'd like to remind you that neither of us won our golf game. Obviously, I would have been the most likely winner. But events intervened, so we'll never know for sure.'

'It has nothing to do with your marker,' he says. 'I understand the rules surrounding those as well as the next person. And I didn't send the boys here today to ask you to come with us. But I'm very glad they did.'

'So is Isabella,' says Toby. 'She's been in a hot air balloon, but she's never been ziplining. And now she can!'

I look at him in some amusement. 'So, you and Ollie have actually done me a huge favour by including me in your expedition?'

'That's right,' he agrees, the sarcasm flying over his head and hitting the opposite wall. 'And don't forget we can canoe on the lake.'

'It's all I've been able to think about for the past two minutes. That, and the opportunity of sharing my sleeping environment with a variety of wild animals and vicious insects.'

'We'll show you how to zip up your tent,' promises Ollie.

'Absolutely,' says Jon. 'Isabella has been kind enough to offer to accompany us, so it's our duty to return her in one piece at the end of the trip. Plus or minus a few scrapes and bruises.'

'You could have mentioned that when you were making your pitch,' I tell him. 'I feel as though I've been the subject of mis-selling. Like those people who persuade you to buy a timeshare for ten times its actual value.'

'Don't you want to go camping?' asks Ollie.

I relent. 'Try to stop me! I won't be happy unless I fall off the zipline, get stuck in a flume, overturn my canoe, and have to be rescued by the local lifeboat crew.'

'Cool!' he says happily. 'I can't wait.'

Chapter Twenty-Six

We leave rather earlier than I would have chosen on Saturday morning. Georgia insists on being there to see me off.

'I'd like to think this is a gesture of sisterly support,' I say as I struggle to fasten the straps on my backpack. 'But I can't help suspecting you have some ulterior motive.'

'You always think the worst of me,' she complains. 'I'm here to wish you well for the trip. And to enjoy the spectacle of my sister preparing to encounter the great outdoors.'

'That sounds rather more likely. Why won't this backpack close?'

'You've packed too much into it?'

'Thanks, Einstein.'

She pokes it with her foot. 'What have you got in there?'

'A grand piano and a hi-fi system. Have you never been camping?'

'Not since I was a child. Matt suggested it once.'

'And?' I ask as she breaks off and stares into space.

She looks surprised by the question. 'I dumped him.'

'Of course, you did. But that isn't a solution in this case. Jon and I aren't dating, so that course of action isn't available to me.'

'Are you sure?' she asks.

'Quite sure. You can't dump someone you aren't in a relationship with. It's in the manual. It may seem unfair, but those are the rules.'

'I mean, are you sure you aren't dating him? Let's look at the evidence. You went out with him last weekend.'

'The boys arranged that, and the tickets had already been bought. Jon was simply getting value for his money. Anyone would have done the same.'

'And now you're going away with him for three nights,' she says.

'That's quite a spin to put on things. Again, this has been arranged for the boys' benefit, not ours. They're desperate to go on this trip, and they needed an extra person to accompany them.'

'And of all the adults in all the world, it had to be you?'

'Of all the adults available at short notice who don't mind spending several days huddled inside an inadequate tent in the lashing rain,' I say. 'Only darting out between downpours to fly down mountains, supported by nothing more than an inadequately secured clip, before racing to the lake to overturn their canoe.'

'And with a man who's clearly besotted with you,' she adds.

'That's ridiculous. Jon and I are friends. We're also sparring partners. Both of us are highly competitive and want to win at any cost.'

'Is that right?' she asks. 'Try letting him know something is important to you, and see how quickly he lets you win.'

'I don't have time for an argument right now. You'll have to leave it until I get back.'

'If you come back,' she says. 'Many things can go wrong on this sort of trip. My friend went camping once and was bitten by a horse.'

'I've met Caroline. Was the horse alright?'

'And rain may be the least of your problems weather-wise,' she goes on. 'It's unusually hot at the moment. There may be forest fires.'

'We aren't camping in the middle of a forest.'

'That makes no difference. They travel very quickly.'

'They'll have to travel across a large lake. I think we'll be fine.'

'How large?' she asks. 'Is there any chance of something nasty lurking in its depths?'

'If you're talking about the Loch Ness Monster, she lives in Scotland. And none of the pictures of her look too scary. If there's a monster in this lake, it's probably a friendly one. And I don't know why you're so worried about potential hazards. If I mysteriously disappear while wandering alone by the shores of the lake one evening, you'll get my bedroom.'

'The thought had crossed my mind,' she says. 'But it would be easier all round if you just moved out in the normal way. How's saving for a deposit going?'

'Fine, thanks. But before you assume you're my next of kin if I get lost on this camping trip, I should tell you I've made a will leaving everything to my goddaughter and her brother.'

She sighs. 'That's my pension plan blown. I'll have to find a rich man to marry after all.'

'In the meantime, you'll be covering all my shifts while I'm gone,' I say. 'You'll have to work twice as hard as usual to make up for my absence.'

'As far as I can see, all I have to do is sit around telling everyone what to do and eating lots of cake. I can do both those things standing on my head.'

'You'll choke if you do,' I warn her. 'Lily is pretty good at basic first aid, but she tends to lose her head in a crisis. You'd better hope some of the Silver Surfers are there if it happens. Mabel in particular is excellent at dislodging pieces of cake lodged in the windpipe as a result of talking and eating at the same time. Or so I hear.'

'I'll bear it in mind,' she promises. 'Seriously, Issy, thanks for the job. You didn't have to offer it to me, and I'm very grateful.'

She looks at her watch. 'Why are you hiding up here when they'll be arriving at any moment? Are you trying to wriggle out of this trip? Just say the word, and I'll push you downstairs and break your other leg. It would be no trouble at all.'

She follows me down the stairs and out onto the drive. 'Is that them now?'

I watch the blue car crunching over the gravel. 'It looks like it. I was praying Jon would get a flat tyre on his way over here. Several, if possible.'

'You should have told me,' she says. 'I've slashed the odd tyre in my time. But it's too late for that now. Off you go, and don't keep them waiting. Send me a postcard!'

Jon jumps out of his car to greet me. 'Can I help with your bags?'

'Bag singular,' I say. 'You instructed me to pack lightly, so I only brought the one backpack.'

I wave to the boys, sitting next to each other on the back seat and beaming at me.

'Don't let them climb out!' says Jon. 'I only just managed to fit everything in this morning. It was like playing a particularly complicated game of Tetris. I'm not sure we can allow the boys to get out when we arrive at the campsite. They may have to stay where they are for the next few days in case everything explodes out of the car.'

'Men always make such a fuss about the smallest things,' I tell him. 'I'd have packed this car in a few minutes and still left enough room left for us to pick up a hitchhiker along the way.'

'Please don't suggest that to the boys! I've only just made them understand that someone handing out free cookies isn't necessarily your new best friend.'

I sling my backpack into the boot, causing him to wince as it crushes a canvas bundle.

'I hope your bag isn't too heavy,' he says, closing and locking the boot. 'That was your tent it landed on. If you've buckled the cross pole, it won't stay up for long.'

'No problem,' I say, opening the door and climbing into the passenger seat. 'I'll swap with you. Hello, boys. How are you both on this fine summer day?'

'Ollie gets car sick on long journeys!' says Toby with relish.

I recoil. 'That isn't quite the answer I was looking for. I was hoping for something more along the lines of, "Good morning, Isabella! We've brought enough snacks for twenty people."'

Jon starts the car. 'Don't wind her up, Toby. Ollie only gets sick on twisty roads, and we'll be on fairly straight roads until the last few miles.'

He sets off down the drive, and I turn to look at the boys. 'Why is it only Ollie that gets carsick?'

'Because I'm awesome!' says Toby at once.

'I'm asking why only one of you suffers from car sickness if you're twins.'

'We aren't identical,' he says. 'We're just normal brothers who happen to be the same age. That was your sister, wasn't it?'

'The one who waved to you? Yes, it was. I usually try to deny the relationship, but you saw us come out of the same house.'

'Are you and she alike?' asks Ollie.

I give an artistic shudder. 'We're like chalk and cheese. No, that isn't a good analogy. Some cheeses taste exactly like chalk. We're like day and night or winter and summer.'

I catch Jon's amused look and add. 'You barely know her. You don't get to have an opinion.'

'Fine,' he says. 'I'll concentrate on my driving and remember my place.'

I turn back to the boys. 'If Ollie insists on being sick, I shall demand your uncle pushes him out and leaves him by the side of the road before turning around and bringing me straight back home. Is that clearly understood?'

They nod but don't look too worried. Children never seem to take what I say as seriously as they should.

'I've made us a playlist,' says Jon, reaching into the dash pocket and handing me his phone. 'Just switch on the player and check it's connected to Bluetooth.'

'Excellent,' I say. 'I love a good playlist to set the tone of the journey. I'm intrigued to discover what you've chosen for a camping holiday – Life is a Highway or Summer Holiday?'

One corner of his mouth twitches. 'Things are a little different when you're travelling with children. This was their favourite band when they were younger, and they demanded it today for old times' sake.'

There's a burst of introductory music, and several male voices start singing in unison about a big, red car. When I look in my mirror, I see both boys singing along at the top of their lungs.

No sooner have the last notes of this charming ditty died away than the music starts again and we're launched straight into the middle of a song about Fruit Salad. It seems to extol the virtues of healthy eating. That's all very well in its way, but I hope Jon hasn't included it to signal the sort of food he plans to serve over the next few days. I may not be an experienced camper, but I'm reasonably sure the only way to get through a trip like this is by consuming vast quantities of sausage and bacon, finished off with roasted marshmallows.

By the time we stop for lunch, my musical education has been considerably broadened.

'Are you regretting offering to accompany us?' asks Jon, pulling into the motorway services and switching off the car.

'Less of an offer than an ambush,' I say.

'I can drop you off at the nearest train station if you like.'

'No, thank you. When I start things, I like to see them through to the end, however bitter it may be. And it's far worse for you than for me. Ollie and I will be enjoying ourselves ziplining while you and Toby do your best to soak through every item of clothing you possess. You'll have to spend the rest of the trip freezing cold and regretting your life choices.'

'Shall we leave these two in the car so all the bags and cases stay in place?' he asks. 'Or risk the entire edifice collapsing by allowing them to climb out and stretch their legs?'

'We should let them out,' I decide. 'I wouldn't put it past them to drive away while we're eating our lunch.'

'Good thinking. Out you get, boys! Hopefully, we'll be able to fit you in again. If not, one of you will have to ride on the roof for the last part of the journey.'

'Bags me!' shouts Toby.

'That's not fair!' says Ollie. 'We should take it in turns.'

'We'll toss a coin for it,' promises Jon.

The boys are still arguing about this when we return to the car half an hour later. Toby is claiming precedence on the grounds he was born twenty minutes earlier, while Ollie is making the rather dubious case he has a better head for heights. Both of them seem disappointed when we successfully rearrange the bags and camping equipment in a way that allows them to resume their original seats.

'You've packed an awful lot for three nights,' I say as we drive away. 'I see now why you told me to bring as little as possible, but it feels slightly hypocritical on your part.'

'Have you ever camped before?' asks Jon.

'Only once with the girl guides. That was shortly before I was asked to leave on the grounds that I required more supervision than a mere three leaders could provide.'

'I'd like to hear that story sometime,' he says. 'Although possibly not when the boys are around. I've been trying to persuade them to join their local cub troupe, and I don't want you giving them any ideas.'

'I wouldn't dream of mentioning it to them. It's one of the episodes in my early life of which I'm not entirely proud. Thankfully, those episodes are few and far between.'

'Am I to understand you've led a blameless life in all other respects?' he asks.

'Absolutely. You can ask anyone who knows me. I could provide you with at least fifty written references if need be. How many other people do you know who could say that?'

'That's most impressive. I assume your sister wouldn't be among those lining up to tell the world in two hundred words or fewer exactly what an addition you are to the local community?'

'Possibly not,' I admit. 'Although I wouldn't bet as much on that as I would have even a month ago.'

'What's brought about her change of heart?'

'It's more of a slight shift in the tectonic plates of her lifelong negativity towards me.'

'You must have something in common,' he says. 'If only a shared set of parents.'

'Poor Mum and Dad. When most people decide to go on and have a second child, it's because the first one was so awful they want to try again for a better model –'

'I must remember to mention that theory to my sister,' he murmurs.

'But in my parent's case, it was clearly because they had such a perfect child right out of the gate, and they hoped for a similar result the second time. I expect they told each other they would be the envy of all their friends, and that herds of child behavioural experts would descend upon Compton, all eager to write the seminal book on parenting.'

'Herds?' he asks. 'Is that the term for a group of psychologists?'

'Unless they choose to go with the more dated "coven". Imagine my parents' horror when, instead of a replica of their perfect first born, Georgia arrived. They must have wondered whether there'd been a clerical error in the hospital nursery and they'd received the wrong baby.'

'She looks remarkably like you. I don't expect they remained in doubt for long.'

I glance back at the boys, who have their heads together over a game involving some sort of dancing fruits and aren't listening to a word we're saying. 'How about those two? Toby has informed me several times they're nothing like each other. It seems important to him.'

'It's important to both of them. And I can vouch for the fact they're very different. They spend half their time squabbling, but if there's even a hint of either of them being in trouble, they close ranks quicker than you can blink.'

He points to the road sign. 'We take the next exit. After that, it's only twenty minutes before we should start seeing signs for the campsite. We'll have plenty of time to put up our tents and explore the area before we set you to work gathering wood for the campfire.'

'I'm not much of a wood-gatherer,' I say. 'I see myself more as a director of wood-gathering activities. It's important to get these things settled before we start.'

'I should point out that most, if not all, of our meals will be cooked over the campfire,' he says. 'Portions will be allocated according to how much the director of operations – that's me – decides the junior members of staff – that's you three – have contributed. Just something to bear in mind.'

'You are a tyrant and a bully,' I inform him. 'Any wood-gathering in which I'm forced to participate will be under strong protest.'

'Duly noted,' he says. 'Keep a sharp eye out for that turning or we'll find ourselves lost in the middle of the Welsh countryside, and you won't get any kind of dinner this evening, let alone one cooked over a blazing campfire.'

Chapter Twenty-Seven

We arrive at the campsite fifteen minutes later and unload the car.

'We should put up Isabella's tent first,' says Jon. 'In an ideal world, she'd do it herself. But as she's a newish camper, I think you two should do it for her.'

'I'm happy to supervise,' I say. 'That's my favourite part of working at a bakery. I enjoy keeping an eye on my colleagues and giving them measured yet honest feedback on their performance.'

'Your favourite part?' he asks.

'You're right. It isn't my absolute favourite. But it comes a close second to sampling all of our products the moment they're out of the oven.'

We've been directed to a good-sized pitch. Jon assures me there's plenty of room for both tents and offers me a choice of location.

'You can sleep on the side closest to the shower block to save you thirty seconds in the morning,' he says. 'Or you may wish to select the space between our tent and the car.'

'That one!' I say with decision. 'It will give me the chance to sneak away and drive home in the event I'm not enjoying myself. It will also offer some much-needed cover if we're attacked by bears in the middle of the night. If I sleep between you and the car, with any luck the bears won't even notice me.'

'There are no bears in Wales,' says Ollie.

'I wish I could believe you were right,' I say. 'But I'm not convinced. And don't get me started on the subject of wolves.'

I remember Jon mentioning Ollie's tendency to sleepwalk when stressed and wish I hadn't said this. To my relief, both the boys burst out laughing.

'Wolves don't live in the British Isles anymore,' says Ollie. 'Our teacher told us there used to be lots of them, but they died out.'

'That's disappointing,' I say. 'How about werewolves?'

He rolls his eyes. 'They aren't real.'

'I feel as though I've been brought here on false pretences,' I tell Jon. 'An absence of bears and wolves is bad enough. But now I hear there are no mythical creatures either, and I was hoping to get a photo of a unicorn.'

'We can make one for you in Photoshop,' offers Toby. 'All we need is a picture of a horse, and we'll do the rest.'

'That's an impressive talent. Remember to include it on your CV. Meanwhile, are you planning to put up my tent or will you be doing that in Photoshop too?'

'Time us!' says Ollie, grabbing a canvas bag and tugging at the zip. 'We've been practising all week in Uncle Jon's garden.'

Their practice has obviously been to good effect as they put it up in less than ten minutes. Despite Jon's gloomy warnings, I'm pleased to see the ridge pole hasn't been damaged. It's a small, one-woman tent, but it doesn't give the impression of a tent that's planning to collapse on its occupant during the night.

'Welcome to your new abode,' says Jon. 'This will be your home for the next three nights. Please keep it clean and tidy, and don't forget to ask the concierge if there's anything we can do to make your stay more comfortable.'

'Does the concierge have any spare toothbrushes?' I ask. 'I'm worried I've forgotten to pack mine.'

'He says there's a camp shop over there that stocks every possible necessity. Why don't you unpack your bags while the boys and I tackle our tent?'

Half an hour later, their tent is up too. Jon is flexing a bruised finger, and Toby has a small cut on the side of his face, but they all seem cheerful enough.

'What now?' I ask. 'It must be almost dinner time.'

'It's half past three,' says Jon. 'Is that when you usually eat dinner?'

'No, because the bakery doesn't close until five thirty most days. But we generally stop for a light-to-medium-sized snack at half past three.'

He reaches into his tent and tosses me a bag of peanuts. 'I came prepared.'

'Thanks,' I say, ripping it open and offering it to the boys. 'You only have yourself to blame for this. Next time we take a road trip, don't make a playlist all about food. I've been thinking about fruit salad and mashed potatoes for the past two hours.'

'Will those keep you going while we have a look around or do you need something more substantial?' he asks.

'I came here prepared to suffer in a good cause. I can hold out for a couple more hours.'

The campsite is delightful. It's set at the edge of a pine forest and near a large lake. It looks peaceful enough – not at all the sort of body of water anyone would suspect of concealing a large, prehistoric creature with malign intent.

'The lake is fed by the river coming down from the hills over in that direction,' says Jon, pointing. 'That's where Toby and I will be whitewater rafting.'

'While we enjoy a far more civilised afternoon skimming over the treetops and enjoying the view,' I say, smiling at Ollie.

We wander through the forest, climbing higher and higher until at last we emerge into sunlight at the top of the hill. The view is magnificent. Rolling green hills stretch out in every direction. The silver ribbon of river winds through the valley below us, catching the light like a necklace. In the far distance, the mountains rise in soft, blue-grey ridges, hazy in the late afternoon warmth. Nearby, a buzzard circles lazily overhead, and the air smells faintly of warm earth and pine trees.

'I'm becoming more reconciled to this trip by the minute,' I say. 'You have excellent taste in holiday destinations, Jon. How did you find this place?'

'I used to know the area quite well. I was at university with someone who came from a village only a few miles from here. I stayed with him several times during the holidays.'

'I can't believe anyone who grew up here would ever want to leave. I love where I live, but this is something extra special.'

'Charlie didn't leave,' he says. 'He got a job a few miles from here after he graduated, and he's been here ever since. He lives just down there.'

He points down the valley to a small village. I can just about make out a church tower, but not much else.

'So, is he away from home this week?' I ask.

'What makes you ask that?'

'You told me I needed to come on this trip because otherwise Ollie couldn't go whitewater rafting with you. But if you know someone local, you could have asked him to pop over and look after Ollie for a few hours.'

'I don't think …' he begins, then clears his throat. 'I'd forgotten he … I mean it didn't occur to me that …'

I can't help laughing. 'You owe me an extra-large dinner for that. And not just dinner. I expect to be offered second helpings of everything while we're here. And to be excused all washing-up duty.'

'It's a deal,' he says. 'Sorry about that. I really had forgotten about Charlie that day the boys invited you.'

'When did you remember?'

'About five minutes after we'd left the bakery. But you'd agreed to come with us by then, and the boys were so excited that –'

'Any uncle who blames his nephews for his disgraceful behaviour should be ashamed of himself,' I tell him severely.

The boys haven't been listening. They're too busy picking up sticks and trying to build a fire.

'You know the rules,' says Jon. 'Fires are to be lit in designated areas only. We don't want to set the entire forest alight.'

'But we wanted to see whether we could make a flame by rubbing two sticks together!' protests Ollie.

'And so you shall. Just not here. Leave them where they are. It's time we were getting back to the campsite to start dinner. If Isabella passes out with hunger, you'll have to carry her down the hill.'

'You've done a beautiful job,' I tell them. 'It looks like a tiny wigwam. Some forest creature will be glad to sleep in there tonight, especially if it rains.'

'A baby bear?' asks Jon. 'Or just a wolf?'

'You may laugh, but you can't prove I'm wrong. A stoat or a weasel may be weaving their way home after a late-night party. They'll be more than thankful to stumble across such a perfectly constructed shelter. They may even move their entire family in or turn it into an Airbnb.'

'It isn't only the boys who have a vivid imagination,' says Jon. 'But you're right. I can't prove that won't happen. Let's agree it's a likely scenario and leave the sticks where they are.'

'I'd like it to be a fieldmouse,' says Ollie. 'We learned about them in school, and they're really cute.'

'It's just the right shaped wigwam for a fieldmouse,' I say. 'I shouldn't wonder if that's exactly what happens. We could come up here tomorrow and look for signs of habitation.'

'First, we need to get you back to the campsite,' says Jon. 'I doubt you'll stay on your feet for much longer without further sustenance.'

'You don't know as much about me as you think you do,' I tell him. 'Come on, boys – I'll race you down the hill. Your uncle can follow on behind. Last one home is a rotten egg!'

Chapter Twenty-Eight

I sleep surprisingly well. I expected to lie awake half the night listening to all the unfamiliar noises around me, but no sooner do I climb into my sleeping bag than I fall into a dreamless sleep for nine hours.

I wake to the sound of subdued chatter and the smell of bacon. My first thought is that I need to jump out of bed and rush downstairs before Georgia eats the last of it. Then I realise I'm lying on a groundsheet. Any attempt to run down a flight of stairs will prove more difficult than I anticipate and most likely result in bruises.

I unzip the tent flap and peer out. The boys are perched on a nearby log, watching Jon flipping strips of sizzling bacon in a large frying pan.

Ollie looks up and waves when he sees me. 'We're having breakfast!'

'I can see that,' I say. 'What I don't understand is why you're having it without me. What was the plan – to cook it secretly and eat it in silence before I woke up?'

'Uncle Jon said we should let you sleep,' says Toby.

'I'll bet he did. If I didn't have such a keen sense of smell that I can detect bacon frying half a mile away, you'd have eaten the lot and disappeared for the day, leaving me here all by myself with no provisions.'

'No, we wouldn't!' he says. 'Ollie and I would have woken you in time to go swimming.'

Jon looks up from the pan and grins at me. 'Good morning. I hope you got some sleep?'

'I slept like a log, thank you. Although I've never understood why logs are supposed to be so sleepy.'

He gestures to the boys. 'They were starving. Like you, they seem to exist in a permanent state of hunger. They're always either eating a meal, telling me how much they enjoyed the meal they've just eaten, or asking plaintively when their next meal will be.'

'That sounds about right,' I agree. 'Do I have time to wash before they've devoured all the bacon and eggs?'

'Take as long as you want. There are two more packets of bacon in the cooler.'

I locate my towel and wash bag and pull on a sweatshirt before setting off for the shower block. It's much nicer than I expected. This whole campsite is. I could get used to holidaying outside if everywhere was like this.

I arrive back at our pitch to find the boys arguing over which activity to do first.

'Move along and make some space for me on that log,' I instruct them. 'What appears to be the problem?'

'I want to go swimming, and Toby wants to go to the playground,' Ollie tells me.

'That's easy enough. You aren't supposed to swim right after a meal. Or that's what they told us when I was a child. So, maybe we should check out the playground first and then go for a swim?'

Jon hands me a plate piled high with sausage, bacon, and eggs. 'Between the three of you, we'll never be far enough away from a meal to swim.'

'Your uncle can be extremely rude,' I tell the boys. 'Criticising people's eating habits is unacceptable. Besides, he's overlooking the concept of midnight feasts. I hope we'll be having at least one of those.'

'Great idea!' says Ollie through a mouthful of toast. 'Can we do that, Uncle Jon?'

'You aren't turning out to be the steadying influence I hoped for when I invited you to join us,' Jon tells me.

I help myself to a piece of only slightly charred toast. 'My grandmother always told me to be careful what you wish for.'

He smiles. 'Lots of people say that.'

'Then you should have known better than to invite me on this trip.'

'I'm very glad I did.'

'Me too!' says Ollie.

'And me!' says Toby. 'Will you go down the flumes with us, Isabella?'

'I came here with no other purpose. Flumes are my speciality. My sister and I perfected the art of them one summer when we were young. The secret of winning a flume race is to twist yourself into an aerodynamic shape.'

'There will be no flume races today,' says Jon. 'There's only room for one person at a time on those slides.'

'That's what the pool attendant told us,' I admit. 'Shortly before saying we'd be thrown out if we tried anything like that again.'

We finish our meal and clear up.

'I've been excused from washing-up duty during this trip,' I say. 'What should I do instead?'

'You and Ollie could collect some more wood,' says Jon. 'I foresee a pressing need for it over the next two days. Six meals a day requires an enormous amount of fuel. Toby can stay here and help me clean up.'

'Why has Isabella been excused washing-up duty?' asks Toby.

'Because your uncle has to do penance for being less than forthright,' I say, grinning at Jon.

'What does that mean?' asks Ollie.

'It means you and Isabella will be collecting wood this morning,' says Jon.

We set off to the play area half an hour later. It's a wonderfully designed playground – the kind you dream of as a child. There are lots of people here, as you would expect during the school summer holidays. But there's enough space for everyone, and there are plenty of activities to prevent boredom.

Jon and I take turns on the flying fox with the boys and hold a competition to see which of us can swing the highest on the rubber tyres. The boys quickly make several new friends, leaving us free to find a nearby bench and observe proceedings.

'This parenting thing is a doddle,' I say, leaning back and relaxing in the warm sunshine. 'I'm always telling Lily she makes far more fuss than necessary about looking after her two. I've never had the least difficulty in amusing them by thinking up new games for us all to play.'

'I can believe that,' he says. 'Do you really think childcare is easy?'

'Of course not. But don't tell Lily I said that. One of my favourite things is telling her how straightforward it all is and how I don't understand why parents of young children complain about being tired. I usually add that it's all a matter of organisation. She particularly enjoys that one.'

'I can imagine,' he says. 'For my part, I can't think of anything more exhausting. I only look after the boys part-time, and I fall asleep at the same time as they do on the days they're with me. That's why I don't want Ali taking on too much before she's ready.'

'How's she doing?'

'A lot better, thanks. But clinical depression doesn't disappear overnight, even when the medication starts to do its job.'

'I don't imagine it does. What does she do for work?'

'She's an occupational therapist. She was at Southampton hospital before David died. I think she's hoping to start working privately by the end of the year so she can choose her own hours while the boys are at school.'

'That's a good idea,' I say. 'I imagine it takes a long time to figure out your new reality after something as devastating as that.'

'She'll get there. She's doing better every day. The key is to let her go at her own pace and pick up the reins again when she's ready. She knows I'm always there for her.'

I gesture towards the boys, who are now climbing as fast as they can to the top of what looks like a giant spider's web made of ropes. 'I'm sure she does. It isn't every brother who would give up his free time to make sure his nephews had an experience like this.'

'I enjoy it,' he says. 'That's the one good thing to come out of this whole terrible business. I've come to know the boys a lot better than I did before. I used to think there was plenty of time for that sort of thing, but our family has learned the hard way that isn't always the case. So, I plan to spend as much time as possible with them all.'

'It's difficult to argue with that. It's a shame my sister and I seem to have drifted apart. And we have far less excuse than your family. We live under the same roof.'

'I imagine that comes with its drawbacks,' he says. 'You can have too much of a good thing.'

'That's true in my case. But it's a constant mystery why Georgia doesn't consider it an honour and a privilege to have me living on site the entire time. The fact she can't see that says a lot about her, and none of it good.'

He laughs. 'I never know how serious you are when you talk about your sister. You always talk as though the pair of you are at permanent loggerheads. But I doubt you'd have offered her a job in your bakery if that were really the case.'

'Much though I'd like to contradict you, I have to admit you're right. I suppose I'm quite fond of her deep down. Very, very deep down. I wish we could communicate better, but at our age that ship has probably sailed.'

'Ali and I have grown closer since David died,' he says. 'Don't assume it's ever too late to put things right.'

'I hope we never go through something like that. But one of us should make the effort, and it will have to be me. Georgia seems to view me as someone who only tells her what she's doing wrong with her life.'

'Is she right?'

'Maybe a little,' I admit. 'I can't help worrying about her lack of direction and want to offer the odd piece of advice. Not so much recently because we see so little of each other, or we did until she started working at the bakery. But I always tried to get her to take things more seriously while we were growing up.'

'That surprises me. You don't strike me as someone who has the most serious outlook on life.'

'I try my best not to,' I say. 'But discovering the thing you want to do and having fun doing it is one thing. Not taking anything seriously and never finding your direction in life is quite another.'

'I know plenty of people who work to live rather than live to work. They find their purpose in life outside the work environment. I'm one of those people. My job is fine, but it doesn't define my every waking moment.'

'I'm not sure Georgia takes either approach,' I say. 'But it's difficult to tell what's going on in someone else's life. Especially someone as uncommunicative as my sister.'

'There's one way you could find out,' he says, waving to the boys and tapping his watch.

'What's that?'

'You could ask her.'

He smiles at my look of surprise. 'Only a suggestion. I've always found it the easiest way to get the information I need about something.'

He waves to the boys again, who reluctantly jump down from the rock wall they've been climbing and run over to us.

'Time for a quick swim before we eat,' Jon tells them. 'And we'd better make it a good lunch. We're going canoeing this afternoon, and we don't want Isabella passing out before we even reach the lake.'

Chapter Twenty-Nine

I wake the following morning to the sound of excited whispers outside my tent. I sit up, rubbing my eyes. The whispers have stopped. Maybe they weren't whispers at all but the rustle of the wind among the pine trees on the edge of the forest.

Hopefully, it doesn't signal the start of a storm. I'm grateful this tent has kept me warm and dry so far, but I don't have much faith in its ability to protect me if a hurricane hits. Or a tornado. I'd be whirling through the sky in seconds, waving to all the other campers as they flew by and trying to hold on to my ruby slippers.

The whispers start again. It's definitely not the wind unless it's learned to speak overnight. I smile as I hear the boys trying to squabble with each other as quietly as possible.

'You've put too much butter on it!'

'No, I haven't. I used just the right amount. Don't drop that plate!'

I'm about to poke my head out and enquire what's going on when I hear a soft thump on the outside of my tent, and the canvas shakes.

I unzip the door and lower my voice to a growl. 'Abandon hope all ye who enter here!'

There's a stifled giggle before Ollie speaks. 'Room service!'

'He means tent service!' says Toby. 'We've been cooking your breakfast, Isabella. You can eat it in bed if you like.'

'Only we don't have a tray,' adds Ollie. 'So you'll have to balance it on your knees.'

He holds out a plate. I'm touched to see how eager they both look and how proud they are of what they've produced.

I unzip the door more fully. 'I can't believe you've done this for me. It feels like staying in a five-star hotel. Better, in fact, because there's a rock-climbing wall almost outside my bedroom door.'

Jon appears and waves to us. 'Good morning. The boys insisted on cooking your breakfast all by themselves. I'm a little envious. They've never done anything like that for me.'

'We wanted to make you some toast too,' Ollie tells him. 'But we used up all the butter on Isabella's. She might share some of hers with you.'

'You're very kind,' says Jon. 'But I'll have to pass. I've already eaten my scrambled eggs, and I'm full.'

'Your loss,' I say, taking the plate Ollie hands me. 'Are you two coming inside? There's just enough room, as long as we all take it in turns to breathe. Toby, why don't you start? Nice, deep breath, then hold it while Ollie has his turn. Then you can let it out while I breathe in, and so on. It should work.'

'It isn't that small in here,' says Ollie, wriggling through the door and perching on the end of my sleeping bag. I hastily remove my feet. I've suffered enough broken bones for one year.

They watch as I inspect the breakfast they've produced.

'The eggs were tricky,' says Ollie. 'But we fished out most of the bits of shell.'

'And the toast would be a lighter brown if Ollie hadn't held it too close to the fire,' says Toby.

'You pushed me!' says Ollie.

'Did not, either!'

'If you two can't stop arguing, you'll have to leave my tent,' I tell them. 'Breakfast should be a peaceful meal. If I have to listen to much more of your bickering, I'll end up with indigestion and be forced to stay in my sleeping bag all day.'

'I'll be ok,' says Toby. 'Uncle Jon can still take me whitewater rafting.'

'You're mistaken,' I tell him, winking at Ollie. 'I will hold Uncle Jon responsible for the whole thing and insist he hangs around the campsite all afternoon in case I need him to fetch me some indigestion tablets or call a doctor.'

'Did I hear my name?' asks Jon's voice outside the tent.

'You may have been mentioned,' I tell him. 'And now I'd like you to take these two heavy lumps out of here before my feet become too numb for me to walk to the ziplining station.'

'But you haven't eaten your breakfast!' says Toby.

'Very true.'

I pick up the nearest piece of toast and turn it around, searching for the least charred area. Finding none, I nibble at the crust and chew hard, praying I don't break a tooth, or Jon will be searching for a dentist too.

The pair of them watch me with eager expressions. They look just like Daisy whenever we pass an ice cream shop. I swallow my mouthful, feeling it scrape over where my tonsils used to be on its way down.

'Excellent!' I pronounce. 'I doubt they could do better at the Ritz hotel. You two should set up a toast stand outside your local train station for the morning commuters. You'll be millionaires before you're thirty.'

'That's really old!' says Toby. 'Uncle Jon is thirty-eight.'

'Some people are old by twenty-eight,' I say. 'Others are still young at seventy.'

'Seventy!' says Ollie in horror. 'That's even older than Grandpa.'

'Grandpa is seventy-five,' comes the voice from outside. 'And he can give both of you a run for your money. Now, please leave Isabella to enjoy her breakfast and help me wash the dishes before we leave.'

'I usually enjoy company while I'm eating,' I tell them. 'But there's something about eggs – especially scrambled ones – that makes me want to appreciate this meal alone.'

The boys scramble out of the tent. A minute later, I hear plates being crashed together and much splashing of water. I hope Uncle Jon had the forethought to provide us with extra crockery. He seems to have packed everything but the kitchen sink, so he probably has. Otherwise, I can see myself being sent on an expedition to forage for large yet non-poisonous leaves to act as plates.

I'm starting to regret having negotiated an exemption from the horrors of washing up. It would be far safer than crashing through the undergrowth, clutching my copy of *The Ladybird Guide to Not Dying While on a Camping Trip*.

'Knock-knock,' says a voice.

'Who's there?' I ask, although I recognise the voice perfectly well.

'Jon.'

'Jon who?'

'Jon Phillips. Who do you think?'

'That isn't much of a punchline. Couldn't you have said something like Jon me for dinner – I've brought snacks?'

'If that were my name, I suppose I could,' he says. 'Remind me why we're having this conversation?'

'How should I know? I'm not the one telling knock-knock jokes.'

There's a long pause.

'May I come in?' he asks at last.

'There isn't much room in here, but half of you can.'

His head and shoulders appear in the doorway. 'Give me your plate.'

'I haven't finished!'

He hands me a second plate piled high with golden slices of toast and a mound of creamy, perfectly scrambled eggs.

'We only have a couple of minutes before the boys arrive back from the shop where I've sent them to buy an unnecessary box of Band-Aids.'

He reaches over and takes the plate the boys brought me. 'I'm afraid I must remove this on health and safety grounds.'

'But they cooked it especially for me!' I protest.

'And you've gone above and beyond the call of duty in eating as much of it as you have. But we need you in good shape today. We can't have you flying down the mountain, moaning and clutching your stomach as the pieces of broken eggshell do their work.'

'I've been eating my breakfast without complaint,' I say. 'Not as fast as usual, I admit, but I'm getting there.'

'No, you aren't. What on earth possessed you to risk food poisoning?'

He peers at the plate more closely. 'I'm not sure how they've managed to both undercook and burn these eggs at the same time. It's an art form of sorts.'

'They aren't too bad,' I say, feeling a wave of loyalty towards the boys. 'And I need to eat something before we set off on another round of death-defying activities.'

'And so you shall. I'll nip out and dispose of this breakfast while you get stuck into the new one. You can emerge from your tent twenty minutes from now and hand us your empty plate, and honour will be satisfied on all sides.'

He slips out of the tent while I do as he suggests. Given that he cooked this at top speed over a campfire, it's an impressive effort.

There's a sound of running feet just as I'm finishing the last delicious mouthful, and I hear both boys talking at once.

'Why don't you knock and ask her?' says Jon's voice.

I unzip the door and hand them my plate. 'Perfect timing. Thank you so much. That was one of the best breakfasts I've ever tasted.'

The boys beam at each other.

'We can make you another one tomorrow,' says Ollie.

'I'm taking us all to the cafe tomorrow morning for hotcakes,' says Jon. 'If there's one thing I've learned over the course of my worryingly large number of years, it's that you should never try to reproduce a triumph. Enjoy it for what it was, and move onto something new. You can never go back.'

'He's right,' I say. 'But that doesn't mean you can't repeat your triumph at a different time and under different circumstances. I suggest you cook your uncle's breakfast for him every morning once you get home. It would be a lovely gesture to thank him for bringing you on this trip.'

'I appreciate your thoughtful suggestion,' says Jon. 'I'll have to think of a way of repaying it at some future date.'

I brush the toast crumbs off my sweatshirt. 'Give me ten minutes to shower and dress, and I'll be ready for anything.'

'I didn't have to shower this morning,' says Toby. 'Uncle Jon said I'd be soaked to the skin in a couple of hours, so there was no point.'

'That was your choice,' I tell him. 'Those of us who have chosen a more civilised way of enjoying the afternoon – by which I mean the more intelligent members of our party – live by different rules. If I don't wash off all these toast crumbs, I'll be itching all day and extremely bad tempered. Believe me, you don't want to experience that.'

Apparently they don't, as no one objects. I shower as quickly as possible and arrive back at our pitch in record time.

'What time is your death-defying spin through the rapids?' I ask Jon.

'Two o'clock. I thought we could spend the morning on the go-karts if no one has any objection.'

Ollie gives a whoop of delight and high-fives Toby. They race off towards the go-kart track, leaving us to bring up the rear in a more sedate fashion.

'I'm afraid to run,' says Jon. 'There's nothing like being around a pair of nine-year-olds to make you feel your age.'

'Age is just a number,' I say. 'I'll bet both of us could beat those two at all kinds of things.'

He smiles. 'I asked my parents whether there was something wrong with the boys to make them so hyperactive. My dad laughed for about five minutes, then told me it was called payback. Apparently, I was exactly the same at their age. I'll have to take his word for it, but I don't remember being on the move from dawn till dusk. And well into the night, if allowed.'

'My parents say the same thing about me as a child. I'm sure they're exaggerating. Most of the stories they recount about me seem most unlikely.'

'Somehow, I'd be inclined to believe them,' he says. 'There are very few stories anyone could tell me about your childhood that I'd find any difficulty believing.'

'I'll take that as a compliment. There's very little point in taking it as anything else.'

He smiles down at me. 'You're quite safe to take it as a compliment. You're an unusual person, Isabella Campbell, and one I'm delighted to have met.'

'Can you mention that to some of my customers the next time you see them? My reputation is often unfairly maligned around Honeywell.'

'I think your customers like you very much,' he says. 'I've seen enough to know how popular you and Lily are with the entire village. But I'm happy to sing your praises at any time. And you don't even need to give me a free cookie to do so.'

'That's good to hear because Lily has forbidden me to hand out any more free products until I show her this month's accounts. Now, please stop talking about your premature ageing and obsessing about free cookies. The boys are waving for us to hurry. The best way we can show them we're still young and sprightly is to knock several seconds off their lap times.'

Chapter Thirty

We set off in different directions after lunch – Jon and Toby to the far end of the lake, and Ollie and me to the hill on the far side of the valley.

The sun is beating down strongly, and I'm glad to think I've packed a bottle of water. Or rather, Jon has packed one for each of us. He's also included a variety of snacks to keep up my strength during the coming ordeal.

'You can share them with Ollie if you like,' he tells me, dropping a bottle of sunscreen into my backpack. 'But don't feel any obligation. He'll survive a two-hour stint of starvation. He's young and healthy.'

'I'd prefer you not to follow that sentence to its logical conclusion,' I say. 'It won't end well for me. Of course, Ollie and I will share. It's important for us both to keep up our strength in case one of us needs to run for help.'

He smiles. 'What do you imagine will happen this afternoon?'

'It's difficult to say. But intrepid adventurers like us don't leave anything to chance.'

'Uncle Jon and I are having an adventure too,' says Toby.

'Sitting in an inflatable raft floating gently down a stream doesn't compare to what we're about to attempt,' I tell him. 'Will there be photographers waiting to document our epic flight, I wonder?'

'Maybe one or two,' says Jon. 'But most of them will have gathered to watch the boat launch. They should get some incredible action shots of our boat flying through the foam as we go down the mountain.'

He looks at his watch. 'We must get going. We don't want to miss our launch time. Look after Isabella, Ollie. She has a tendency to trip over if someone isn't watching her. And keep an eye out for any loose tree roots. She won't notice them until it's too late.'

'What a pity no one thought to build a cable car here,' I tell Ollie as we climb the hill ten minutes later. 'Although, contrary to what your uncle pretends to believe, I'm in no danger of tripping over anything. Are you doing alright? Do you need a lie down?'

He gives an excited skip. 'I'm fine! Are you really tired?'

'Just the usual elderly person stuff,' I say in a feeble voice, allowing my legs to buckle slightly.

'You and Uncle Jon aren't really old,' he says. 'We just meant you're –'

'Another sentence I'm begging a member of your family not to finish. Come on, you ridiculous child. Even I can make it up a hill like this, and I've only recently recovered from a broken leg.'

We reach the ziplining station twenty minutes later. There's a welcome breeze up here, and I pull off my hat to enjoy it. I take out a scrunchie and tie my hair back all ready for the flight. The cool air feels wonderful on the back of my neck.

'You had cream in your hair the first time we met you,' says Ollie.

'I prefer not to remember that occasion, and neither should you. Try to erase it from your memory and think of me instead as the woman who hands out free cookies whenever you appear.'

'Uncle Jon likes your hair,' he says. 'I heard him talking to Mum about you. She asked what you looked like, and he told her you had very nice hair.'

'Maybe he was talking about someone else,' I suggest.

'No, he wasn't. He also said you had bright blue eyes. That must be you, don't you think?'

'It may narrow it down a little. Well, that was kind of Uncle Jon. I feel as though I should say something nice about his hair in return. It's difficult to think what that should be without time to prepare. His hair suits the shape of his head. That's the best I can do at such short notice. Are you ready for your maiden flight?'

'My what?' he asks, replacing the lid on his water bottle and handing it back to me.

'It's what people call someone's first flight. More accurately, they say it about an aircraft, but it counts for us too. Let's do this!'

The operator checks each of us, making sure our harnesses are fitted tightly, our carabiners clipped into place, and our helmets adjusted properly. He gives us a quick demonstration – instructing us to keep our arms tucked in, our knees slightly bent, and let the zipline do the work.

'Who's going down first?' he asks.

'Ollie,' I say. 'I don't like the idea of him going faster than me and catching me up.'

'It doesn't work like that,' he says. 'No one sets off until the person ahead has safely landed. If you'd like to go first, I can send this chap down once you've arrived.'

'And if I get stuck halfway down, you can send him down to dislodge me, rather like getting a cork out of a bottle. Is that alright with you, Ollie?'

He nods. 'Uncle Jon told me to keep an eye on you. I can't do that if you're up here and I'm down there.'

I take a deep breath. 'Here I go! If I scream and burst into tears during my journey, I'd be grateful if you didn't mention it to anyone. I'll do the same for you in return.'

'Are you really scared?' he asks.

'Not very. But it adds to the thrill. My sister always calls me a drama queen. I'm just trying to live up to it.'

I step up to the edge of the platform and grip the harness. Taking a deep breath, I push off, hoping for the best. The zipline hums as it pulls me forward, the world drops away beneath me, and suddenly I'm weightless, soaring above the treetops.

A rush of air fills my ears, and my heartrate increases along with the speed. It's faster than I expected, but somehow liberating. The ground seems very far away, and I catch glimpses of a small stream making its way down to the lake. For a moment, I feel as though I'm truly flying – gliding through the sky thinking of nothing but the sound of the wind and the thrill of the ride.

The trees blur past in flashes of green and brown, and I laugh out loud as I skim over them, stretching out my arms like wings. The platform at the far end grows closer, the cable stretches taut, and I instinctively slow myself by pulling my knees in. The braking system engages with a soft click, and I come to a stop just inches from the platform, landing smoothly with a small bounce.

I turn to see Ollie launch himself off the top platform and swoop towards me. I watch him as he descends, grinning widely. He lands safely, breathless with excitement, and I help him off with his harness.

'Can we go again?' he begs.

'Are you sure? I was certain you'd have had enough after the first ride.'

'I don't mind going by myself if you didn't enjoy it.'

'I loved it,' I assure him. 'I'm just teasing you. But you may have to help me back up that hill. I made it up there once, but I'm not sure I can manage it twice.'

'I'll push you,' he promises.

'Then, let's get going!'

The second ride is, if anything, even more fun than the first. I'm no longer worried about Ollie deciding halfway down this ziplining lark isn't for him after all and having a panic attack. I launch myself more enthusiastically off the ledge this time and enjoy every moment of the downward flight. I imagine myself as a bird skimming over the canopy of trees, but without the fear of a larger bird deciding it's lunchtime and that I'd make an excellent entrée.

I unclip my harness and turn to watch Ollie gliding towards me, his face a picture of pure joy as he exists entirely in the moment, all other thoughts forgotten.

'Your little boy has really taken to this,' says the operator.

'He hasn't had the easiest year,' I say. 'Something like this is exactly what he needed.'

He nods. 'We all need a break from everyday life from time to time.'

Ollie arrives at the platform in a final swooping rush and beams at us.

'You looked exactly like a hawk coming in to land,' says the operator as he unclips the harness.

Ollie's face is glowing with excitement. 'I just saw an eagle! I think it was a golden eagle. I watched a nature programme with Dad, and there was a whole flock of them.'

'I don't think there are any eagles in Wales –' begins the man, but I nudge him and shake my head slightly.

He smiles at Ollie. 'A group of eagles is called a convocation. Don't ask me why.'

'This wasn't a convo … conversation,' says Ollie. 'It was all by itself. It flew out of sight almost at once, but I'm sure that's what it was.'

'I took plenty of photos of you coming down the wire,' I tell him. 'Maybe we can enhance them and see it in the background. Not many people can say they've been photo-bombed by a golden eagle!'

We thank the man and set off for the campsite. Ollie doesn't say much for the first few minutes, and I leave him to enjoy his memories in peace.

'My dad would have loved ziplining,' he says suddenly.

I feel a flash of panic as I realise how woefully unprepared I am for this sort of conversation. Neither of the boys has talked about their father since I've met them. I've assumed the subject is too painful. But the worst thing I could do is brush it off and change the subject.

So, I smile back at him. 'Did your father enjoy outdoor sports?'

'He liked football. He supported Southampton, and he took us to see them sometimes when they had a home game. We played football with him in the garden too. Uncle Jon plays with us now, but he isn't as good as Dad.'

'What else did your father like to do?'

'He liked cooking and building things. He made the best spaghetti bolognese in the world. He used to let me and Toby help chop the mushrooms, even though we weren't very good at it. And he built us a treehouse in the big oak tree at the end of the garden. It took him ages, but he didn't mind. He said important things are always worth doing properly.'

He keeps talking about David, and I drop in the odd question as we make our way back to the campsite. His face lights up as he tells me how his father used to take them biking through the woods, racing down the trails so fast that Ollie thought they might lift off the ground. And how David liked to swim in the sea, even in winter, and how he helped the boys build a ramp for their scooters and encouraged them to climb every single tree they saw.

'Where did he and your mum meet each other?' I ask as we walk across the grass towards our tents.

'They were in the same chemistry class at university. Mum broke a test tube, and Dad said it was him. But that was because he wanted her to like him.'

This is obviously a story he's heard many times before.

'He must have liked her quite a bit if he was prepared to take the blame for something he hadn't done,' I say.

'I suppose so. Mum says she hadn't noticed him until then, but she thought it was cool of him.'

'It was extremely cool of him. Your dad sounds like a nice man. Did he like ice cream?'

'He liked chocolate, but he didn't like strawberry. Mum likes salted caramel.'

'All excellent flavours,' I say. 'This talk of ice cream is making me hungry. What do you think about visiting the cafe and seeing which flavours they serve?'

'What about Uncle Jon and Toby?' he asks.

'There's no point waiting for them. It's quite likely their boat had a puncture coming down the rapids, and they're helping to carry what's left of it back down to the cars. I vote we go over to the cafe and see how much ice cream we can eat before they get here.'

Jon and Toby arrive just as we're finishing our first cones.

'How did you know where to find us?' I ask Jon when they walk in.

'It didn't take a great deal of detective work. You weren't in the tents when we arrived back. So, we guessed you were either stuck halfway up the hill, dangling precariously from a wire, or you'd returned before us. In that case, there was only one place you were likely to be.'

'A lucky guess. Now you're here, would you both like an ice cream while we exchange war stories from this afternoon? I can recommend the raspberry sorbet. And, judging by the speed with which Ollie demolished his chocolate hazelnut ripple, I think we can safely say that flavour met with his approval.'

'Why didn't you wait for us?' asks Toby accusingly.

Ollie wipes his mouth on his sleeve. 'Isabella said you'd probably punctured your boat and wouldn't be back for ages.'

'Did she indeed?' says Jon. 'Funnily enough, I was saying the same thing about you while we drove back. Not a puncture, of course, but I wouldn't have been at all surprised if Isabella had tangled herself up in the zipline, and they'd had to call out the engineers to fix it.'

'What high opinions we share of each other,' I say.

He smiles. 'I have a very high opinion of you.'

'You'd lose it fairly quickly if you'd seen me screaming at the top of my voice this afternoon. Ollie put me completely to shame. He handled the whole thing like a pro. One member of staff compared him very favourably to a member of the hawk family.'

'I saw a golden eagle!' says Ollie. 'I was about halfway down the hill when I looked up and saw it flying behind some trees.'

'Your dad liked those, didn't he?' asks Jon. 'I can see why. They're magnificent birds.'

'How about you?' I ask Toby. 'Were you compared to a trout or a salmon by your tour guide?'

He grins and shakes his head. 'No, but it was awesome! Uncle Jon almost fell out of the boat at one point.'

'What did I tell you while we were driving back?' Jon asks in an exasperated tone.

'Not to mention that you almost fell out,' says Toby. 'Sorry, I forgot. Can I have an ice cream too?'

'Of course,' I say. 'What do you think – banana splits all around?'

'Sounds good,' says Jon. 'But I'll get them. You've done us a huge favour by coming on this trip.'

'Nonsense. It was the boys that did me the favour. I would never had thought of going ziplining if Ollie hadn't kindly invited me. And now I'm addicted. The least I can do is stand you all a round of ice creams.'

We take our banana splits outside and sit in the warm afternoon sunshine to eat them while Jon and Toby tell us about their hair-raising ride.

'It looked quite a calm sort of river to me in the brochure,' I say when they've finished. 'It sounds as though you're making a fuss about nothing. Ollie and I had a real adventure. We flew fearlessly down the mountain without the slightest fuss.'

'The river was a lot rougher than you'd think,' says Toby. 'Why do you think Uncle Jon almost fell out?'

'Because he has a poor sense of balance,' I say. 'I believe it's something to do with the middle ear. It's the reason so many elderly people have falls.'

'Elderly I may be,' says Jon, 'but I still have enough energy for a game of crazy golf before dinner. What do you all say?'

I push back my chair. 'I was thinking of having another banana split, but it's best not to eat too much before a game of golf, especially a grudge match. I can celebrate my win with an extra-large meal this evening. Who wants to be on my team?'

'Me!' say the boys in unison.

'We'll have to toss a coin,' I tell them. 'Loser gets Uncle Jon.'

Chapter Thirty-One

We sit around the campfire after dinner, talking about our day. 'It feels like several days rolled into one,' I say, accepting the stick Jon hands me and picking up the bag of marshmallows. 'I thought my everyday life at the bakery was busy. But that was before I realised it was possible to go-kart in the morning, fly down a mountain in the afternoon, then finish with a triumphant round of golf before dinner.'

'One point!' says Jon. 'You and Ollie beat us by one point!'

Ollie and I high-five each other.

'One point is enough,' I say. 'To be honest, we could have beaten you by a much bigger margin. But this is your holiday too, and we didn't want to spoil it for you.'

'It was the bridge,' says Toby. 'If Uncle Jon hadn't taken five shots to get over that, we'd have won.'

'You're lucky he only took five shots,' I say. 'The last time I played golf with him, he almost concussed a clown.'

'Can we play again before we leave tomorrow?' asks Ollie.

'We have to check out by ten,' says Jon. 'But as long as we're packed and ready to go by nine o'clock, I don't see why not. Will we stay with the same teams or mix it up?'

'Same teams!' says Ollie.

'That's not fair!' says Toby. 'You're only saying that because Isabella is better than Uncle Jon.'

'You aren't supposed to say that out loud,' I tell him. 'You'll hurt your uncle's feelings. Extremely old people can be surprisingly sensitive about their golf scores.'

'I'm immune to insults by now,' says Jon. 'The boys are always telling me I don't run fast enough or save as many goals as I ought. I've made my peace with it.'

'You aren't bad at golf,' says Ollie. 'It's just that Isabella is a bit better.'

'She certainly talks a lot when her opponents are trying to concentrate,' says Jon. 'We'll stick with the same teams tomorrow so Toby and I can have our revenge. But that depends on us being up early. It will take a while to pack these tents and reload the car. You two need to get ready for bed now.'

The boys wander off towards the shower block, grumbling.

'I should supervise them,' says Jon. 'I won't be long. Try not to finish the entire bag of marshmallows before I get back. The camp shop is closed, and they're the last ones we have.'

They all return twenty minutes later. The boys are in their pyjamas, with freshly washed hair.

'Good job!' I say when they arrive back at the campfire. 'How long will this unnatural state of cleanliness last?'

'Hopefully, until we get home,' says Jon. 'We don't want to give their mother too much of a shock.'

'What happens now?' I ask the boys. 'Does Uncle Jon tuck you into your sleeping bags and sing you a lullaby? I'd offer, but I don't have the greatest singing voice. I could manage a rap if you like. Or I could tell you a ghost story. I know some truly terrifying ones!'

'Mum made Uncle Jon promise not to tell us any ghost stories,' says Toby. 'She's worried about Ollie sleepwalking.'

'No problem,' I say. 'I can tell them on the journey home instead. It will make a pleasant change from songs about cold spaghetti.'

We say goodnight to the boys, and they disappear into their tent. I listen to them whispering and giggling together, but the sound quickly dies away.

'There's one thing to be said for sleeping outside in the fresh air,' says Jon. 'They're both asleep in minutes. As for Ollie sleepwalking, I doubt he'd have the energy. He hasn't moved a muscle either of the nights we've been here.'

'I don't think I have either, although it's difficult to be one hundred percent sure without CCTV everywhere. It's possible I've been climbing out of my sleeping bag each night and wandering all over the campsite, but I doubt it.'

He laughs. 'As far as I'm aware, there have been no reports of a dark figure moving from tent to tent, foraging for food.'

'Like a bear?' I ask.

'Exactly like a bear! Or one of these fictional monsters you're so fond of mentioning right before the boys go to bed on the grounds that you made no such promise to their mother.'

'Not necessarily fictional,' I say. 'I'm almost certain the Campsite Chomper is real. And the Flashlight Phantom.'

'Don't tell him I mentioned it, but Toby was peering over the edge of the boat this afternoon, hoping to see the Waterfall Weirdo.'

I laugh. 'Was he really? I'll have to tell Lily and Georgia all about these monsters when I get home. I expect we have one in our bakery too.'

'You do. I've heard about the Bakery Bandit from several primary sources, so it must be true. Apparently, it roams the bakery from early morning to early evening, seeking what it may devour. There are often no signs of its presence except for steadily diminishing stock levels.'

'Fascinating,' I say. 'I doubt these primary sources are as accurate as you'd like to believe. I would definitely have met this mythical beast at some point. I spend a lot of time in that place.'

'I'm confident of my sources,' he says. 'They're quite reliable.'

'If you're talking about Lily, no she isn't. She'll come up with any old nonsense after one too many cappuccinos. And don't forget I do the books in our bakery. I'd know in a second if our stock records didn't match our actual inventory. But I like the idea of a bakery monster. It gives us a competitive edge.'

There's a strange rattling sound nearby. I make an instinctive grab for the bag of marshmallows, and he laughs. 'Always good to see someone's priorities. It's Toby snoring.'

I retain my grip on the bag just in case. 'I was worried it was a minor earthquake. I'd better not put down the bag in case of aftershocks.'

'I can't rule it out,' he says. 'But I'm fairly sure my explanation is the correct one. He was snoring last night too. He has an appointment with a specialist soon. Ali says she wouldn't be surprised if he needs to have his tonsils removed.'

'Poor Toby,' I say. 'Let me know if he does, and I'll pop around with ice cream.'

'I will. By the way, Ali asked me to thank you very much for coming on this trip with us. She's keen to meet you sometime.'

'Please tell her she's very welcome. Her brother can be tough to take, but her delightful children more than make up for it.'

'Ollie mentioned you'd talked with him about David,' he says. 'I'm glad you did. The boys don't talk about him to everyone. They must trust you.'

'I hope so. I wasn't sure what to say. I mostly just listened.'

'Which is the best thing anyone can do,' he says.

'He chatted about some of his dad's interests and what they used to do together. David sounds like a nice man.'

He stares into the fire. 'He was a very ordinary, very decent man. And he loved his family very much. It was an absolute tragedy for them all.'

'For you too,' I say. 'I know you're doing everything you can to help everyone else. But don't forget your loss too.'

'It seems tiny in the scheme of things.'

'Maybe so, but it's still a part of your story, and it's alright to acknowledge that.'

He smiles at me. 'You're a very wise woman, Isabella Campbell.'

'Again, can you please mention that to my customers and co-workers?'

'If you like. But I'm sure they know it already.'

'You wouldn't say that if you heard the way they talk about me! And they don't always wait until I've left the room.'

To my surprise, he reaches over and takes my hand. 'If they don't realise by now how lucky they are to have you working with them, there's no hope for them.'

'I'm lucky to be working with them too,' I say, not pulling my hand away, although I'm not much of a hand holder in general.

He studies my face for a long moment before leaning forward and gently kissing me.

He pulls back a little and looks into my eyes. 'Is this ok?'

For some reason, I seem to have lost the power of speech – a definite first for me. So, I just nod.

He touches my cheek. 'I wanted to kiss you the very first time I saw you.'

'You can't have done. My face was covered in cream.'

'Not entirely covered. A large part of it was dairy free. I looked up from Simon's boring blueprint and saw an incredibly beautiful woman standing in the doorway, her hair shining in the sunlight.'

'That was my hat. Nathan made me wear it. But you're right – it was incredibly shiny.'

'My heart stood still for a split second,' he says.

'After which, I hurled the cakes across the room and landed on top of them, like all true romantic heroines.'

'And blamed me for the whole thing,' he agrees. 'And that still wasn't enough to put me off you.'

'None of this adds up,' I say. 'If you were so taken with me, why did you refuse the very tiny favour I asked of you?'

'Because I had no authority to do anything else.'

'We knew that really, but the Silver Surfers said they trusted to my powers of persuasion.'

'I can see why,' he says, pulling me closer and putting his arm around me. 'You're extremely persuasive under the right circumstances. Just not that time.'

'I wish you had been able to help us,' I say. 'The arts centre is an amazing project. We just need to get it over the line.'

The fire crackles between us, casting flickering shadows across his face as we sit in comfortable silence. The warmth of the flames mingles with the cool night air, and I can feel someone's heart beating faster than usual. I'm not entirely sure whether it's mine or his. It's difficult to tell without pulling away from him, and I don't want to do that.

I glance at him, his eyes soft in the firelight, a smile tugging at the corner of his mouth. The tension between us has been building all weekend, despite all my efforts to ignore it, and now it feels as though the moment is finally here. I know I should put a stop to this before it begins, but my body has given up listening to the signals my brain is trying to send it.

Before I know it, his lips are on mine again, warm and gentle at first. This time, it's definitely my heart that's racing. He deepens the kiss, and my hand flies to his shoulder, gripping his fleecy jacket. I can feel the heat of him pressing against me, and all my logical thoughts start to slip away, like the last embers of a fire fading into the night. Time to call a halt before I get so carried away I can't think straight.

I draw back and take a deep gulp of air. 'I'm not sure this is a good idea.'

He doesn't release me. 'I think it's an excellent idea.'

'That's because you haven't thought it through. You've had an adrenaline-filled day, followed by an evening under the stars. You saw me in the firelight and decided it was all extremely romantic. So, you kissed me.'

'I'd have been happy to kiss you in the sunlight or the rain or even in the middle of a howling blizzard.'

'That shows a poor grasp of priorities,' I say. 'If we're hit by a sudden snowstorm, you should be busy building an igloo rather than thinking about kissing me.'

He smiles and gently touches my cheek. 'I'm saying the firelight is irrelevant. It may light up your hair and make your eyes shine –'

'It would have made my hard hat shine even more effectively.'

'You can bring it with you the next time we go camping, and we'll find out. I'm trying to tell you our current situation has nothing to do with the way I feel about you.'

I move away from him and wrap my arms around my knees. 'I think it has to.'

'What do you mean?'

I nod towards the tent, where a faint rumbling can still be heard. It sounds like a baby dinosaur settling down after a good meal. 'You aren't a free agent.'

'The boys? They're a huge priority for me, but that doesn't mean I have no room for other priorities in my life.'

'You of all people should know that life has a way of throwing us curve balls,' I say. 'Some of them less pleasant than others. You can't predict how much they'll need you in the future.'

'What happened to David was unexpected and shocking,' he says. 'But no one can protect themselves entirely against that kind of thing. You didn't expect to break your leg, and David didn't expect to be killed in a car crash. All we can do is play the hand we're dealt and move on.'

'I agree. And I can't tell you how much I admire you for doing that. Ali and the boys are so lucky to have you. The thing is –'

'It isn't the hand you were dealt?' he asks.

'In a way. I might have the luxury of giving this a go, but the boys don't. They've already lost one parent. It isn't a good idea for someone to become a part of their life who isn't certain she'll stay. I think if you and I were to start anything, it would have to be all or nothing. And my track record with relationships isn't great. I've never been in one that's lasted for longer than six months. Which means that right now, neither of us can commit to its being more than a short-term thing.'

He attempts a smile. 'That's a definite no, isn't it?'

'It's a reluctant no. I really like you, Jon, and I don't want to waste time hoping you'll reappear at some future point and offer me something we can both live with. I'd prefer to chalk it up to bad timing and let us both move on.'

'I understand,' he says. 'I can't say I'm not disappointed. But I appreciate your honesty. And your care for the boys. For what it's worth, you've been a valuable part of their lives, whether or not you realise that. You stepped up when they needed you. Not everyone would have done that.'

'I'm sorry things haven't worked out for us,' I say. 'But I remember my mother once telling me that people come into your life for different reasons and for different lengths of time. And those people whose journeys only join with yours for a few steps can be just as important as those who walk with you the entire length of the path.'

He leans over and kisses my cheek. 'I can't help wishing our journey together had been more than a few short steps. But I'm happy we've had that at least.'

I release his hand, then look down at the smouldering logs in dismay. 'Is that my bag of marshmallows?'

He follows my gaze. 'I believe so. How did you come to drop those?'

'I remember letting go of the bag when you kissed me, but I thought I'd dropped it onto the grass.'

We survey the melted plastic and blackened lumps of what used to be delicious pink and white marshmallows.

Jon bows his head briefly. 'I'm very sorry for your loss.'

'I'm glad we're going home tomorrow,' I say. 'I couldn't bear to look at what might have been.'

His gaze flickers over me for a second before he gives a painful smile. 'Me neither.'

Chapter Thirty-Two

I don't sleep as well as I did the first two nights here. I keep dozing and waking, thinking I've heard a wild animal howling in the distance. Whatever it is, it doesn't come down and prowl around the campsite. I open my eyes at seven o'clock to hear the boys talking in what they imagine are hushed tones.

'Why can't we make her breakfast again? She ate it all yesterday.'

'I've already told you,' says Jon's voice. 'I'm taking us for hot cakes.'

'Isabella prefers our cooking,' says Ollie.

I unzip my tent door and poke my head out before the culinary wars get started.

'I would, of course, prefer your homemade breakfast,' I tell the boys. 'But I promised your uncle I'd try the hot cakes he keeps talking about. We won't have time to do both, especially not if we want to fit in a game of golf before we leave.'

We pack the car and walk over to the cafe for breakfast. The hot cakes are excellent, but I struggle to finish my portion. I see Jon glance at me once or twice, and I'm relieved he doesn't comment.

We play one last game of golf, which Ollie and I lose by two points. He tries to demand a rematch, but Jon refuses.

'We need to return our clubs before checkout time,' he says, 'or they might decide to charge me for another night.'

'Cool!' says Toby. 'I don't want to go home. Do you, Isabella?'

'The idea of a long, hot bath is quite appealing,' I say. 'But it's been a wonderful weekend. I hope you can all come here again next summer.'

'Will you come with us?' asks Ollie. 'You're a lot more fun than Grandpa.'

Jon laughs. 'I won't tell him you said that. It's time for us to go if we want to be home in time for dinner. Your mum is getting back from Cornwall this afternoon, and she'll want to hear all about your big adventure.'

Neither Jon nor I have much to say on the way home. I'm happy to switch on the music after the first half hour, even if it does mean listening to songs about food and cars.

They drop me off outside the bakery just before five o'clock. The boys climb out, despite their uncle's desperate pleas for them to remember the rules of Tetris and the possible consequences if they move more than a couple of inches. To my surprise, both boys hug me tightly before climbing back into the car.

'Thank you for a lovely trip,' I tell Jon. 'I had a great time.'

'Me too,' he says. 'And those two clearly did. I should get them home. Their mother will want to dump them in the bath for several hours to make sure every single layer of mud is removed.'

The last thing I hear as they drive away is both boys insisting they're perfectly clean, and no baths are required. I watch until the car is out of sight, then open the bakery door.

'I didn't expect to see you today!' says Lily.

I drop my bag next to the nearest table and sink into a chair. 'I decided to stop in and check how everything has gone in my absence. Has Georgia called in sick each day?'

'Hey!' says a voice, and Georgia appears from behind the counter where she's either been counting our stock or eating it. I know which one my money is on.

'My goodness!' I say. 'I was almost sure you'd have taken the opportunity of me being out of cell phone range to develop some mysterious illness – severe enough to keep you away from work, but not bad enough to prevent you going out with friends for the day.'

'That's most unfair,' says Lily. 'She's been the perfect employee. I couldn't have managed without her.'

'Lily was just telling me that if you went away again, she'd barely notice,' says Georgia. 'According to her, of the two of us, I get far more work done.'

I give Lily a hurt look, and she laughs. 'That isn't quite how I remember it. You and your sister appear to share the same flexible memory. You're more similar than either of you is prepared to admit.'

'So, everything has run smoothly in my absence?' I ask.

'Very smoothly. Business has been brisk, the eclairs haven't disappeared at quite the same rate as usual –'

'That's because I prefer meringues,' says Georgia.

'And the building work is going on well,' finishes Lily.

'At the arts centre?' I ask. 'We still haven't raised all the money we need to complete the work. What will happen when our funds run out? Surely, the builders aren't planning to stop and leave it half-finished?'

'I don't know all the ins-and-outs of the finances. But Mrs Ogilvie and Mabel were in here earlier, and they said there was enough money to finish the job. I asked them where it came from, and they told me Mavis had it all in hand.'

'Maybe she's found a secret benefactor,' I suggest. 'Someone to whom a couple of thousand pounds means no more than the price of a latte.'

'Either they didn't know or they weren't saying. The main thing is that the arts centre will be finished on schedule. Mavis has arranged a party of volunteers to do the decorating once the builders have left. So, we're still on for the grand opening at the end of August. It should be a great day. The bakery will provide the catering at a reduced price. There'll be a bouncy castle behind the pub and lots of stalls. And the school band is booked to play. My two are very excited about the whole thing.'

'Shall I close up the shop now?' asks Georgia.

'Would you mind making me a cappuccino first?' I ask. 'I've missed them while I've been away.'

'Don't they have coffee in Wales?' asks Lily.

'They have plenty of coffee, but somehow it doesn't taste the same when the water has been boiled over a campfire and there are bits of leaves and twigs in the mug. By the end of the second morning, I was starting to value Georgia more and more.'

'It's taken you long enough,' says Georgia. 'How are you getting home? Would you like a ride?'

'That's very kind of you, but I was hoping to have a quick catch up with Lily if she has time.'

'Jack is picking up the children from my parents today,' says Lily. 'I'll text him to say I'll be half an hour late. I can drive you home when you're ready.'

Georgia hands me a mug, turns the sign on the door to Closed, grins at us both, and disappears.

I give a choke of laughter when I see she's made a picture of a tent on my foam.

'Did you and she really get along alright?' I ask Lily.

'Of course. It was nice getting to know her better. You should give her a chance sometime. You may just find you like her.'

I take a sip of my drink. 'As a matter of fact, she and I have been inching along that road for a few weeks now. I'm willing to admit I may not always have been the perfect sister. I'm also willing to admit Georgia definitely hasn't been.'

'That's very gracious of you,' she says. 'Is that what you wanted to talk to me about?'

'Goodness, no! I have better things to discuss than my relationship with my sister. I thought we could chat about my camping trip. I forgot to send you a postcard, so I decided to fill you in face to face.'

'Abby reminded me before she left that the coconut slices need to be sold by tomorrow evening,' she says. 'Shall I bring you a plateful of those?'

'I'm good, thanks.'

She turns an astonished gaze on me. 'Did you just refuse a cake?'

'I suppose I did. I'm not terribly hungry.'

'I'll get the first aid kit from the kitchen.'

'Hilarious. Out of interest, which of its components were you planning to use?'

'No idea,' she says. 'This particular medical emergency hasn't arisen before. What do you suggest?'

'I'm not the one calling in the crash team.'

She stops smiling. 'Are you alright, Isabella? You don't seem like yourself.'

I pull myself together with an effort. 'I'm a little tired. I didn't sleep too well last night, and it was a long journey home.'

'How was the camping part of it?'

'Much better than I expected. Jon and the boys brought everything I could possibly need, and they looked after me beautifully.'

'That's good. How did the ziplining go? That's the reason you were invited, wasn't it?'

'So I was led to believe. But it appears there would have been other available options if I'd said no. Jon has an old friend living in the area he could have asked to help out.'

'Why doesn't that surprise me?' she asks. 'I never believed it was all the boys' idea. I suspected all along that Jon had an ulterior motive for inviting you.'

'I'm afraid he did. I found myself acting as the getaway driver when he and the boys held up the burger stand at the motorway services on our way there. It was quite a shock, I can tell you!'

'Nice try,' she says. 'But there was nothing on the news about any burger stand raids. I'd have remembered that.'

I cradle my mug in my hands. It feels pleasantly comforting.

'It's exactly the sort of item they put in the round-up section at the end of the local news. "And finally, on to this afternoon's bun-believable heist at a burger stand. Sadly, the police are in a real pickle. They have been unable to ketchup with the perpetrators and have no suspects to grill." It would be far more exciting than reporting on a parrot who's managed to learn its owner's phone number.'

'Which leads me to think this particular crime didn't occur,' she says. 'Why don't you tell me what did?'

'The usual camping stuff. We swam, canoed, and played crazy golf. And Ollie and I went ziplining while the other two were on the boat. We made a campfire each night and roasted marshmallows.'

I don't mention the fate of last night's marshmallows. It might lead to awkward questions.

'It all sounds very romantic,' she says.

'Romantic? It was a camping trip.'

'Come on, Isabella. It's as clear as day that Jon likes you. Did he communicate that to you at any point? I need details. There's a lot of money riding on this.'

I almost drop my mug. 'Riding on what?'

'How long it will take for the two of you to get together.'

I bite my lip and look past her at the shiny coffee machine. Georgia really has been pulling her weight while I've been gone.

Lily stops smiling. 'Are you ok?'

'I'm fine. You aren't serious about the money?'

'The Silver Surfers are running a book on it. But don't mention that to Mavis or she'll shut it down. She doesn't approve of gambling.'

'Running a book on me and Jon?' I ask.

'That's right. Most people bet you'd get together during the first evening. But there were several outliers. Mabel said it wouldn't be until after the ziplining. She thought you'd come flying down the mountain, screaming and terrified, and Jon would scoop you up in his manly arms and tell you everything was alright now he was there.'

'She did not!'

Lily laughs. 'I think she reads too many romances from the library van. Mrs Ogilvie surprised everyone by saying she didn't believe you'd get together until after you returned from the camping trip. She said it would take a few days for you both to realise your true feelings. But Jon would call you the moment he arrived home and ask you out to dinner. It was a bold guess, but Phyllis gave her excellent odds. And Bernie bet –'

I hold up my hand to stop her. 'You've jumped the shark there!'

'It's true!' she protests. 'Admittedly, Mrs Ogilvie placed his bet for him, but the syndicate allowed it. He's apparently planning to buy a year's supply of biscuits with his winnings.'

She looks at me expectantly. 'Don't leave me hanging? Which option was it?'

'How do you know it was any of them?'

'Of course, it was. All we need to know is when Jon told you how he feels about you. There were a few side bets on exactly where the denouement would take place, so it would be helpful if you could give us an exact location. Barb and Phyllis wanted to run a bet on Jon's actual words, but they decided that would be impossible. Your reputation for putting a spin on the truth precedes you.'

'Very wise of them,' I say, picking up my handbag. 'I should be getting home. I have a lot to do this evening. You wouldn't believe how smoky all my clothes are. I'll have to wash them several times to get rid of the smell. I assume Georgia isn't working tomorrow?'

'She offered, but I told her she should take a well-deserved day off. Are you sure you don't want to stay and talk some more?'

'I'll tell you the rest of my exciting adventures over our morning coffee,' I say. 'It won't be as good as Georgia's, but it should be drinkable enough.'

She follows me towards the door. 'You still haven't given me an answer about Jon. What happened between the pair of you?'

I force myself to smile as I hold open the door for her. 'I'm sorry to disappoint you, but all your bets are null and void. Nothing happened.'

'That can't be true.'

'It's lovely of you all to believe no man can be within a half mile radius of me without succumbing to my charms. But we appear to have found the exception that proves the rule.'

She looks so crestfallen that I almost want to laugh. Almost, but not quite.

'But you and he are so perfect for each other,' she says at last.

'We really aren't. If I were you, I'd get your money back before Mabel finds out the awful truth. Spend it on wild nights and riotous living. Otherwise, you can tell Mavis Sotherby what's going on. She'll insist everyone's money is refunded at once.'

'I can see you'd rather not talk about it,' she says. 'Don't worry, I'm not planning to badger you about it all the way home. But I'm leaving my bet exactly where it is. They always say it isn't over until the fat lady sings, and my intuition tells me there may still be a surprising third act twist.'

Chapter Thirty-Three

It's good to get back to work the next day. Holidays are all very well and a welcome break from reality, but they aren't real life. Real life is what you choose to do every day. In my case, that's the bakery, and I'm lucky to do something I enjoy so much.

Georgia is enjoying what my mother describes when I see her at breakfast as a well-deserved lie-in.

'She's been working so hard for the past few days,' she tells me, setting a plate of toast in front of me and handing me the butter dish.

'About time,' I say. 'The words Georgia and hard work aren't often associated with each other.'

'She's perfectly capable of putting in the effort. She just hasn't found the thing that motivates her.'

I roll my eyes. 'In other words, the thing that motivates her hasn't wandered up our drive and knocked on the door? You have to go out and look for it, not wait for it to find you. Think of all the old fairy tales. Those young men were always setting out to seek their fortunes. The stories never began, "Nathaniel was sitting around at home one day, waiting to see who would rock up and offer him a job he might deign to accept." Even Puss in Boots slipped on some uncomfortable-looking footwear and set out to find himself a few ogres to eat.'

Mum only laughs. 'Don't be late for work. I'd hate to inform Georgia her mentor and role model was so busy complaining about her sister that she missed opening the bakery.'

I cram the last piece of toast into my mouth and push back my chair. 'Never let it be said that a member of the Campbell clan failed in their duty to provide the public with sustenance. I'd never be able to hold up my head again. By the way, thank you for mine.'

'You're very welcome,' she says. 'I realise I may not be making your toast for much longer. You've been saying for a while now you're ready to move out.'

'It's way past time. I'm so grateful to you and Dad for letting me stay here for as long as you have. I'm almost sure my rent hasn't covered everything I've eaten. And I know for a fact Georgia's hasn't. But it's helped me to save up a decent deposit, so I'll be out of your hair as soon as I've found the right place. Sadly, that will leave you to deal with Georgia all by herself. But none of us can expect to have everything in life exactly the way we'd have chosen. Into each life some rain must fall, and all that.'

'Off you go,' she says. 'Before I put your rent up.'

'Consider me gone!'

I arrive at the bakery to find Lily and Abby engaged in a discussion about the opening of the arts centre.

'Good morning!' I greet them. 'Lily was able to verify my safe return with her own eyes yesterday evening, but I know Abby will be delighted to see for herself that her favourite colleague has come to no harm in the wilds of the British countryside.'

'Hi, Isabella,' says Abby, not looking quite as relieved as I'd hoped. 'I hear you had fun on your camping trip.'

'Fun is not the word! I crushed it. There was no real doubt I would, but it's always nice to be proved right. I felt sorry for the pair of you being cooped up in here while I launched myself off mountain tops and set new records in the swimming pool.'

'You mean the three of us?' asks Lily.

'Two and a half at most. It's still difficult for me to believe my sister did anything except create more work for you. But I'm back now and ready to put right whatever she messed up.'

'I'm sorry to be the one to break it to you,' says Abby, 'but Georgia is very popular with our customers. Not only does she prepare their drinks just the way they like them, but she comes up with creative combinations for the cakes and coffees. Word has got around, and I've heard several customers ask for her pairing recommendations.'

'Like a sommelier?' I ask.

'Exactly. According to Georgia, you should always pair a latte with a brownie because the flavours don't fight. And an Americano is apparently the perfect drink to bring out the flavour of a lemon tart. We're thinking of producing a menu called Georgia's Gourmet Gobbles.'

'I also overheard her giving directions to a couple of tourists who'd got lost and found themselves in Honeywell,' adds Lily. 'She was recommending things for them to see in the area. They ended up chatting with her for so long that they stayed for a cream tea.'

'Which she talked them into pairing with a pot of hibiscus tea,' says Abby. 'Apparently, she'd have made a different suggestion if they'd chosen the apricot instead of the raspberry jam.'

I'm ninety-five percent sure they're winding me up, but there's a small possibility they aren't. A five percent chance, in fact. Not for nothing did I undergo my rigorous accountancy training.

'So,' says Lily, 'you have large shoes to fill now you're back.'

'Like Puss in Boots,' I agree. 'Which, coincidentally, I was talking about with my mother this morning, although in a slightly different context. This is a day of wonders indeed. I'm delighted my sister appears to have acquired some sort of work ethic since she and I first met. Maybe there's hope for her after all.'

'Here comes Bernie with his two servants,' she says. 'I wonder whether they'll turn and walk away once they realise it's you working here today and not your sister.'

I draw myself up to my full height. 'Our customers have too much sense not to appreciate what they've got.'

I open the door, and Bernie bounds inside.

'Welcome!' I say. 'What a pleasure to see you all on this fine day.'

'Darn!' says Mabel. 'I was looking forward to a lovely picture of a tree on my morning coffee.'

I refuse to catch Lily's eye. 'No problem at all. What kind would you like? I expect I could manage a pine tree.'

'I'd like a silver birch,' she says. 'With just the beginnings of the new spring leaves, but still with a few late buds. Late March, say, or early April.'

'I've just remembered Lily is on drinks duty this morning,' I say. 'I have some paperwork to catch up with in the office.'

Mabel laughs. 'I'm only teasing you. From what I can gather, you and your sister are extremely competitive with each other.'

'Competition is only a factor when there's any kind of equality, which isn't the case with me and Georgia. But I'm glad to know she hasn't driven all our regular customers away.'

Mrs Ogilvie smiles at me. 'I think you're rather like me and Mabel. She pretends that everything I do annoys her, but she's very fond of me really.'

'Fond is a strong word,' says Mabel. 'But Edie and I tolerate each other surprisingly well these days. Maybe you and your sister will do the same by the time you're our age.'

'If you ask me,' says Lily, 'they'll get there long before that. The pair of them rub along fine whenever Isabella forgets they're supposed to be at loggerheads. And no one asked her to offer Georgia a job here. That was all her own idea.'

'We all make mistakes,' I say. 'The thing is to recognise them and learn from them.'

'If you admit that employing Georgia at the bakery wasn't a mistake,' says Lily, 'I'll make the drinks.'

I hesitate. I like the idea of not having to create pictures on the foam in line with Mabel's exacting specifications.

'She's doing fine,' I say. 'I'm glad we gave her a chance.'

'Good enough,' says Lily. 'What can I get you both to drink?'

'Two pots of Earl Grey, please,' says Mabel with a wink at me.

'Unfair!' I tell her. 'If you hadn't implied you were after a milk-based beverage, I would never have made that damaging admission.'

'I'm aware of that. But it's good for all of us to do something we dislike once in a while. On that subject, how did the camping trip go?'

I fix her with a steely gaze. 'I know exactly what's going on here. Lily lost her nerve and told me everything. I can tell you right now that no one is getting anything out of me, so you can all stop risking your pensions making flippant bets about my personal life.'

'Not just pensions,' she says. 'Lily placed a bet too. Quite a high one, if I remember correctly.'

'That's because Jack and my parents wanted a piece of the action too,' says Lily. 'Each of us chipped in ten pounds and bet you'd arrive home with a blushing Jon in your train. I'll admit the pair of you don't appear to have made much progress over the weekend. But we were smart enough to place a two-way bet.'

I eye her suspiciously. 'What was your second guess?'

'She can't tell you that,' says Mabel. 'All the participants have been told not to discuss their bets with you, so there's no chance of anyone accidentally changing the course of events.'

'You have a remarkably high opinion of yourselves,' I say. 'I doubt most of you could even change a lightbulb. Anyway, I can't sit around discussing your failings all day. I have work to do.'

I give them all my most gracious smile and wander off to my office, leaving Lily to make whatever picture she chooses on Mabel's cup of tea.

Chapter Thirty-Four

I was planning to tell Lily more about the camping trip after we closed the shop for the day, but she has to rush off at three to collect Ethan from preschool. It's just as well. Anything I tell her about Jon will conflict with the oath of secrecy Mabel has forced everyone to take.

It feels strange to be the subject of a bet rather than the instigator. I've organised plenty of bets in my time – most recently the one about how I broke my leg. But as far as I remember, none of them has involved someone else's love life. They've been more concerned with guessing how long it will be before Wendy Protheroe tries to return one of our products or what new complaint Mabel will make about Bernie.

I drive back to Compton, trying to decide which variety of pizza to order for dinner. I'm very keen on quattro formaggi, but I might make an exception if the local pizzeria is offering one of its anchovy specials.

My parents have left for an evening out with friends. With any luck, I will have the house to myself. I'm looking forward to some peace and quiet and the uncontested possession of the remote control.

To my surprise, I find Georgia waiting for me in my bedroom.

'I'm not planning on moving out for a while yet,' I say. 'If you're measuring up my room to see whether your horrible furniture will fit, let me assure you that both our rooms are the same size. I remember Mum picking up a tape measure to demonstrate that fact when you were complaining about me having the largest bedroom when you were twelve. I pointed out very kindly and helpfully that your room only seemed smaller because you insisted on dumping piles of rubbish everywhere. I'm all for people adopting their own decorating styles, but I couldn't help wondering whether yours worked as well as it might.'

'I'm not here to measure up your room,' she says. 'I was waiting for you.'

'Five words to make even the stoutest heart quail. Did you need something in particular?'

'I wanted to say thank you.'

She sees my look of surprise and laughs. 'It isn't a trick. I'm not looking for a loan or anything.'

'That's good because I don't have any money. My savings are sitting in a high-yield account ready for me to buy somewhere to live. The rest of my financial assets are tied up in the bakery.'

'Thanks for the warning, but I'm not after anything. First, I wanted to let you know how grateful I am you gave me this job.'

She sees the look on my face. 'I mean temporary job. Don't worry. I have no intention of hanging around for long. But the fact remains you did something nice for me when I needed it. I'll do the same for you if you're ever in a similar situation.'

'I appreciate that,' I say. 'But there's no need for you to feel that way. Lily and I have often discussed getting in some part time help to give us both a bit more flexibility. You came along at just the right time.'

'No, I didn't. You went out of your way to help me. I don't know why that's so difficult for you to admit.'

I'm not sure how to answer this. It's true that I'd rather not make a big deal of it, but that's because it isn't.

'What's the other thing you wanted to thank me for?' I ask.

'Mum told me what happened.'

'You've lost me. What happened when?'

'When we were small. She told me about that car almost hitting me and you pushing me out of the way just in time.'

I sit down abruptly on the bed. 'Why did she tell you about that? She and I agreed it was best to forget all about it.'

She sits next to me. 'She told me that too. She said you wanted to put it behind you, so she and Dad agreed to go with that. You didn't seem too upset about the whole thing, and they didn't see any reason to scare me with it. But I wish I'd known.'

'Why?' I ask. 'What good would it have done?'

'Because it might have helped me to understand a few things.'

'Such as?'

'Why you've always felt so responsible for me.'

I shake my head. 'You have that all wrong.'

Her voice is uncharacteristically gentle. 'No, I haven't. You were always checking up on me when I was younger.'

'You mean bossing you around?'

'That's how I saw it. But I'm wondering now whether there was something else behind it all. Was there?'

I stare at the carpet, trying to pick out a pattern in the cream and beige blocks. 'I suppose it's possible. But I almost never think of that day, so it's unlikely.'

'What happened?' she asks.

'Didn't Mum tell you?'

'She told me what she saw. I'd like to hear what it was like for you.'

I'm not sure how it helps to talk about things like this, but I know my sister. When she's determined to do something, she usually does it. I may as well save us both some time.

'It was a blazing hot summer's day,' I say slowly. 'You were about four, and I was six or seven. We were driving up to Scotland to stay with Mum's family for the holidays. Halfway there, we got a puncture. It was a quiet stretch of road, so Dad pulled over to the hard shoulder and told us to get out of the car while he called Roadside Assistance. Mum opened the door nearest to the verge and told us to climb out and stand on the grass. Before either of us could stop you, you'd darted past her and run around the back of the car into the road. I jumped out and ran after you just as a car came flying around the bend. You were standing right in its path, and you froze. I grabbed your collar and dragged you back just as it went past, almost hitting the side of our car.'

She's silent for a moment before asking, 'Would that car have hit me?'

'Yes.'

There's an even longer silence. 'Would it have killed me?'

'Possibly.'

I don't add anything. There's nothing more to say. She asked what happened, and I told her. I hope she doesn't regret it.

She takes my hand and squeezes it. 'Thank you.'

I squeeze it back. 'You're welcome. You'd have done the same for me.'

'We'll never know. But we do know you did it for me. Why didn't you want me to know about it?'

'How would it have helped anything? You were only four, and you got the biggest telling off of your short life – once Mum had stopped crying and hugging you. If you'd understood what had really happened, you'd have had nightmares for the rest of your life.'

She nods. 'But what about you?'

'I didn't get told off.'

'That's not what I'm asking. How did it affect you?'

'I was upset when it happened. But we were off to Scotland, which was always one of my favourite places. I soon forgot about it all.'

'I wonder,' she says. 'Mum said she and Dad talked about getting you some therapy. But you didn't bring it up again, and you seemed fine. So, they decided to let you move on in your own way.'

'I think they were right. I haven't thought about it for years. I don't blame you for what happened, if that's what you're thinking. You were very young, and you didn't stop to think what you were doing. It was just one of those things. And we had a happier outcome than some people.'

I think of David, Ali, and their boys, and the happy little family that disintegrated in one split second.

'But you didn't get over it entirely,' says Georgia, breaking into these thoughts.

'I'm pretty sure I did.'

'I don't think so, and neither does Mum. We talked about it the night you went away. I told her about you giving me a job even though you disapprove of every single one of my life choices.'

'Is that what you think?' I ask, considerably taken aback.

'Of course. I grew up with you telling me I ought to be doing my homework and making better choices of friends and thinking about my future. I always thought you were just being obnoxious.'

'Maybe I was.'

'You weren't like that all the time. Most of the time you were my cool big sister. All my friends thought I was lucky to be related to Isabella Campbell.'

I roll my eyes. 'That's because all your friends were idiots.'

She doesn't say anything – just waits.

'Oh!' I say as the penny drops. 'That's the kind of thing you're talking about.'

'Pretty much. It felt as though you'd appointed yourself as guardian for my moral and educational welfare, and I never understood why. Talking to Lily, it sounds as though you've done the same thing for several of your staff members. Not their moral welfare, but you've sorted out most of their love lives for them.'

'Lily likes to exaggerate,' I say. 'It's one of her greatest faults. But I put up with it because she has so many redeeming qualities.'

'I'm serious, Issy. Maybe it's time for you to think about what you need instead of what everyone else needs. And to put a little faith in other people to look after themselves without your help.'

I turn to face her. 'Are we still discussing your schooldays and non-existent career path?'

'I'm talking about Jon.'

She feels me pull away and tightens her grip on my hand. 'I know you'd rather not discuss him, but you have no choice. I was invited to place a bet, but I refused.'

'I'm glad you have better things to do with your money.'

'I refused because Mabel was telling everyone they mustn't talk to you about Jon or she'd tear up their betting slip and keep their money. She said it constituted insider trading and would be frowned on by the Turf Club.'

I laugh. 'That sounds like Mabel. But I don't plan to discuss Jon with you, so you could have joined in.'

'You don't have to talk about him,' she says, 'but I'm going to. If I had placed a bet, it would have been that Jon would tell you how you felt, and you would immediately pull away and started overthinking it. You'd worry about his boys and their future and end by second guessing yourself into a complete tailspin. After which, you'd tell yourself you'd done the sensible thing by backing away, and everyone would be better off for the decision you'd made.'

This time, it's shock that keeps me speechless. I never think of my sister as being sensitive. But by some means or other, she's come remarkably close to the truth.

'You aren't completely wide of the mark,' I say at last. 'Although if you were as sensitive and empathetic as you like to think, you'd also have bet on me dropping a bag of marshmallows into the fire and destroying them. But this situation is more complicated than you're making out. Jon and I aren't teenagers. Other people depend on us to make good decisions.'

'Maybe it's time you started being responsible for your own happiness,' she says. 'And allow other people to be responsible for theirs.'

'I was tempted,' I admit. 'But I don't want to hurt those boys if this doesn't work out.'

'That isn't the real reason,' she says.

'Of course, it is. I've never been in a long-term relationship, which suits me just fine. I'm not looking for any man to complete me. But in this situation, I have to consider what the boys need too. And I'd hate them to be hurt if Jon and I don't work out.'

She shakes her head. 'You aren't worried about the boys being hurt if they lose you. You know Jon is a good man and will protect them if that happens. You're worried that losing the boys will hurt you.'

'It comes to the same thing.'

'Not quite. You're frightened of getting close to those children because you aren't sure they'll stick around. I think what happened when we were young left you feeling you could lose someone close to you at any point, and it terrifies you to realise you can't control that. So, you've decided it's safer not to commit to anything for too long in case you get hurt.'

'I know perfectly well no one has any control over bad things happening,' I say. 'Look what happened to those boys.'

'But you've never quite believed it,' she says. 'You've always tried to make sure things go right for the people around you – starting with me.'

'And you wish I hadn't?'

'If I'd known why you were doing it, I might not have pushed you away so hard. And you might have learned to let go and think more about what you want and less about what everyone else needs.'

'I don't know what to say,' I tell her. 'But I'll give it some thought.'

'You'd be wise to do so. One of your customers told me the other day I had remarkably good judgement. If you aren't careful, they'll be signing a petition for you to take early retirement so they can appoint me in your place.'

'Let's not get carried away. You've given me something to think about. You haven't turned into the Dalai Lama overnight.'

She jumps to her feet. 'I have to go. Jeremy is taking me out to dinner.'

'Whereas I'm stuck at home all by myself, making do with a two-for-one pizza deal.'

'That's your choice. Make a different one if it isn't what you want.'

She pauses in the doorway and looks back at me. 'It's ok to be happy, Issy. It really is.'

I wipe my eyes on my sleeve. 'Thanks, Georgia. You should get going before Jeremy changes his mind and goes without you.'

'He wouldn't dare. But in case he takes me somewhere swanky, with those annoyingly small portions, could you order me a pizza too? I'll prepare all the drinks tomorrow to make up for it. Even if Wendy Protheroe comes in.'

'Fine,' I say. 'I'll order three.'

'You're the best!' She blows me a kiss and disappears.

I hear her run downstairs and slam the front door behind her. I pull out my phone and scroll through the pizza toppings. I'll wash my face while I wait for it to arrive, then settle down for some well-deserved peace and quiet. It looks as though I have a hard evening's thinking ahead of me.

Chapter Thirty-Five

'Have you seen Abby's plans for the opening ceremony?' Lily asks me a few days later. 'Mavis isn't sure how many people will turn up, so we've had to make a rough estimate of numbers and hope for the best. The beauty of its being so close to the bakery is that we can pop back here for extra supplies if need be.'

'She ran them past me yesterday evening,' I say. 'They look great. It should be a wonderful afternoon.'

Georgia appears from the kitchen holding a tray of lemon meringue tarts. 'Abby says she would like these to last until at least this afternoon. I told her it depended on how she defined the word afternoon.'

'I usually tell her it's always afternoon somewhere,' I say. 'Did you mention that you and I would have to run our usual quality control tests?'

She lays down the tray, walks over to the coffee machine, and switches it on. 'No need. She's aware of our highly-tuned process.'

'It's an inspiration to watch the pair of you work,' says Lily. 'If it doesn't cause a disturbance in the force, I think I'll join you today. Ethan was being difficult this morning, and I ended up missing breakfast.'

'What do you think?' I ask Georgia. 'Would it be too disruptive to allow an amateur to interfere with our system?'

Lily picks up a tart. 'Amateur or not, I own half this bakery. I like to think of myself as fairly easy-going, but even I have my limits.'

'She makes a fair point,' I tell Georgia. 'Two cappuccinos, please. And whatever you're having.'

I arrange the tarts in the display cabinet, reserving two for me and Georgia. They look rather forlorn sitting by themselves on their plate, so I add a couple of doughnuts.

'Here you are!' says Georgia, setting down my mug in front of me. 'I used the Christmas tree stencil for our chocolate powder today. Christmas is only five months away, which is almost nothing.'

'Very festive,' I approve. 'I didn't know we owned special stencils.'

'Grace used them when she was working here,' says Lily. 'Don't you remember? She had a heart, a Christmas tree, and a candy cane. I think she bought them from the Christmas market. Abby found them in the kitchen recently, and Georgia's been using them to wow our customers ever since.'

'I made a special one for Ivy's birthday last week,' says Georgia. 'She sings in the local choir, so I cut out a treble clef and used that. She seemed quite pleased.'

I survey her over the top of my mug. 'Who would have predicted this – Georgia Campbell – model employee?'

'It comes as a surprise to me too,' she admits. 'Is there some sort of employee of the month programme? And does it come with a cash bonus?'

'No, and no. But we could probably run to an extra eclair for your post-lunch snack.'

'That works for me.'

'I'm intrigued by the sight of the two of you working together in relative harmony,' says Lily. 'You should have come to work here much sooner, Georgia.'

Georgia finishes her tart and picks up a doughnut. 'That's very kind of you. But until recently, I was unavailable due to my almost single-handedly propping up the Christchurch fashion scene.'

'How is Cath getting on without you?' I ask.

'I haven't enquired. It would be too painful if she had to hear from me and remember what she's lost. But I went to visit Lucinda yesterday. She had her baby last week. They've called him Arthur.'

'That's a lovely name,' I say. 'Pass on my congratulations!'

'I already did. And she said to thank you and Lily for the basket of muffins.'

'I told Georgia you would have been the first to suggest sending one,' says Lily, 'if you hadn't been risking life and limb in some remote location.'

'And Mark has been offered a new job,' adds Georgia. 'So, Lucinda can stay at home and enjoy her maternity leave after all.'

'What did she say about Cath?' I ask.

'She and Mark are suing her for unfair dismissal. It couldn't have happened to a nicer woman.'

'Are you joining in with the lawsuit?'

She shakes her head. 'Lucinda suggested it, but I don't need the hassle. If I'm being totally honest, Cath didn't get great value out of me. My heart wasn't entirely in that job. I'm surprised I lasted there for as long as I did. I've decided to put it all behind me and move on.'

'That's very mature of you,' says Lily. 'But I hope Lucinda wins her case.'

'I expect she will,' says Georgia. 'There are all sorts of laws about discriminating against pregnant women. There aren't so many about discriminating against unmotivated employees who resent having to do any work.'

'That's true,' I say. 'Lily and I are extremely clued up on employment law. Is that why you've been so obliging and helpful ever since you arrived here?'

'No, it's because I like working here. If I'd realised how much fun you all had each day, I'd have forced you to give me a job far sooner.'

Abby puts her head around the kitchen door. 'I'm just running over to ask Shelley about using her freezer. We're about to run out of space in ours, and she offered to help out if she could.'

'Say hi to Victoria for me,' I tell her.

'Have you been down to see the arts centre?' Lily asks me.

'I haven't had time.'

'That doesn't usually stop you. Generally, you take every opportunity to be near The Red Lion around lunchtime. By which I mean anytime between the hours of ten a.m. and three p.m.'

'I've been too busy catching up here,' I say. 'You know how it is when you've been away for a few days. You come back to find your inbox is full of emails that only you can deal with.'

'I checked your computer while you were away in case there was something important,' she says. 'There was a non-urgent note from our suppliers and another reminding you to renew your subscription to the chocolate of the month club. I noticed you were a platinum member.'

'Is that Choc-a-lot?' asks Georgia with interest.

'No, Truffle Time.'

'I looked at that one, but Choc-a-lot gives you more free extras, so I went with them.'

'And the pair of you still insist you're nothing like each other?' says Lily.

'We aren't!' I say, horrified.

'Not even a little bit,' agrees Georgia. 'You're confusing our vague physical resemblance with the concept of possessing similar personalities.'

Lily laughs. 'Whatever you say. We should do some work now we have four mouths to feed instead of three. And don't forget two of those are Campbell mouths. It's a heavy responsibility for any small to medium-sized business.'

'I won't be here for lunch,' says Georgia. 'That ought to save you some money. I finish work at lunchtime today, so I'll be eating at The Red Lion. Would either of you like to join me?'

'I can't,' I say quickly. 'I have to do next week's orders.'

'Couldn't you do them this afternoon?' asks Lily.

'I could, but I don't like to put things off.'

'Is this because you don't want to go to the arts centre?' she asks.

'Possibly.'

'Because of Jon?'

'I haven't seen him since the camping trip, and he hasn't contacted me.'

'Have you contacted him?' she asks.

'My phone is probably tapped. If I go within a hundred metres of his house or workplace, a member of the betting syndicate is bound to follow me. I can't risk upsetting the delicate balance of the odds calculations. Mabel would never forgive me.'

'In other words, you're scared to go and talk to him,' says Georgia.

'Not scared, exactly. But I haven't yet decided what I want to say to him.'

'That makes a change. You aren't usually lost for words. You're the poster girl for acting without thinking.'

'Generally long before thinking,' I agree.

'So, why are you taking so long to come to a decision?' she asks.

'Maybe because this one is important to her,' says Lily. 'It's easy enough to wander through life, not looking more than one step ahead, when nothing matters very much. It's more complicated when you encounter something you sense may be rather more important. I have a theory about why Isabella is finding it so difficult to think straight about this particular man.'

'Could I pay you not to share it with us?' I ask.

'No need,' says Georgia. 'I'll bet it's the same theory as mine.'

'Couldn't you both track down Mabel and have this conversation with her?' I beg. 'You can place your bets on whatever this ridiculous theory may be and leave me out of it.'

'I've already told you I'm not placing a bet,' says Georgia. 'It would be a most unsisterly thing to do. Besides, I don't have any money. But I know I'm right.'

'Me too,' says Lily. 'You don't want to lose Jon and the boys if everything goes wrong. Am I right?'

'Possibly,' I say. 'Although it isn't as simple as that.'

'And he's the first person who's ever said no to you,' says Georgia with an evil grin. 'That must have been quite a shock. But it's good to know he's capable of standing up to you if you ever do get together.'

'Georgia's right about you and men,' Lily tells me. 'The first time I met you, you were dating my ex-boyfriend. I really wanted to hate you, but you made that impossible. I watched you very carefully, and it was obvious you had Stephen wound around your little finger. He never changed his plans when I was with him. But you said jump, and he asked how high? It's been the same ever since. I've watched a long line of men queuing up to go out with you, and none of them has lasted for more than a few dates. At first, I thought it was because you weren't looking for anything serious. Eventually, I realised not a single one of them ever stood up to you. They were so keen to get a date with you that they allowed you to walk all over them. Some women would like that, but not you.'

'She's right,' says Georgia. 'You want a relationship of equals, and most men aren't offering that. It comes of having the excellent Campbell genes. For all your faults – and they are many and various – you aren't quite as unfortunate looking as you might be. And that's attracted all the wrong kinds of men.'

'Even accepting you're correct,' I say, 'which I'm very far from doing, it doesn't follow that Jon and I are right for each other. Don't forget he comes with a lot of baggage. Very cute and adorable baggage, but still baggage.'

'That's just something you're hiding behind,' says Lily. 'You know as well as I do that none of this is insurmountable if you make up your mind to do it. You're using it as an excuse not to take a risk. I think Jon has the capacity to hurt you, and that's why you're hesitating. Not because he has a couple of nephews he's helping through a bad patch.'

Georgia pulls off her apron. 'I have to go. I want to see whether the new roof is finished, then ask Victoria about the game pie situation. You're quite safe to go down and take a look, Issy. Shelley told me yesterday that Jon isn't on site this week. I'm not even sure he'll be coming to the grand opening unless he's specifically invited.'

'Why were you there yesterday?' I ask.

'I told you. I'm interested in what's happening over there. See you later!'

She tosses the apron onto the nearest table and skips off down the street.

'If she can afford game pie two days running,' I tell Lily, 'we're paying her too much.'

'I think Victoria gives her a discount.'

'She doesn't offer me a discount!' I say. 'And I used to be her employer.'

'You aren't helping to decorate the arts centre.'

'Neither is Georgia,' I say.

'She's been going there after work most days. And she was there all day yesterday. Didn't she mention it to you?'

'Not a word. Miracles will never cease. It's been strange enough to see her doing some actual work to earn her living. I didn't expect to hear she was offering her services for free.'

'People can surprise us,' she says. 'You surprise me almost daily. Georgia is just living up to the Campbell tradition.'

'It would appear so. Hand me that cloth, and I'll finish wiping those tables before the lunchtime rush starts.'

'And while you're doing that, you can consider what Georgia and I have told you,' she says.

I lift up a vase of flowers and carefully wipe the table before replacing it. 'I make no promises. I still need some time to think things over. But I'm very grateful to both of you for caring enough to say it.'

Chapter Thirty-Six

I decide to take Georgia's advice and go to the arts centre after work. She and Lily are quite right to say I've been avoiding Jon, but it seems there's no danger of meeting him today. I know I can't avoid him forever, and it would be less awkward if we met again sooner rather than later. But for some reason, it's something I'm not ready to face. I've never felt the slightest embarrassment bumping into exes. And Jon isn't even an ex. He's just a 'might have been but for various excellent reasons never was.'

Something has changed recently, and I suspect that something is me. Perhaps I'm starting to take life more seriously. It's a dreadful thought, and I hope it isn't true. But there may be something in what Georgia said about making a choice to be happy and putting some faith in those around me to deal with their own choices. It would make life a lot simpler if I didn't feel responsible for anyone else's path in life.

I find Georgia clutching a paint roller and wearing a paint-splashed shirt over the T shirt she wore to work today.

'That shirt looks awfully familiar,' I say. 'If it weren't for the fact it's covered in paint, and the one I'm thinking of is safely tucked away in my wardrobe, I'd almost think it belonged to me.'

'You never wear it,' she says. 'And the colour doesn't suit you.'

'True. I can't think why I bought it. Would you like some help with that? I could easily run home and find something to protect my clothes. It wouldn't take me a moment to go through all your things.'

She points to a pile of shirts in the corner of the room. 'You can use one of those. Someone brought in a load of old clothes for the volunteers to use.'

'And yet you still looked through my wardrobe? The workings of your mind have always been a mystery to me.'

'They weren't here when I started helping out,' she says impatiently. 'So, I put this one in my bag before I left home. Why do you always have to make such a fuss about everything?'

'It's a mystery,' I say, picking up a man's shirt and pulling it on. 'This should keep me clean enough. The last time I was here, I ended up covered in cream. I could have done with this shirt that day.'

She shows me where the rollers are kept, and we set to work. I stop after half an hour to ease the kinks out of my aching back.

'I must say it's a revelation to see you working not one but two jobs on a single day,' I tell Georgia.

'I could say the same thing to you.'

'But with far less cause. Seriously, I'm impressed. I wasn't sure how things would work out at the bakery, but you've really got stuck in there. Our customers love you. Admittedly, they love anyone who provides them with cake, but they appear to be fonder of you than anyone could have predicted.'

She reaches up and rolls paint into the corner. 'I would have predicted it. Why wouldn't they love me? I'm very lovable.'

'You have your moments,' I admit. 'But this painting isn't a part of earning your daily crust. What led you to become involved with all this?'

'Lily and I came to The Red Lion for a drink the day you went camping. Victoria showed us what was going on here, and they both told me about your idea for the arts centre. It seemed like a worthwhile thing, so when Mavis Sotherby mentioned they needed volunteers to decorate the place, I signed up.'

I pick up my roller again. 'Good for you. What I don't understand is how they've finished all the building work so quickly. Was there really a secret benefactor? It's surprising word hasn't got out if there is. You know what our customers are like. Especially the Silver Surfers. They're the human equivalent of an electronic messaging service.'

'You should ask Mavis,' says Georgia.

'That would be the simplest solution, but I'd prefer to exhaust all other possible solutions before doing that. She can be quite terrifying at times. I'm always on my best behaviour when I'm around her. She makes me feel as though I'm back at school, and someone has given me a detention for using a Bunsen burner to heat up a Pop-Tart in the chemistry lab. Does she have that effect on you too?'

'No, because I'm an adult. You toasted Pop-Tarts at school?'

'Of course not! It was just a random example. There's no need for you to go prattling on to Mum and Dad about it.'

'I'll try,' she says. 'But it may not be possible. You know what a chatterbox I am. Once I start talking, I find it difficult to stop.'

'You can keep that shirt,' I offer.

'I've already told you it doesn't suit you. And you and I have the same colouring. Besides, it's covered with paint. How about lending me that blue evening dress the next time I ask for it?'

I frown. 'It feels rather unfair to be blackmailed into lending you my favourite dress in order to stop you from telling our parents about something I very definitely didn't do. But it would be more of a shame to sow even the smallest seed of suspicion in their minds that I'm not quite as perfect as they've always believed. You have a deal.'

We continue to paint for the next hour until Victoria arrives.

'Great job!' she tells Georgia, looking at the freshly painted walls. 'You've been here for hours. You must be hungry. Hi, Isabella. I didn't realise you were here too.'

'That's because I'm camouflaged,' I say, looking down at my shirt. 'Between me and the wall, it's difficult to tell which of us is wearing the most paint.'

'It's definitely you,' she says. 'How was the camping trip?'

'Wonderful!' I say before Georgia can speak. I don't want her airing her theories about me and Jon for a second time. Victoria is a busy woman and doesn't need irrelevant information cluttering up her brain.

'I came to ask whether you'd like to come over to the pub for dinner,' she says. 'Shelley told me to say it's on the house.'

'Are you talking to Georgia?' I ask. 'Or both of us?'

'She only mentioned Georgia, but that's because we didn't realise anyone else was here. I'm sure she'd have included you if she'd known.'

I pull off my shirt and drop it back onto the pile. 'I've been coming to this pub since I was a toddler, and not once has Shelley or anyone else offered me a free portion of game pie. Yet the moment my sister wanders in, everyone is falling over themselves to give the stuff away. Life is most unfair.'

'We're offering it to all our lovely volunteers,' she says. 'So, you know what to do if you want free pie in the future.'

She looks around the room. 'It seems you've almost finished in here. The poker club has done most of the upper floor with the help of various members of the gardening club. And the bell ringers painted the hallway and stairs last week. It hardly seems possible that when I first arrived in Honeywell, this was only an idea in Isabella's extremely fertile brain. And now we have an almost fully-fledged arts centre.'

'It was one of her better ideas,' admits Georgia. 'We'll be over for dinner once we've cleaned these rollers. Or rather, once I've supervised Isabella doing it. It's a highly skilled task, and it's time she learned how to do it.'

We finish cleaning up and wander over to The Red Lion to claim our free meal.

'I used to wonder why you raved about their pie so much,' says Georgia. 'But I'm forced to admit you have a point.'

'What will we do if Victoria only has one portion left?' I ask.

'She'll give it to me! I was here for several hours, whereas you rocked up at the last minute and took all the credit. The least you can do is offer me the game pie and order the fish and chips.'

'I'll give you points for quantity of work,' I say. 'But I brought the gift of quality. They're two very different things.'

'I combined the two. My painting is of a very high standard. Nathan complimented me the other day on the quality of my cutting-in.'

'What's that?' I ask.

'I'm not entirely sure. But apparently, I did it beautifully.'

'I expect he was right. I'm just surprised you're doing it at all. Joking aside, this isn't the sort of thing I'd have expected you to get involved with. Why did you?'

'Working in the bakery had something to do with it,' she says. 'All your customers seem so involved in everything that's going on in the village. And you and Lily are right there in the middle of everything. You say you never expected to find me painting a room voluntarily. I could just as easily say that I never expected to find you running your own bakery.'

'I know what you mean. It surprised me too. But one thing just led to another. First, I met Lily, and we became friends. Then I realised the bakery would close once Mr Mason retired, and the idea just popped into my head. To tell you the truth, I never thought it would take off the way it did. I thought we might get it back on its feet, then sell it on to someone else so they could continue running it. But we both loved it so much that never happened. Instead, we decided to make a real go of it, and here we are eight years later, actually turning a profit!'

'You're very lucky,' she says. 'I know you've worked hard, but you've found the thing you want to do, which makes a huge difference. I've never done that.'

'That's ok,' I say. 'Not everyone manages to combine their work and their social life in the way Lily and I have. You may have had a slightly chequered employment history, but you've also had a pretty active social life. Maybe you're someone who doesn't mind what they do to earn a living because the important part of their life takes place outside of work.'

'That's what I used to think. But I'm wondering now whether that's how I want to live the rest of my life. I can't believe I'm saying this, but there's a tiny way in which I wish I were more like you.'

'I imagine most people would love to be more like me,' I say, and laugh at her disgusted expression. 'I'm joking. Right at this moment, I'm not sure I want to be very much like me.'

'Seriously?'

'Maybe a bit.'

I look around at the posters on the walls announcing the date of the grand opening. 'It's difficult to explain, but I feel curiously detached from this whole thing, and I don't know why. It almost feels as though I was never a real part of it, which is strange, considering it was my idea in the first place.'

'Is it because I'm involved?' asks Georgia. 'I can easily find something else to do. I'd understand if you felt I was muscling in on your territory.'

'You can't back out now,' I say. 'We need as much muscle as possible. And it isn't that. It's lovely that you and I have got to know each other a little better, and I'm happy to see you becoming a part of this community. Honeywell is a wonderful village, and everyone should have a place like that in their lives. Something else is wrong, but I'm not sure what.'

'You've lost your sense of connection,' she says. 'You had your life exactly as you wanted it, all nice and planned out. And then someone came along with a whole different set of plans and obligations, and you can't think how to combine them. You'd like to, but you're terrified of losing yourself in the process.'

Our game pies arrive, and I don't object when Georgia immediately selects the larger portion.

'Am I right?' she asks through a mouthful of chips.

'I'd like to say you're completely wrong and tell you this is why I never come to you for advice. But you may have a point. A very small and accidental one,' I add quickly before she suggests I employ her as my future life coach and relationship guru.

'That means I'm right,' she says complacently. 'I thought so. What do you plan to do about it?'

'Eat this game pie,' I say, picking up my knife and fork and moving my plate away from her. 'And then ask very nicely and politely whether they have any crème brûlée left.'

'Good answer,' she says, slicing into her pastry and inhaling deeply. 'I suggest we order ourselves a nice cappuccino to follow. Nathan has improved no end since I gave him a few tips about how to get the best out of their new coffee machine. Who would have thought I'd have been such a force for good in your community?'

'I'm still not convinced this isn't some sort of reality television show,' I say. 'There may be hidden cameras around the village, like the ones in The Truman Show.'

She rolls her eyes. 'You really do suffer from main character syndrome when I'm not around to keep you grounded. I can promise there are no hidden cameras, and no microphones. Just me and my incredible wisdom.'

'I wouldn't go that far,' I say. 'But if it makes you feel any better, I'm willing to admit you have, accidentally or not, made a certain kind of sense this evening. Just don't tell anyone I said so.'

Chapter Thirty-Seven

Lily and I have to work extra hours in the days before the arts centre opening. Abby needs more help in the kitchen, and someone has to be in there with her most of the time. Georgia offers to come in each day, and we gratefully accept.

'I think it's only fair we give our parents a break,' I tell Lily. 'I'll be moving out soon, which means they'll be the recipients of the pure, undiluted Georgia. I hope they find a way to cope. Otherwise, she may wake one morning to discover they've sneaked away in the middle of the night.'

'Leaving the house entirely for me?' asks Georgia. 'You haven't thought this through. You'll be living in some tiny little studio flat, whereas I'll be enjoying the run of a four-bedroom house.'

'You'd have to cook for yourself,' I remind her. 'And do all your own cleaning. I don't think you'd enjoy that. And you couldn't employ a cleaner on what Lily and I pay you.'

'I can barely afford to order pizza on what Lily and you pay me. But I could take in a couple of lodgers. They couldn't possibly be as bad as you.'

'Have you two finished bickering about something that's never going to happen?' asks Lily. 'Because Abby wants some help with the mini quiches. I have to leave early today to pick up the children.'

'Do you have a coin?' Georgia asks me. 'We can flip it to choose which of us helps Abby.'

'I have plenty of coins,' I say. 'That's what happens when you own a successful bakery. But it isn't how the employer relationship works. I tell you what needs doing, and you salute and rush off to do it.'

Lily picks up her bag. 'I've never once saluted Isabella, and I don't intend to start. I advise you to follow my example, Georgia. I also hope you've joined a union. I recommend it to all our new employees. Isabella is the kind of employer for whom unions were invented.'

'I'll help Abby in the kitchen,' Georgia tells me, and disappears before I have time to protest.

'I know!' says Lily before I can speak. 'You're giving her a written warning. Could you clean the tables and change the flowers before you do that? And check next week's orders.'

She disappears, leaving me to meditate on the unfairness of life, but also to marvel at the sequence of events that has led to me standing here today as one of the owners of The Sugarloaf Bakery. There's never any point in looking back and wishing you'd done things differently. But it's nice when you can look back and realise you wouldn't have changed a thing.

This place feels like home, and my co-workers like family. This is literally true in Georgia's case. But it's also true for Lily and Abby, and all the women who've worked with us over the past few years. And our customers feel like extended family – Mabel and Mrs Ogilvie, Iris, Phyllis, Barb, Mary, and a host of others. Not forgetting Bernie, our bakery mascot. I have no idea what the future holds, but I never want to forget just how lucky I am to have all this right now.

By Monday morning, I'm willing to change the word lucky to misguided. It's chaos in the bakery. Georgia is serving our customers and making the drinks. Abby is putting the finishing touches to the cake she's been commissioned to make for the grand opening. And I'm busy packing up the cakes and tarts and helping Lily's father pack them into his car.

'I'm so grateful you offered to help with this,' I tell Martin. 'The last time I was tasked with transporting cakes to The Red Lion, only about twenty percent of them made it there in one piece.'

'I'm surprised it was that many,' he says, opening the passenger door and stacking the final few boxes on the seat.

'It wasn't because I ate them. I suffered a terrible accident after I arrived there!'

'If you say so.' He smiles at me and drives away.

'I tripped over an extension cord!' I call after him, but he's already closed his window.

I glance around to make sure no one can hear me shouting at passing cars. But the high street is empty. People must be getting ready for this afternoon's shindig. The opening ceremony starts in less than an hour.

It's tight, but we make it in time. By two o'clock, we've closed the bakery, packed the final batch of scones into Martin's car, and we're standing in front of the makeshift stage waiting for the ceremony to begin.

'Who's cutting the ribbon?' Lily asks me. 'By rights, it should be you. If you hadn't come up with the idea for an arts centre, goodness knows what we'd be doing now. We could be about to hear some local dignitary declare the Groovy Goat open.'

'Or the Boogie Bar,' adds Abby.

'The village would never have rallied around to raise money for a seventies theme pub,' I say. 'Although we wouldn't have needed to. That awful pub chain would have paid for it all themselves.'

'We'd all be standing here today wearing fringed waistcoats and weaving flowers into each other's hair,' says Lily. 'And the band would be playing the Bee Gees' greatest hits.'

I shiver. 'A narrow escape indeed. Here comes Mavis, clutching her ceremonial pair of scissors. I hope she doesn't make too long a speech. Daisy has promised to take me on the bouncy castle.'

Mavis ascends the stage to the strains of the theme tune from Star Wars and holds up her hand for silence. It seems even the tubas and trombones sense her authority, as the band immediately stops playing. She's holding the microphone, although she barely needs it. It's a still day, and her voice carries perfectly without it.

'Good afternoon, and welcome to the new Honeywell Arts Centre!' she says in beautifully enunciated tones, from which even the most experienced royal could learn a thing or two. 'I'm honoured to have been invited to say a few words before cutting this ribbon and declaring the building open for business. As you know, this was always intended to be a village project.'

'Of the village, by the village, and for the village,' I murmur to Victoria, who has just joined us.

'Shhh!' she says. 'Mavis has bat-like hearing, and you know what she's likely to do if she realises anyone else is talking at the same time as her.'

I've had rather too much experience of falling under the shadow of Mavis' displeasure, so I decide to keep quiet.

'From its first inception,' Mavis goes on, 'this arts centre was planned to be a place everyone could visit to learn how to paint, make pottery, enjoy dance classes, or join a community choir. What happens here will be limited only by the imaginations of those who use it.'

'Challenge accepted,' I whisper to Georgia, who grins.

'Honeywell is a community,' Mavis goes on. 'We work together, play together and, above all, we always have each other's backs. I look forward to seeing what we as a community will do with our new arts centre in the years to come. So, without further ado –' she raises the scissors and snips the ribbon Angela Carson is holding taut for her – 'I am delighted to declare the Honeywell Arts Centre well and truly open!'

There's a burst of applause, and the band breaks into a somewhat shaky rendition of Congratulations!

'Isn't she going to smash a bottle of champagne?' asks Abby.

'This is an arts centre, not a ship,' I tell her. 'It would be a good thing for all of us if you could remember that distinction in the future. Otherwise, we may turn up for a batik session one day, only to find we're interrupting a mainsail repair class.'

'Isn't that Toby and Ollie?' asks Lily, pointing towards the bouncy castle.

'I didn't expect to see them here today,' I say in a casual tone.

'I doubt they came by themselves,' says Lily.

'I wouldn't put anything past those two. They're an ingenious pair when they set their minds to something.'

'The million-dollar question is who brought them?' she says. 'Jon or their mother? Did he mention anything about it to you, Isabella?'

'I haven't heard from him lately,' I say in an even more casual tone. 'I should look for Daisy. I promised to buy her and Ethan several ice creams if they behaved well during the ceremony. I didn't hear any shrieks and screams, so I assume they did.'

'Ice cream?' asks Georgia, brightening. 'See you all later!'

'Dad's waiting in line for a pony ride with the children,' Lily tells me. 'You know you can't go on that, Isabella. It's for the under-twelves only.'

'Discrimination at its finest. I think I'll check out the toffee apple stall while I wait. Is anyone coming with me?'

'Not me,' says Victoria. 'I'm working today.'

'And I promised to find Jack as soon as the ceremony was over,' says Lily. 'He and I have barely seen each other this week.'

'It's been the same with me and Chris,' says Abby. 'I can see him over there talking to my parents. See you all back at the bakery.'

She wanders off, leaving me standing by myself, feeling strangely isolated. I'm about to go in search of something to eat when a woman I haven't seen before touches me on the shoulder. 'Excuse me. Are you Isabella Campbell?'

'Guilty as charged. You aren't from Health and Safety, are you?'

'I'm Ali. Toby and Ollie's mum.'

'It's lovely to meet you,' I say. 'I haven't seen the boys yet, but someone mentioned they were here.'

'They're on the bouncy castle with their uncle. I was invited, but I wanted to find you and thank you for everything you've done for my children. I can't think how they talked you into going camping with them, but I was so grateful when I heard you'd agreed. Jon told me he'd be fine, but I know he was a little worried about keeping an eye on them both in a strange place.'

'You're more than welcome,' I say. 'I had a wonderful time. Camping is my new favourite thing. And I'm very fond of your boys. They're a credit to you and their father. I was so sorry to hear what happened last year.'

'Thank you. It was a terrible time, but things are getting easier now we've settled into a new routine. And Jon has been amazing. I'll never criticise younger brothers again.'

'I've been feeling the same way about my younger sister recently,' I say. 'She isn't nearly as awful as she wants me to believe. I like to think either of us would have helped the other out in your situation. Although maybe not to the same extent as Jon has. He's really committed to those boys.'

'He's been a life saver,' she says. 'And the boys adore him. They really like you too. It's been "Isabella this" and "Isabella that" ever since they got back from their camping trip. Ollie told me yesterday that Isabella didn't make him wash his hands before dinner, so he didn't see why I should.'

'I suppose I ought to have done,' I say. 'But when you're sitting on a log next to a campfire, after an afternoon of scrambling around the forest floor searching for beetles, you've made your peace with a bit of dirt.'

'It's good for their immune systems,' she says. 'But don't tell them I said so.'

She hesitates, then adds. 'Did you know Jon would be here this afternoon?'

'No, but it makes sense. He's been involved with the project from the beginning, so it's natural he wants to see how it turned out. He's done an excellent job of overseeing it all. The building looks great both inside and outside.'

'He's always been organised,' she says. 'But he enjoys being around people too. I can see why his work suits him. You own a bakery somewhere around here, don't you? The boys told me you have the coolest job in the world, and they want to own their own bakery when they're older. Or a sweetshop. They don't mind which.'

'I'm living the dream,' I say, laughing. 'Tell them they're welcome to visit us any time they like. You too.'

'I know they'll hold me to that. What about Jon?'

The directness of the question takes me by surprise. 'What about him?'

'I shouldn't have asked that,' she says. 'I'm sorry. It's none of my business. He's been very quiet since he came back from that camping trip, and I wondered a bit. That's all.'

'He may be worn out,' I say. 'It took me several days to fully recover.'

'That's quite likely. I can see you don't want to talk about him, and goodness knows you don't need a complete stranger butting into your private life. And Jon wouldn't say a word to me, even when I asked him. All I wanted to say was that things are going much better for me and the boys now. So, if you were worried that …' She trails off, looking uncomfortable.

'I'm glad things are improving for you all,' I tell her. 'But I'd hate you to think that I or anyone else could ever resent you and the boys needing Jon. Nothing could be further from the truth. Whatever may have happened between me and him has nothing to do with the boys and everything to do with me. I've had to do a lot of thinking about what I want out of life.'

'I won't ask what conclusions you've come to,' she says. 'And I'm grateful you haven't told me to stay out of your business.'

'My best friend tells me I spend most of my time in other people's business. Maybe it's time for me to listen to other people for a change.'

'I have to get back to the boys,' she says. 'I promised I'd take them for a second turn on the bouncy castle. I'm hoping their first round will have burned off some of their energy.'

'The triumph of hope over experience? I've been camping with them. I know how much stamina they have. It almost made me wish I were nine years old again. You're a far more experienced parent than I am, but I've been a godmother for the past six years. My tip is to take them camping every single week. They'll sleep like babies. You will too. Even Toby's snoring won't wake you up.'

'I'll make a note of your advice,' she promises. 'See you later?'

'I hope so. Enjoy your aerial adventure.'

She runs off towards the bouncy castle. I watch her go, my mind racing. She certainly seems to be doing well. I hope that continues. And I'm glad to know she has so many people looking out for her if things ever take a turn for the worse.

I wander towards the refreshment tent to make sure everything is going according to plan. Lily and I offered to help serve the cakes and tea, but the Silver Surfers assured us they had it all covered.

'By which they mean they want the first pick of all the best cakes,' I told Lily, who shrugged.

'Do we care as long as we get a well-deserved afternoon off?'

She was right. It's yet another example of me thinking nothing can go to plan unless I'm there to supervise it. It may be time to sit back and enjoy an afternoon with no responsibility at all. Maybe this is why Georgia always looks so relaxed.

I walk past the face-painting stall and am just about to take a shortcut behind the makeshift stage when I run into Jon coming the other way. We stare at each other for a moment.

'Hi, Isabella,' he says. 'I was looking for you.'

'I thought you were playing on the bouncy castle with the boys.'

'Ali has taken over for a while. What were you doing?'

'Heading for the refreshment tent.'

'Of course, you were! If I'd stopped to think, I could have camped out in there and waited for you to arrive.'

'I was planning to stop at the toffee apple stall on the way,' I say. 'Only it's not where Lily told me it would be – next to the face painting.'

'I'll buy you as many toffee apples as you can eat if you give me five minutes of your time first,' he says. 'I really want to talk to you.'

'I want to talk to you too,' I say. 'I didn't realise you'd be here today or I'd have been better prepared. But now is as good a time as any. Only, I'd prefer not to do it in the middle of the refreshment tent.'

'Five pounds says you've never before uttered those words – and never will again. How about behind this stage? There's no one about. They're all bouncing or galloping around or breaking their teeth on homemade sweets.'

I glance around. He's right. Everyone is busy with all the activities. No one is looking in this direction.

I lean against the back of the stage and take a deep breath. 'If you don't mind, I'd like to go first.'

Chapter Thirty-Eight

He turns to face me, a wary look on his face. 'Go ahead.'

For the first time in my life, when given the opportunity to speak, I find myself at a loss for words.

He seems to realise this. 'Would you like me to start?'

'I'm just collecting my thoughts. As I said, I didn't think you'd be here today.'

'The boys heard about it and insisted on coming. They said it sounded like fun, so Ali and I thought we'd make a day of it. They start school again next week, and it seemed like a good way to round off the holidays.'

He shoves his hands into his pockets and stares down at his feet. 'Also, I hoped I might see you.'

'That was pretty much guaranteed. I wouldn't have missed this for the world.'

'So, what did you want to say to me?' he asks. 'It's too late now to demand a discount. All the work has been completed, and the contractors paid in full.'

'I'm aware of that. As it turns out, you weren't needed at all. We received a last-minute donation from an extremely generous benefactor. Or maybe just a generous one. It's difficult to tell without knowing how rich he or she may be.'

'I'm glad to hear it,' he says. 'Saying no to your request wasn't easy.'

'How can you say that? It took you less than two seconds. And you looked as though you were enjoying every moment of it.'

'I was steeling myself to refuse your request, knowing that my refusal made it less likely I'd see you again. But my professional duty came first.'

'I don't believe a word of it,' I say. 'But that's no longer relevant. The building has been finished without you compromising your professional ethics in any way.'

'Is that what you wanted to talk to me about?' he asks. 'The fact you managed to finish this project despite my lack of cooperation?'

'That wasn't the only thing. But I was diverted by you mentioning the shocking way in which you behaved during our first meeting. I really hoped to see you again so I could give you something.'

I reach into my bag, pull out a smaller bag, and hand it to him with a dramatic flourish.

He looks down at it with a puzzled frown. 'Marshmallows?'

'That's right.'

He turns the bag over in his hands. 'Slightly squashed marshmallows?'

'That's because I've been carrying them around in my bag for the past few days. You can't think how difficult it's been not to eat them.'

'Yes, I can. But why are you giving me a bag of marshmallows?'

'Because the last time you and I were eating marshmallows, you kissed me. And I was hoping you might do it again.'

There's a flash of hope in his eyes. 'Do you mean that?'

'I never joke about marshmallows. I realise there's no campfire here, so we can't continue the tradition by throwing them into the fire. But this stage is made of wood. I could set it alight if you think it would help.'

He drops the bag onto the grass and takes two quick strides towards me. He pauses with his hands on my shoulders. 'What changed your mind?'

'I weighed up the risks of a future with you and one without you, and the second alternative seemed too sad to contemplate. Everyone has been telling me it's time I started putting a little faith in other people and stopped trying to save the world all by myself. I've decided to take their advice.'

I have no chance to say anything else before his arms wrap around me, firm and urgent, pulling me against the solid warmth of his chest. For a split second, he gazes into my eyes, and then his mouth meets mine in a kiss that wipes away every coherent thought.

I lose track of time, of sound, of everything except the steady rhythm of his heartbeat against my chest and the softness of his lips. This kiss isn't rushed or dramatic. It's warm and certain – the kind that makes you feel as though you've kissed each other a thousand times before and will a thousand times again.

I draw back at last and look up at him, my heart racing. 'Do I take it you'd like to give this thing a second chance?'

He smiles down at me. 'That wasn't a goodbye kiss.'

'I hoped it wasn't, but I don't know you well enough to be sure. You may say goodbye to everyone like that. In which case, you and I will be having a talk before long about appropriate greeting etiquettes.'

'I usually shake someone's hand when I leave,' he assures me. 'At the most, I kiss them on the cheek. Let me show you the difference.'

As he pulls me towards him again, the strap of my bag snags on the edge of the stage, causing me to stagger and almost disappear through the velvet curtain. He catches me in time.

'That was a close thing,' I say. 'It would have given the passers-by a bit of a shock if I'd appeared from nowhere like The Wizard of Oz.'

'You could have told them you were looking for your ruby slippers.'

'You've dropped your marshmallows,' I say. 'Not the best start to our new relationship. You'd better pick them up before a passing troupe of ants discovers them and takes them off to their anthill.'

'It's an army of ants, not a troupe. And I'd buy you some more marshmallows if they did.'

'Don't make promises unless you mean them,' I warn him.

'I've never meant anything more. If you like, I'll promise to have a large bag delivered to you every morning by special messenger.'

'That won't be necessary. Just send me the occasional box tied up in a ribbon instead of red roses.'

'It's a deal.'

He draws me close and kisses me again. His lips press against mine, soft but insistent, as his hands move to my back, pulling me deeper into the warmth of his embrace. I respond instinctively, my fingers tracing the line of his jaw.

I'm not sure how long we would have stayed here, locked in each other's arms and lost to the world. A sudden loud cheer makes us jump and pull apart. A moment later, someone pulls back the red curtain, and I see what seems to be the entire village standing on the grass looking at us.

'Finally!' calls a voice.

I peer into the crowd to see Mabel waving at me.

She produces a small notebook and opens it. 'Who guessed it would be during the grand opening?'

'Not me,' says Ivy. 'I had last Tuesday.'

'I wasn't too far off,' says Phyllis. 'I guessed the third week of August.'

'What's happening?' I ask, bemused.

'We're settling the final bets,' says Mabel.

'Are you talking about me and Jon?'

'Who else? You've kept us waiting for long enough.'

'What's going on?' asks Jon.

I gesture towards the crowd. 'This lot have been running some kind of book on the odds of the two of us getting together. I'm sorry to disappoint you all, but Jon and I were simply discussing our recent camping trip. A pair of my socks appears to have ended up in one of the boys' backpacks. He was just returning them to me.'

Lily grins at me. 'That argument would be a lot more believable if the microphone hadn't been on for the past few minutes.'

I glance at the microphone, lying next to the curtain. I must have knocked it off its stand when I crashed into the stage, and somehow it got switched on.

'How much did you all hear?' I ask Lily.

'Enough for Mabel to close the betting and stop offering any further odds on the outcome.'

'I knew I was facing long odds of getting Isabella to change her mind,' says Jon. 'Thank you to everyone who believed in me enough to place your bets.'

'We didn't believe in you so much as we believed in Isabella,' says Phyllis. 'She usually gets there in the end.'

'I appreciate that,' I say. 'I can't help feeling our customers would have ostracised me entirely if I hadn't found the courage to speak to Jon and tell him how I felt. But I didn't count on everyone in the village overhearing our conversation.'

'Not everyone,' says Lily. 'Just enough of us to realise most people have lost their money.'

'If you're expecting me to apologise for that, you can forget it. As a leading member of this community, I must tell you I consider all of your behaviour to be disgraceful. If Mavis Sotherby ever finds out, you'll be in trouble, and I won't lift a finger to save you.'

None of them looks as apprehensive as I hoped when I make this threat.

'She was one of the people who got you together,' says Lily. 'You should be grateful for that.'

'We met when Isabella turned up and threw a box of cakes at me,' says Jon.

She smiles. 'But who sent her to do that?'

'Mavis only suggested I went over there to ask for a discount,' I say. 'She couldn't possibly have known I'd meet Jon and end up with him. To be fair, she didn't instruct me to start hurling cakes. That was all my own idea.'

'True,' says Lily. 'But I still think we should give her some of the credit. And the moment the Silver Surfers saw the pair of you together, they started laying bets on how long it would take for you in particular to realise you'd finally met your match.'

I look at Jon, who's shaking with laughter.

'I don't understand why you find this so amusing,' I say. 'Doesn't it make you feel like a contestant on Blind Date?'

'Why should I care? I've won the prize, which is all that matters to me.'

'Smooth,' approves Mabel. 'Are you really upset with us, Isabella?'

'I suppose not. I'm quite touched you were so keen to see me happy.'

'So am I,' says Jon.

'We weren't so bothered about you,' Mabel tells him. 'But we all love Isabella. We've watched her help so many people during the years, and we thought it was about time she had her own happy ending. If need be, we had several plans up our sleeves for giving you both a nudge. But in the end, you worked things out for yourselves, and we're all delighted you did.'

'That would be more touching,' I say, 'if you hadn't opened a book on the possible results. Lily and her family won't be able to eat for the next few weeks.'

'Jack has promised to take on some overtime if need be,' says Lily. 'Our children won't go hungry.'

Something clicks in my brain. I turn to face Jon.

'The unknown benefactor! The one who made it possible to finish the building work.'

'I heard something about that,' he says casually.

'Was it by any chance you?'

His face doesn't flicker. 'I thought the benefactor was supposed to be anonymous.'

'Quite right,' says Mabel, giving him an enormous wink. 'He or she said they'd withdraw their donation if their identity was ever revealed. So, I guess we'll never know.'

'But –' I begin.

'I'd let it go if I were you,' Phyllis advises me. 'Some mysteries are best left undisturbed. The important thing is that we got over the finishing line. And so did you.'

'Now that's all cleared up,' says Ivy, 'it's time for Mabel to announce who's won this bet.'

Mabel gives a snort of laughter and waves her notebook at us. 'I can't believe I'm about to say this. But it seems as though, contrary to all expectations, the one who made the closest guess is none other than our very own mutt!'

Chapter Thirty-Nine

There's a burst of laughter before Ivy exclaims. 'That can't possibly be true!'

'I'm afraid so,' says Mabel. 'Believe me, if there was any way around it, I'd have found it. But he came the closest, so I'll have to award the prize to him. There's nothing I can do about it. I'll fall foul of the gaming commission if I try to fix the results.'

'And Mrs Ogilvie would contact the RSPCA,' says Lily.

'And all the local newspapers,' agrees Mabel. 'I don't believe there's any possible loophole.'

She turns and scans the crowd. 'Where has Edie got to? The last I saw of her, she was taking the mutt to look at the produce stall.'

'There she is,' says Ivy. 'Edie – over here! Have you heard the news? The mu – I mean Bernie – has won first prize!'

Mrs Ogilvie looks puzzled. 'For what?'

'How many competitions has he entered today?' asks Mabel. 'On second thoughts, don't tell me. I'd prefer not to know. I'm talking about the book we've been running on these two.'

She gestures towards me and Jon, and Mrs Ogilvie's face lights up.

'Have they sorted themselves out?' she asks. 'I'm so pleased.'

'Which is very generous of you,' I say, 'considering you spent the first few years of our acquaintance wondering what on earth Lily had got herself into.'

'Nonsense,' she says with a faint blush. 'And even if that were true, I'm sure this young man will be a steadying influence on you.'

'Don't count on it,' says Jon. 'I couldn't stop Isabella launching herself off a mountain peak and flying with the eagles or red kites or whatever it was Ollie really saw. I refuse to assume the smallest responsibility for whatever she may choose to do in the future.'

'Not the greatest beginning to our relationship,' I say.

'I'll always do my utmost to rescue you from the consequences of your own folly. But I'll never attempt to stop you from doing anything you set out to do.'

'That sounds more than fair to me,' says Ivy. 'Now, about this prize. What was the exact nature of Bernie's guess?'

Mabel gestures towards Mrs Ogilvie, who smiles. 'Bernie doesn't really approve of betting, but he made an exception in this case because he's so fond of Isabella. He bet on it all happening just when everyone had given up hope.'

I can't help laughing. 'He's a very wise dog.'

She beams back at me. 'He is. And he's planning on spending his winnings on a bag of biscuits and a new jacket for the winter with a fur-lined hood.'

'You've never suggested buying me a fur-lined winter jacket,' says Mabel. 'Sometimes, I feel like a second-rate citizen in my own home.'

'Only sometimes?' asks Phyllis. 'So, is that everything? I want to have a go at the coconut shy before it's too late.'

'I'll join you,' says Mabel. 'After which, the mutt can treat us both to tea. It's the least he can do, considering how many walks the pair of us have given him.'

The crowd disperses, leaving me and Jon standing by the stage with Lily and Jack.

'We'll give you some privacy,' she says. 'We need to find our children and make sure they haven't talked their grandparents into adopting a goat from the petting zoo.'

'Some privacy would be most welcome,' I tell her. 'I didn't plan to make my declaration to Jon in front of half the inhabitants of the New Forest.'

'You should know by now that nothing is private in this village. But we do our best. See you both later.'

'Would you like to get out of here so we can talk properly?' Jon asks me.

'Not until we've visited the tea tent. It's thirsty work telling someone how you feel about them.'

'You still haven't told me very much,' he says. 'Just that you've changed your mind about wanting me in your life.'

'Most people would be delighted to hear me say that.'

'And so I am. But if you remember, I had something to tell you too.'

'Please don't tell me you've realised I was right when I said you and I were a bad idea, and you came here today in order to break it to me gently. That would be awkward for both of us. Especially in light of the fact everyone I've ever met was listening in.'

He smiles. 'That wasn't what I planned to say. I wanted you to know you'll never come second in my life. There may be times when the boys need me more than usual, but I'm hoping we can navigate that together.'

'Your sister already told me that when I met her earlier this afternoon. She also said I needn't worry about her boys taking up too much of your time. What neither of you realises is that your boys were never the problem. My only concern was whether I'd be letting them down if I became a part of their lives and things didn't work out for us. But Georgia said she thought I was more worried about losing them than them losing me. And Lily told me I should let you worry about the boys and just decide what I want. After that, everything became very simple. I want all three of you in my life, if you'll have me.'

'If I'll have you?' He pulls me into his arms and kisses me again.

'I still don't plan on having children of my own,' I warn him when I finally emerge. 'So, if you have any ideas of changing my mind, forget it.'

'I don't care,' he says. 'It's you I want, not some mythical future lifestyle.'

'That isn't enough for everyone.'

'It's more than enough for me. Any man who persuaded you to share his life with him would be the luckiest man on the face of the earth. If he had even the smallest grain of sense, he'd spend all his time and energy hanging on to you.'

He takes my hand. 'Let's check out the tea tent before all the food has gone.'

'There's plenty more hidden back at the bakery,' I say. 'This isn't our first professional gig.'

We wander towards the tent. As we pass the tombola stall, I notice Ollie and Toby standing in line with their mum.

'Hi, boys,' I say. 'Are you having a good time?'

'Why are you holding Isabella's hand?' Ollie asks Jon.

'In case she gets lost,' he says. 'I'm taking her to find something to eat, and I don't want her wandering off.'

'Can we come with you?' asks Toby. 'I'm tired of waiting here. We can come back later, and I'm hungry.'

'I heard what happened,' says Ali. 'Sadly, I wasn't close enough to hear for myself, but someone called Mabel stopped me and told me all about it.'

'All about what?' asks Ollie.

'Are you Uncle Jon's girlfriend?' Toby asks me suddenly.

I smile at him. 'Would you mind if I said yes?'

'No, I think it's a very good idea.'

'Me too,' says Ollie. 'You can take us camping all the time now.'

'No one mentioned that was one of a girlfriend's duties,' I tell Jon. 'I may have to rethink a few things.'

'If the pair of you refrain from putting my new relationship in jeopardy before it's even started,' he tells the boys, 'I'll buy you both a doughnut.'

'They're very good,' I say. 'Abby made them only a few hours ago, and they're extremely full of jam. I should know. It was my turn to do the taste tests.'

The boys high-five each other and race off towards the tea tent.

Ali laughs as she watches them go. 'Imagine having an uncle who's dating the owner of a bakery. That really is the dream. I'm very glad we'll be seeing more of you, Isabella, and I look forward to getting to know you better. I should go and see what those two are up to.'

'I'm sorry about all this,' says Jon when she's gone. 'I hope you aren't feeling too overwhelmed by my relatives?'

'Not in the slightest. I've survived many years of Georgia without crumbling. I can handle those two with one arm tied behind my back. I could also beat you at crazy golf the same way.'

'I don't believe that,' he says. 'But I hope to have many opportunities to prove you wrong.'

He reaches into his pocket and pulls out a crumpled piece of paper.

'What's that?' I ask. 'A list of all the tiny future requests I might make that you intend to refuse without discussion? Because I received that message loud and clear the very first day I met you.'

'It's the score sheet from our first ever game of crazy golf,' he says.

'The one with the clown?'

'That's right.'

'Why did you keep it?' I ask, and my heart turns over at the look in his eyes.

'I never got your marker,' he says, folding it carefully. 'So, this felt like the next best thing.'

'I'll give you my marker right now if you like. I'm finally ready to hand it over.'

'Are you sure?' he asks. 'It's a pretty big deal. That's the thing about markers – you never know what someone will ask for.'

'As long as it isn't the last eclair, we'll be fine.'

'Even I know my limitations,' he tells me. 'I promise never to fight you for the last cake on the plate.'

I smile back at him. 'I'm not saying I won't share it with you fifty-fifty. And you're the first person I've ever considered doing that with.'

He puts his arms around me and looks down into my eyes. 'Fifty-fifty sounds good to me. As for everything else – we'll figure it out along the way.'

Thank you for reading!

If you would like to read a free short story telling you how Lily and Isabella came to buy the bakery, go to this link to request your free copy.

rosemarywhittaker.com/a-new-start

A Tale of Two Christmases

Annie never comes home for Christmas. There's too much chance of running into Alex. He broke her heart, and she never wants to speak to him again. Alex always comes home for Christmas. He's desperate to talk to Annie about what went wrong between them.

Join the fun in the first book of the ***Christmas in Honeywell*** series.

A Tale of Two Christmases is available now in paperback and Kindle e-book.

Books by Rosemary Whittaker

All available now in paperback and Kindle e-book

The Sugarloaf Bakery series

A Sugarloaf Valentine
A Sugarloaf Mix-Up
A Sugarloaf Surprise
A Sugarloaf Christmas
A Sugarloaf Easter
A Sugarloaf Secret
A Sugarloaf Summer
A Sugarloaf Appeal
A Sugarloaf Adventure

The Christmas in Honeywell series

A Tale of Two Christmases
A Boxful of Christmas
The Christmas Cookie Club

The Year Away series

The Cinnamon Snail
Sunshine State
The Wattle Birds
The Feijoa Tree
The Villa Mimosa

Short Reads

All available now in Kindle e-book

Making the Effort

Made in United States
Cleveland, OH
10 July 2025

18402503R10164